SAINT OVERBOARD

FOREWORD BY
MICHAEL HIRST

THE ADVENTURES OF THE SAINT

SAINT OVERBOARD

LESLIE CHARTERIS

SERIES EDITOR: IAN DICKERSON

Text copyright © 2014 Interfund (London) Ltd.
Foreword © 2014 Michael Hirst
Publication History and Author Biography © 2014 Ian Dickerson
All rights reserved.

Published by Thomas & Mercer, Seattle

www.apub.com

ISBN-13: 9781477842751
ISBN-10: 1477842756

Cover design by David Drummond, www.salamanderhill.com

Printed in the United States of America.

To
H. C. Ryland
Who had the nerve,
B. H. Robinson
Who had the money, and
Richard L. Mealand
Who helped from the beginning—this result
Of their widely different encouragement is
Very gratefully dedicated

PUBLISHER'S NOTE

The text of this book has been preserved from the original edition and includes vocabulary, grammar, style, and punctuation that might differ from modern publishing practices. Every care has been taken to preserve the author's tone and meaning, allowing only minimal changes to punctuation and wording to ensure a fluent experience for modern readers.

FOREWORD TO THE
NEW EDITION

Let's face it, every Saint novel is essentially the same. In fact, that's a large part of their appeal: the same rhythms and verbal tropes, the purple passages, and the inevitable, implausible plot devices. The insouciant, raffish hero—an alter ego if ever there was one—is, of course, always and necessarily the same, and the large cast of his antagonists are in reality a handful of rather stock villains with interchangeable names. The plots creak dreadfully, women are always desirable and shapely but not really attainable, and the Saint, to be frank, wouldn't last more than five minutes in the dark, violent underworld he is supposed to inhabit.

And yet . . .

Is it nostalgia or something even more powerful that continues to make these novels not only readable but entertaining and satisfying? Nostalgia, now, there certainly is. Simon Templar's talk of honour, his romantic gestures, seem more and more old-fashioned, like a fading photograph. And the whole world of the novels—its entire reality— has very obviously disappeared.

But even so, the Saint's chivalrous code of behaviour, his very reason for being, still manages to resonate. In this wonderful, rickety novel—which I urge you to dive into—Charteris has several stabs at trying to define it. "You're kind," she said simply, "and you want so much that you can never have. You have an honour that honest people couldn't understand. You're not fighting against laws; you're fighting against life. You'd tear the world to pieces to find something that's only in your own mind, and when you've got it you'd find it was just a dream . . ." Elsewhere, the Saint reflects that "He had always been mad, by the Grace of God. He still was." He believes himself to be among the high elect of "divine lunatics."

Placing the Saint within a literary and romantic tradition that goes back to medieval prototypes (Simon, after all, is a Knight Templar) is not only clever of Charteris—who I had the great pleasure of meeting—but also helps to ensure his character's immortality. Despite the fact that his near-contemporary James Bond has gone on to greater fame and fortune, the fact is that Bond is a much shallower, more vulgar, less realized character. Bond also displays too many of his author's unpleasant psychological traits: he is a misogynist for whom women must be brutally possessed before being gratuitously and often deviantly dispensed with.

The Saint, as his name suggests, doesn't have a deviant bone in his body. Charteris would love to think of him as a dangerous, edgy, and lawless "outlaw," but he's as much—and as little —a real outlaw as Robin Hood. And like Robin Hood, he is surely a national treasure.

We need to go on embracing and reading about him, or lose whatever platonic ideal he still seems to represent.

—Michael Hirst

SAINT OVERBOARD

PREFACE

When this book was first published, it appeared with the following preface:

For the diving sequences in this story I am deeply indebted to Messrs. Siebe Gorman & Co., of Westminster Bridge Road, London, the well-known submarine engineers, who most kindly made it possible for me to obtain the first-hand experience of diving without which the latter part of this book could not possibly have been written.

For the idea of the story I am indebted solely to history. I have become so used to seeing the adjective "incredible" regularly used even in the most flattering reviews of the Saint's adventures, even when I have taken my plots from actual incidents which may be found in the files of any modern newspaper, that I almost hesitate to deprive the critics of their favourite word. But I have decided, after some profound searchings of heart, that in this case it is only fair to give them warning. For their benefit, therefore, and also for that of any other reader who may be interested, I should like to say that the facts mentioned on pages 23–25 may be verified by anyone who cares to take the trouble, and I submit that my solution of one of the most baffling mysteries of the sea is as plausible as any.

Obviously, this was long before the invention of the Aqualung brought "skin diving" to replace many of the cumbersome procedures described in some sequences in this story, to say nothing of special kinds of miniature submarine which can now cruise, observe, and perform certain sampling and pick-up operations at depths which seemed fantastic when Professor Yule invented his "bathystol."

That seems to be the trouble with writing any story that hinges on some fabulous invention, in the days we live in. Once upon a time, as with the imaginative predictions of Jules Verne, progress moved with enough dignity and deliberation to allow the book to become a quaint old classic, and the author to pass on to his immortality, before making his incredible creations merely commonplace. Today the most preposterous contraption a fictioneer can dream up is liable to be on sale in the neighbourhood drug store or supermarket while he is still trying to flog his paperback rights.

This is a trap I have fallen into a number of times, and I think I must now resolve to write no more stories of that type. I shall attempt no more adventurous predictions of what some mad (or even sane) scientist will come out with next.

But I am certainly not going to withdraw this story, or any other, simply because technology has outstripped many of the premises and limitations that it was based on. I think it still stands up as a rattling good adventure, and that should be enough for anybody's money. Including my own.

—Leslie Charteris

CHAPTER ONE:
HOW SIMON TEMPLAR'S SLEEP WAS
DISTURBED AND LORETTA PAGE
MADE AN APPOINTMENT

1

Simon Templar woke at the shout, when most men would probably
have stirred uneasily in their sleep and gone on sleeping. It was distant
enough for that, muffled by the multiple veils of white summer fog
that laid their fine prints of mist on the portholes and filled the night
with a cool dampness. The habit of years woke him, rather than the
actual volume of sound—years in which that lightning assessment and
responses to any chance sound, that almost animal awareness of events
even in sleep, that instantaneous leap to full consciousness of every
razor-edged faculty, might draw the thin precarious hair-line between
life and death.

He woke in a flash, without any sudden movement or alteration in
his rate of breathing. The only difference between sleep and wakefulness
was that his eyes were open and his brain searching back over his
memory of that half-heard shout for a more precise definition of its
meaning. Fear, anger, and surprise were there, without any articulate
expression . . . And then he heard the sharp voice of a gun, its echoes
drumming in a crisp clatter through the humid dark; another fainter
yell, and a splash . . .

He slid from between the blankets and swung his long legs over the side of the bunk with the effortless natural stealth of a great cat. The moist chill of the fog went into his lungs and goosefleshed his skin momentarily through the thin silk of his pyjamas as he hauled himself up the narrow companion, but he had the other animal gift of adapting himself immediately to temperature. That one reflex shiver nicked over him as his bare feet touched the dew-damp deck, and then he was nervelessly relaxed, leaning a little forward with his hands resting on the weatherboard of the after cockpit, listening for anything that might explain that queer interruption of his rest.

Overhead, according to the calendar, there was a full moon, but the banks of sea-mist which had rolled up towards midnight, in one of those freakish fits of temperament that sometimes strike the north coast of France in early summer, had blanketed its light down to a mere ghostly glimmer that did no more than lend a tinge of grey luminance to the cloudy dark. Over on the other side of the estuary St Malo was lost without trace: even the riding lights of the yacht nearest to his own struggled to achieve more than a phosphorescent blur in the baffling obscurity. His own lights shed a thin diffused aurora over the sleek seaworthy lines of the *Corsair*, and reached no further beyond than he could have spun a match. He could see nothing that would give him his explanation, but he could listen, and his ears shared in that uncanny keenness of all his senses.

He stood motionless, nostrils slightly dilated almost as if he would have brought scent to his aid against the fog and sniffed information out of the dank saltiness of the dark. He heard the whisper of ripples against the hull and the faint chatter of the anchor-chain dipping a link or two as the *Corsair* worked with the tide. He heard the sibilant creak of a rope as the dinghy strained against the side of a craft moored two berths away, and the clanking rumble of a train rolling over the steel ways somewhere behind the dull strip of almost imperceptible luminousness that was Dinard. The mournful hooting of a ship groping towards harbour, way-out over the Channel towards Cherbourg, hardly more than a quiver of vibration in the clammy stillness, told him its own clear story. The murmur of indistinguishable voices somewhere across the water where the shout had come from he heard also, and could build up his own picture from the plunk of shoe-heels against timber and the grate of an oar slipping into its rowlock. All these things delineated themselves on his mind like shadings of background detail on a photographic plate, but none of them had the exact pitch of what he was listening for.

He heard it, presently—an ethereal swish of water, a tiny pitter of stray drops from an incautiously lifted head tinking back into the oily tide, a rustle of swift movement in the grey gloom that was scarcely audible above the hiss and lap of the sea under his own keel. But he heard it, and knew that it was the sound he had been waiting for.

He listened, turning his head slightly, ears pricked for a more precise definition of the sound. Over in the fog where the voices had been muttering he heard the whirr of a lanyard whipped from its coiling, and the sudden splutter and drone of an outboard motor taking life jarred into the fine tuning of his attention. Then he cut it out again, as one tunes out an interfering station on a sensitive radio receiver, and touched on that silent dragging cleave of the water once more, that sluicing ripple of an expert swimmer striving to pass through the water quickly but without noise. Nearer, too. Coming directly towards him.

Still Simon Templar did not move, but his immobility had an electric tension about it, like that of a leopard about to spring. Whatever might be happening out in that steamy darkness was not strictly any concern of his, except in the role of public-spirited citizen— which he was not. But it was for just that blithe willingness to meddle in affairs which did not concern him that he had come by the *Corsair* herself and all his other outward tokens of unlimited wealth, and which made certain persons think it so epically absurd that he should go about with the nickname of the Saint. Only for that sublimely lawless curiosity, a variegated assortment of people whose habitats ranged from the gutters of Paris to the high spots of Broadway, from the beaches of the South Pacific to the most sanctified offices of Scotland Yard, could see no just reason why he should be taking a millionaire's holiday at Dinard instead of sewing mail-bags in Larkstone Prison or resting in a nice quiet cemetery with a stomachful of lead to digest. But the roots of that outlaw vigilance were too deep for cure, even if he had wished to cure them; and out there in the vaporous twilight something odd was happening of which he had to know more. Wherefore he listened, and heard the outboard chuffing around in the murk, and the swimmer coming closer.

And then he saw her. A shift of the air moved the mist-curtains capriciously at the very limit of his vision, and he saw her suddenly in the down-seeping nimbus of his riding lights.

Her.

It was that realisation of sex, guessed rather than positively asserted by the dimly-seen contour of her features and the glistening curve of a green bathing cap, which sent a skin- deep tingle of intuition plunging into profound and utter certainty. If it had been a man, he would not have lost interest, but he could have produced half a dozen commonplace theories to assimilate that final fact, with a regretful premonition that the adventure would not be likely to run for long. But a girl swimming stealthily through a fogbound sea at three o'clock in the morning could not be associated with yells and shooting in the dark by any prosaic theory, and his pulses, which up to that moment had been ticking over as steadily as clockwork, throbbed a shade faster at the knowledge. Somewhere out there in the leaden haze big medicine was seething up, and inevitably it was ordained that he must dip his spoon in the brew.

He was standing so motionless, half cloaked by the deep shadow of the deckhouse, that she had taken three more long strokes towards the ketch before she saw him. She stopped swimming abruptly, and stared up—he could almost read the wild thought tearing through her mind that she was caught in a trap, that in such a situation he could not help challenging her. And then, as the monotonous chugging of the outboard circled round and came closer, he caught in her upturned eyes a frantic forlorn-hope appeal, a desperate voiceless entreaty that placed the ultimate seal on his destiny in that adventure.

He leaned over the side and grasped her wrist, and her first revelation of his steel-wire strength was the amazing ease with which he lifted her inboard with one hand. Without a word he pushed her down on the floor of the cockpit and unhitched a fender, dipping it in the water to repeat the faint splash she had made as she came out.

At that moment the outboard loomed up through the mist and coughed itself to silence. Dropping the fender to water level once again, so that there should be no doubt left in any interested minds about the origin of whatever noise had been heard from that quarter, he adjusted it under the gunwale of his dinghy and made it fast to the stanchion from which he had slipped it. The other boat was gliding up under its own momentum while he did so, and he was able to make a swift summary of its occupants.

There were three of them. Two, in rough seamen's jerseys, sat in the stern sheets, one of them holding the tiller and the other rewinding the starter lanyard. The third man was sitting on one of the thwarts forward, but as the boat slid nearer he rose to his feet.

Simon Templar studied him with an interest that never appeared more than casual.

From his position in the boat, his well-cut reefer jacket and white trousers, and the way he stood up, he was obviously the leader of the party. A tallish well-built man with one hand resting rather limply in his coat pocket—a typical wealthy yachtsman going about his own mysterious business. And yet, to the Saint, who had in his time walked out alive from the bright twisted places where men who keep one hand in a side pocket are a phenomenon that commands lightning alertness, there was something in the well-groomed impassivity of him as he rose there to his full height that touched the night with a new tingling chill that was nevertheless a kind of unlawful ecstasy. For a couple of seconds the Saint saw his face as the dinghy hissed under the lee of the *Corsair*, a long swarthy black-browed face with a great eagle's beak of a nose.

Then the beam of a powerful flashlight blazed from the man's free hand, blotting out his face behind its dazzling attack. For a moment it dwelt on Simon's straightening figure, and he knew that in that moment the dryness of his hair and his pyjamas were methodically noted and reduced to their apparent place in the scheme of things. Then the light swept on, surveyed the lines of the ketch from stern to bow, rested for another moment on the name lettered there, and went flickering over the surrounding water.

"Lost something?" Simon inquired genially, and the light came back to him.

"Not exactly." The voice was clear and dispassionate, almost lackadaisical in its complete emptiness of expression. "Have you seen anyone swimming around here?"

"A few unemployed fish," murmured the Saint pleasantly.

"Or are you looking for the latest Channel swimmer? They usually hit the beach further east, towards Calais."

There was a barely perceptible pause before the man chuckled, but even then, to the Saint's abnormally sensitive ears, there was no natural good humour in the sound. It was simply an efficient adaptation to circumstances, a suave get-out from a situation that bristled with question marks.

"No—nothing like that. Just one of our party took on a silly bet. I expect he's gone back."

And with that, for Simon Templar, a flag somewhere among the ghostly armadas of adventure was irrevocably nailed to the mast. The mystery had crept out of the night and caught him. For the tall hook nosed man's reply presumed that he hadn't heard any of the other sounds associated with the swimmer, and, presuming that, it stepped carefully into the pitfall of its own surpassing smoothness. More—it attempted deliberately to lead him astray. A swim on a foggy night that included gun-play and the peculiar kind of shout that had awakened him belonged to a species of silly bet which the Saint had still to meet, and he couldn't help being struck by the fact that it disposed so adequately of the obvious theory of an ordinary harbour theft, and the hue and cry which should have arisen from such an explanation. Even without the glaring error of sex in the last sentence, that would have been almost enough.

He stood and watched the search party vanishing on their way into the fog, the flashlight in the hook nosed man's hand blinking through the mist until it was lost to sight, and then he turned and slid down the companion into the saloon, switching on the lights as he did so. He heard the girl follow him down, but he drew the curtains over the portholes before he turned to look at her.

2

She had pulled off the green bathing cap, and her hair had tumbled to her shoulders in a soft disorder of chestnut rippled with spun gold. Her red mouth seemed to be of the quality that triumphs even over salt water, and the purely perfunctory covering of her attenuated bathing costume left room for no deception about the perfection of her slender sun-gilt figure. Her steady grey eyes held a tentative gleam of mischief, soberly checked at that moment and yet incorrigibly seeking for natural expression, which for one fleeting instant worked unpardonable magic on his breathing.

"A bit wet in the water tonight, isn't it?" he remarked coolly.

"Just a little."

He pulled open a drawer and selected a couple of towels. As an afterthought, he detached a bathrobe from its hook and dropped that also on the couch.

"D'you prefer brandy or hot coffee?"

"Thanks." The impulse of mischief in her eyes was only a wraith of itself, masked down by a colder intentness. "But I think I'd better be getting back—to collect my bet. It was awfully good of you to—understand so quickly—and—and help me."

She held out her hand, in a quick gesture of final friendliness, with a smile which ought to have left the Saint gaping dreamily after her until she was lost again in the night.

"Oh, yes." Simon took the hand, but he didn't complete the action by letting go of it immediately as he should have done. He put one foot up on the couch and rested his forearm on his knee, and the quiet light of amusement that twinkled in his sea-blue eyes was suddenly very gay and disturbing. "Of course, I did hear something about a bet—"

"It—it was rather a stupid one, I suppose." She took her hand away, and her voice steadied itself and became clearer. "We were just talking about how easy it would be to get away with anything on a foggy night, and somehow or other it got around to my saying that I could swim to Dinard and back without them finding me. They'd nearly caught me when you pulled me on board. I don't know if that was allowed for in the bet, but—"

"And the shooting?"

Her fine brows came together for a moment.

"That was just part of the make-believe. We were pretending that I'd come out to rob the ship—"

"And the shouting?"

"That was part of it, too. I suppose it all sounds very idiotic—"

The Saint smiled. He slipped a cigarette out of a packet on the shelf close by and tapped it.

"Oh, not a bit. I like these games myself—they do help to pass away the long evenings.

Who did the shooting?"

"The man who spoke to you from the dinghy."

"I suppose he didn't shoot himself by mistake? It was a most realistic job of yelling." Simon's voice expressed nothing but gentle interest and approval; his smile was deceptively lazy. And then he left the cigarette in his mouth and stretched out his hand again. "By the way, that's a jolly-looking gadget."

There was a curious kind of thick rubber pouch strapped on the belt of her swim suit, and he had touched it before she could draw back.

"It's just one of those waterproof carriers for cigarettes and a vanity case. Haven't you seen them before?"

"No." He took his foot down again from the couch, rather deliberately. "May I look?"

The note of casual, politely apologetic inquisitiveness was perfectly done. They might have been carrying on an idle conversation on the beach in broad sunlight, but she stepped back before he could touch the case again.

"I—I think I'd better be getting back. Really. The others will be starting to worry about me."

He nodded.

"Perhaps they will," he admitted. "But you can't possibly go swimming about in this mess. You don't know what a risk you're taking. It's a hundred to one you'd miss your boat, and it's cold work splashing around in circles. I'll run you back."

"Please don't bother. Honestly, the water isn't so cold—"

"But you are." His smiling eyes took on the slight shiver of her brown body. "And it's no trouble."

He passed her with an easy stride, and he was on the companion when she caught his arm.

"Please! Besides, the bet doesn't—"

"Damn the bet, darling. You're too young and good-looking to be washed up stiff on the beach. Besides, you've broken the rules already by coming on board. I'll take you over, and you can just swim across if you like."

"I won't go with you. Please don't make it difficult." "You won't go without me."

He sat down on the companion, filling the narrow exit with his broad shoulders. She bit her lip.

"It's sweet of you," she said hesitantly. "But I couldn't give you any more trouble. I'm not going."

"Then you ought to use those towels and decide about the brandy and/or coffee," said the Saint amiably. "Of course, it may compromise you a bit, but I'm broad-minded. And if this is going to be Romance, may I start by saying that your mouth is the loveliest—"

"No, no! I'm not going to let you row me back."

"Then I take it you've made up your mind to stay. That's what I was talking about. And while we're on the subject, don't you know that it's immoral for anyone to have legs like yours? They put the wickedest ideas—"

"Please." There was a beginning of reluctant anger creeping into her gaze. "It's been nice of you to help me. Don't spoil it now."

Simon Templar inhaled deeply from his cigarette and said nothing.

Her grey eyes darkened with a scrap of half-incredulous fear that clashed absurdly with the careless good humour of his unvarying smile. Then, as if she was putting the ridiculous idea away, she came forward resolutely and tried to pass him.

One of his long arms reached out effortlessly and closed the remainder of the passage. She fought against it, half playfully at first, and then with all her lithe young strength, but it was as immovable as a bar of iron. In a sudden flash of panic savagery she beat at his chest and shoulders with her fists, but it was like hitting pads of toughened rubber. He laughed softly, without resentment, and she became aware that his other hand had been carefully exploring the form of the curious little pouch on her belt while she fought.

She fell back quickly, staring at him.

"I thought it clunked," he murmured, "when I pulled you in. And yet you don't look as if you had a cast-iron vanity."

Her breath was coming faster now, and he knew that it was not only from her exertions.

"I don't know what you're talking about. Will you let me out?"

"No."

He liked her spirit. The trace of mischief in her eyes was gone altogether, by this time, frozen into a sparkle of dangerous exasperation.

"Have you thought," she asked slowly, "what would happen if I screamed?"

"I suppose it couldn't help being pretty musical, as screams go. Your ordinary speaking voice—"

"I could rouse half the harbour."

He nodded, without shifting his strategic position on the companion. "It looks like being a noisy night."

"If you don't let me go at once—"

Simon Templar extended his legs luxuriously and blew smoke-rings.

"Sister," he said, "have you stopped to consider what would happen if I screamed?" "What?"

"You see, it isn't as if this was your boat. If I'd swum out and invaded you at this hour, and you'd been wearing pyjamas instead of me, and more or less the same argument had taken place—well, I guess you could have screamed most effectively. But there's a difference. This tub is mine, and you're trespassing. Presumably you couldn't put up a story that I kidnapped you, because then people would ask why you hadn't screamed before. Besides, you're wearing a wet bathing costume, which would want a whole lot more explaining. No— the only thing I can see to it is that you invited yourself. And the time is now moving on to half-past three in the morning. Taking it by and large, I can't help feeling that you'd be answering a lot of embarrassing questions about why you took such a long time to get frightened. Besides which, this is a French port, with French authorities, and Frenchmen have such a wonderful grip on the facts of life. I am a very retiring sort of bloke," said the Saint shyly, "and I don't mind telling you that my modesty has been outraged. If you make another attempt to assault me—"

The grey eyes cut him with ice-cold lights.

"I didn't think you were that sort of man."

"Oh, but I am. Now why don't you look at the scenery, darling? We could have quite a chat before you go home. I want to know what this gay game is that starts shooting in the night and sends you swimming through the fog. I want to know what makes you and Hooknose string along with the same crazy story, and what sort of a bet it is that makes you go bathing with a gun on your belt!"

The last fragment of his speech was not quite accurate. Even as he uttered it, her hand flashed to the waterproof pouch, and he looked down the muzzle of a tiny automatic that was still large enough to be an argument at point-blank range.

"You're quite right about the gun," she said, with a new glacial evenness in her voice. "And, as you say, Frenchmen have such a wonderful grip on the facts of life—haven't they? Their juries are pretty easy on a woman who shoots her lover . . . Don't you think you'd better change your mind?"

Simon considered this. She saw the chiselling of his handsome reckless face, the bantering lines of devil-may-care mouth and eyebrow, settle for a moment into quiet calculation, and then go back to the same irresponsible amusement.

"Anyway," he remarked, "she does give the fellow his fun first. Stay the night and shoot me after breakfast, and I won't complain."

The magnificent unfaltering audacity of him left her for a moment without words. For the first time her eyes wavered, and he read in them something that might have been an unwilling regret.

"For the last time—"

"Will I let you go."

"Yes."

"No."

"I'm sorry."

"So am I," said the Saint gently. "From the brief gander I had at Hooknose just a little while back, he looked like a man's job to me. I know you've got what it takes, but these games can get pretty tough. Tough things are my job, and I hate being jockeyed out of a good fight."

"I'm going now," she said. "I mean it. Don't think I'm afraid to shoot, because I'm ready for accidents. I'll count five while you get out of the way." The Saint looked at her for a second, and shook his head.

"Oh, well," he said philosophically. "If you feel that way about it . . ."

He stood up unhurriedly. And as he stood up, one hand slid up the bulkhead with him and touched the light switch.

For the first instant the darkness in the cabin was absolute. In the sudden contrasting blackness that drenched down across her vision she lost even a silhouette of him in the opening above the companion. And then his fingers closed and tightened on her wrist like a steel tourniquet. She struggled and tripped against the couch, falling on the soft cushions, but he went down with her, and her hand went numb so that she had no power even to pull the trigger while he took the automatic away. She heard his quiet chuckle.

"I'm sorry, kid."

As they had fallen, his lips were an inch from hers. He bent his head, so that his mouth touched them. She fought him wildly, but the kiss clung against all her fighting, and then suddenly she was passive and bewildering in his arms.

Simon got up and switched on the lights.

3

"I'm Loretta Page," she said.

She sat wrapped in his great woolly bathrobe, sipping hot coffee and smoking one of his cigarettes. The Saint sat opposite her, with his feet up and his head tilted back on the bulkhead.

"It's a nice name," he said.

"And you?"

"I have dozens. Simon Templar is the only real one. Some people call me the Saint." She looked at him with a new intentness.

"Why?"

"Because I'm so very, very respectable."

"I've read about you," she said. "But I never heard anything like that before." He smiled.

"Perhaps it isn't true."

"There was a Professor Vargan who—got killed, wasn't there? And an attempt to blow up a royal train and start a war which went wrong."

"I believe so."

"I've heard of a revolution in South America that you had something to do with, and a plot to hijack a bullion shipment where you got in the way. Then they were looking for you in Germany about some crown jewels. I've heard that there's a Chief Inspector at Scotland Yard who'd sell his soul to pin something on you, and another one in New York who thinks you're one of the greatest things that ever happened. I've heard that there isn't a racket running that doesn't get cold shivers at the name of a certain freelance vigilante—"

"Loretta," said the Saint, "you know far too much about this life of sin."

"I ought to," she said. "I'm a detective."

The immobility of his face might have been carved in bronze, when the light-hearted mockery left it and only the buccaneer remained. In those subtle transformations she saw half his spell, and the power that must have made him what he was. There was a dance of alertness like the twinkle of a rapier blade, a veneer of flippant nonchalance cored with tempered steel, a fine humour of unscrupulousness that demoralised all conventional criterions.

And then his cigarette was back in his mouth and he was smiling at her through a haze of smoke, with blue eyes awake again and both wrists held out together.

"When arrested," he said, "the notorious scoundrel said, 'I never had a chance. My parents neglected me, and I was led astray by bad companions. The ruin of my life is due to Night Starvation. Where are the bracelets?'"

She might not have heard him. She sprang up, stretching her arms so that the sleeves of the bathrobe fell back from her wrists.

"Oh, no! . . . It's too perfect. I'm glad!" The mischief was in her eyes again, matching his own, almost eclipsing it for that moment of vibrant energy. "You're telling the truth, I know. The Saint could only have been you. You would go out and take on any racket with your hands. Why didn't you tell me at once?"

"You didn't ask me," answered the Saint logically. "Besides, modesty is my long suit. The threat of publicity makes me run for miles. When I blush—"

"Listen!"

She wheeled and dropped on the berth beside him, and he listened.

"You've stolen, haven't you?"

"With discretion."

"You've tackled some big things."

"I pick up elephants and wring their necks."

"Have you ever thought of stealing millions?"

"Often," said the Saint, leaning back. "I thought of burgling the Bank of England once, but I decided it was too easy." She stirred impatiently.

"Saint," she said earnestly, "there's one racket working today that steals millions. It's been running for years, and it's still running. And I don't mean any of the old things like bootlegging or kidnapping. It's a racket that goes over most of the world, wherever there's anything for it to work on, and it hits where there's no protection. I couldn't begin to guess how much money has been taken out of it since it began."

"I know, darling," said the Saint sympathetically. "But you can't do anything about it. It's quite legal. It's called income tax."

"Have you heard of the *Lutine*?"

He studied her with his gaze still tantalising and unsatisfied, but the eagerness of her held him more than what she was actually saying. He was discovering something between her soft-lipped beauty and her fire of anger; something that belonged equally to the lurking laughter of her eyes and the sober throb of persuasion in her voice, and yet was neither of these things; something that made all contradictions possible.

"It sank, didn't it?" he said.

"In 1799—with about a million pounds' worth of gold on board. There've been plenty of attempts to salve the cargo, but so far the sand's been too much for them. Then the Lutina Company took over with a new idea: they were going to suck away the silt through a big conical sort of bell which was to be lowered over the wreck. It was quite a simple scheme, and there's no reason why it shouldn't have worked. The company received a few letters warning them not to go on with it, but naturally they didn't pay much attention to them."

"Well?"

"Well, they haven't tried out their sand-sucker yet. The whole thing was blown sky- high in 1933—and the explosion wasn't an accident."

The Saint sat up slowly. In that supple movement the buffoonery slipped off him as his dressing-gown might have slipped off, and in the same transformation he was listening intently. Something like a breath of frozen feathers strolled up his spine—an instinct, a queer clairvoyance born of the years of inspired filibustering.

"Is that all the story?" he asked, and knew that it was not.

She shook her head.

"Something else happened in the same year. An American salvage ship, the *Salvor*, went out to search a wreck off Cape Charles. The *Merida*, which sank in 1911 and took the Emperor Maximilian's crown jewels to the bottom with her—another million-pound cargo. They didn't find anything. And fish don't wear jewellery."

"I remember the Terschelling Island fireworks—the Lutine. But that's a new one."

"It's not the only one. Two years before that another salvage company went over the *Turbantia* with a fine comb. She was torpedoed near the Maars Lightship in 1916, and she had seven hundred and fifty thousand pounds' worth of German bullion on her—then. The salvage company knew just where to look for it. But they didn't find it . . . That was quite a small job. But in 1928 the Sorima Company made an official search for a collection of uncut diamonds and other stones *worth more than a million and a quarter*, which were on board the *Elizabethville* when another U-boat got her on her way back from South Africa during the war. Well, they found a lot of ammunition in the strong-room, and thirty shillings in the safe, which didn't show a big dividend."

"And this has been going on for years?"

"I don't know how long. But just look at those three jobs. They average out at over a million pounds a time. Leave out all the other official treasure hunts that are going on now, and all the other millions that may have been sneaked away before the authorised salvage companies get there. Leave out all the other jobs that haven't been discovered yet. Doesn't it tell you anything?"

Simon Templar sat back and let the electric tingles play up his vertebrae and toe- dance airily over the back of his scalp. His whole body felt the pulse of adventure in exactly the same way as a sensitively tuned instrument can detect sounds inaudible to the human ear. And to him the sounds were music.

In that short silence he had a vivid picture of all the far reaches of the sea on which the *Corsair* cushioned her light weight. He saw the lift of storms and the raw break of hungry rocks and death stealing out of the invisible to give the waters their treasure. He saw the green depths, the ultimate dim places under the spume and sapphire beauty, saw the vast whale-shapes of steel hulls sunk in the jade stillness, and the gaunt ribs of half-forgotten galleons reaching out of the fronds of weed. What unrecorded argosies might lie under those infinite waters, no one would ever know. But those that were known, those that the sea had claimed even in the last four hundred years . . . His imagination reeled at the thought. The *Almirante Florencia*, lost treasure-house of the Armada, foundering in Tobermory Bay with two million pounds in plate and jewels. The Russian flagship *Rurik*, sunk on the Korean coast with two and a half million pounds in specie. The sixty-three ships of the Turkish Navy sent to the bottom of Navarino Bay in 1827 with ten million pounds between them. The *Chalfont Castle*, with her steering carried away and her plates sprung below the waterline in the great storm of that very year, drifting helplessly down on to the Casquets to the west of Alderney, and sinking in twenty fathoms with five million pounds of bar gold in her strong-room. Odd names and figures that he had heard disinterestedly from time to time and practically forgotten crept back from the hinterlands of unconscious memory and staggered him . . . And he saw the only possible, the only plausible corollary: the ghost pirate stealing through grey dawns to drop her divers and her steel grabs, the unsuspected gangsters of the sea who had discovered the most pluperfect racket of all time.

He would have thought that he had heard every note in the register of crime, but he had never dreamed of anything like that. The plot to swindle the Bank of Italy by means of one million perfectly genuine 100-lire bills, for his share in which he was entitled to wear the pendant of the Order of the Annunziata in the unlikely event of his ever attending a State function, was mere petty pilfering beside it. Sir Hugo Renway's scheme for pillaging the cross- Channel gold routes was mere clumsy experiment in comparison. And yet he knew that the girl who sat looking at him was not romancing. She threw up the stark terse facts and left him to find the link, and the supernatural creep of his nerves told him where the link was.

Her grey eyes were on him, tempting and challenging as they had been when he first saw her with the lights striking gold in her hair and the sea's damp on her slim shoulders, and in his mind he had a vision of the black expressionless eyes of the hook nosed man who stood up in the boat and lied to him.

"Why?" he said, with a dreamy rapture in his slow deep breath. "Why didn't I know all this before?"

"Perhaps you were too busy."

"Anything else could have waited," said the Saint, with profound conviction. "Except perhaps the Bank of England . . . And is that what you're detecting?"

She took a cigarette from his pack, and a light from the butt between his fingers.

"Yes. I work for the Ingerbeck Agency—we have a contract with Lloyd's, and we handle a lot of other insurance business. You see, where we work, there's no ordinary police force. Where a ship sinks, the wreck is nominally under the protection of the country that covers the water, but if the underwriters have paid out a total loss the salvage rights belong to them. Which means precisely nothing. In the last fifty years alone, the insurance companies have paid out millions of pounds on this kind of risk. Of course they hoped to get a lot of it back in salvage, but the amounts they've seen would make you laugh."

"Is it always a loss?"

"Of course not. But we've known—they've known—for a long time, that there was some highly organised racket in the background cheating them out of six figures or more a year. It's efficient. It's got to be. And yet it's easy. It has clever men, and the best equipment that money can buy. We went out to look for them."

"You?"

"Oh, no. Ingerbeck's. They've been on it for the last five years. Some of their men went a long way. Three of them went too far—and didn't come back." She met his eyes steadily. "It's that sort of racket . . . But one of them found a trail that led somewhere, out of hundreds that didn't, and it's been followed up."

"To here?"

She nodded.

"You see, we came to a brick wall. The men could get so far, but they couldn't go on. They couldn't get inside the racket. Two of those who didn't come back—tried. We couldn't take a chance on anything drastic, because we've no official standing, and we hadn't any facts. Only a good guess. Well, there was one other way. Somewhere at the top of the racket there must be a head man, and the odds are that he's human."

He took in the grace of her as she lounged there in the oversized bathrobe, understanding the rest.

"You came out to be human with him."

The turn of her head was sorcery, the sculpture of her neck merging into the first hinted curve between the lapels of the bathrobe was a pattern of magic that made murder and sudden death egregious intrusions.

"I didn't succeed—so far. I've tried. I've even had dinner with him, and danced at the Casino. But I haven't had an invitation to go on board his boat. Tonight I got the devil in me, or something. I tried to go on board without an invitation."

"Didn't you guess there'd be a watch on deck?"

"I suppose so. But I thought he'd probably be sleepy, and I could move very quietly." She grimaced. "He got me, but he let me go when I fired a shot beside his ear—I didn't hurt him—and I dived overboard."

"And thereby hangs a tale," said the Saint.

4

He stood up and flicked his cigarette-end through a porthole, helping himself to another. The lines of his face were lifted in high relief as he drew at a match.

"You didn't tell me all this to pass the time, did you?" he smiled.

"I told you because you're—you." She was looking at him directly, without a trace of affected hesitation. "I've no authority. But I've seen you, and I know who you are. Maybe I thought you might be interested."

She straightened the bathrobe quickly, looking round for an ashtray. "Maybe I might," he said gently. "Where are you staying?"

"The Hotel de la Mer."

"I wish you could stay here. But tonight—I'm afraid there must be a thin chance that your boyfriend wasn't quite satisfied with my lines when we exchanged words, and you can't risk it. Another time—"

Her eyes opened wider, and he stretched out his hand with a breath of laughter. "I'm going to row you home now," he said. "Or do we have another argument?"

"I wouldn't argue," she began silkily, and then, with the corners of her mouth tugging against her will, she took his hand. "But thanks for the drink—and everything."

"There are only two things you haven't told me," he said. "One is the name of this boat you wanted to look at."

She searched his face for a moment before she answered, "The *Falkenberg.*"

"And the other is the name of the boyfriend—the bloke who passed in the night."

"Kurt Vogel."

"How very appropriate," said the Saint thoughtfully, "I think I shall call him Birdie when we get acquainted. But that can wait . . . I want to finish my beauty sleep, and I suppose you haven't even started yours. But I've got a hunch that if you're on the beach before lunch we may talk some more. I'm glad you dropped in."

The fog was thinning to a pearl-grey vagueness lightening with the dawn when he rowed her back, and when he woke up there were ovals of yellow sunlight stencilled along the bulkhead from the opposite portholes. He stretched himself like a cat, freshening his lungs with the heady nectar of the morning, and lighted a cigarette. For a while he lay sprawled in delicious laziness, taking in the familiar cabin with a sense of new discovery. There she had sat, there was the cup and glass she had used, there was the crushed stub of her cigarette in the ashtray. There on the carpet was still a darkened patch of damp, where she had stood with the salt water dewing her slim legs and pooling on the floor. He saw the ripple of gold in her hair, the shaft of challenge in her eyes, the exquisite shape of her as he first saw her like a shy nymph spiced with the devil's temper, and knew a supreme content which was not artistically rewarded by the abrupt apparition of a belligerent face sheltering behind a loose walrus moustache in the door leading to the galley.

"Lovely morn'n, sir," said the face, and limped struttingly in to plunk down a glass of orange juice beside him. "Brekfuss narf a minnit."

The Saint grinned ruefully and hauled himself up.

"Make it two minutes, Orace," he said. "I had company last night."

"Yessir," said Orace phlegmatically, gathering up cups, and he had retired to the galley again before Simon saw that he had left a second glass of orange juice ostentatiously parked in the middle of the table.

The mist had receded under the sun until it was only a haze on the horizon, and a sky of pale translucent azure lofted over a sea like glass. Simon went up on deck with a towel round his middle and slipped adroitly into the water, leaving the towel behind. He cut away across the estuary in a straight line of hissing crawl, turned and rolled over on his back to wallow in the invigorating delight of cold water sheathing his naked limbs, and made his way back more leisurely to eat bacon and eggs in a deck chair in the spacious cockpit while the strengthening sun warmed his shoulders.

All these things, then, were real—the physical gusto of life, quickened by unasked romance and laced with the wine of danger. Even the privileged cynicism of Orace only served as a touchstone to prove reality, rather than to destroy illusion. It was like the old days— which as a matter of fact were by no means so old. He lighted a cigarette and scanned the other boats which he could see from his anchorage. A cable's length away, towards the Pointe de la Vicomté, he picked a white rakish motor cruiser of about a hundred tons, and knew that this must be the one even before he went down to the saloon for a pair of binoculars and read the name from a lifebelt. *Falkenberg*. Simon's lips twitched in a half-smile that was entirely Saintly. The name of the legendary Flying Dutchman was a perfect baptism for the pirate ship of that hawk-faced black-browed man who called himself Kurt Vogel, and the Saint mentally saluted the Antarctic quality of bravado that must have chosen it. Still using his binoculars from the prudent obscurity of the saloon, he took in the high outswept bows and the streamlined angles of the wheelhouse forward, the clean lines of superstructure dipping to the unusually low flat counter, and credited her with twin racing engines and a comfortable thirty knots. Abaft the saloon there was a curious projection neatly shrouded in canvas—for the moment he could not guess what it was.

He stropped his razor and ran water into a basin, and he was finishing his shave when his man came through with the breakfast plates. Simon rounded his chin carefully and said, "Orace, have you still got that blunderbuss of yours—the young howitzer you bought once in mistake for a gun?"

"Yessir," said Orace unemotionally.

"Good." The Saint wiped his razor and splashed water over his face. "You'd better get out my automatic as well and look it over."

"Yessir."

"Put a spot of oil in the works and load up a couple of spare magazines. And grease the cartridges—in case I take a swim with it."

"Yessir."

"We may be busy."

Orace's moustache stirred, like a field of corn under a passing zephyr. His limp was a souvenir of Zeebrugge Mole and days of authorised commotion as a sergeant of His Majesty's Marines, but it is doubtful whether even in those years of international discord he had heard as many different calls to arms as had come his way since he first took service with the Saint.

"'Ave you bin gettin' in trouble again?" he demanded fiercely. The Saint laughed behind his towel.

"Not trouble, Orace—just fun. I won't try to tell you how beautiful she is, because you have no soul. But she came out of the sea like a mermaid, and the standard of living went up again like a rocket. And would you mind moving off that bit of the carpet, because the comparison is too hideous. She stood there with the water on her, and she said 'Will you let me out?' And I said 'No!' Just like that."

"Did yer, sir?"

"And she pulled a gun on me."

"Go on, did she?"

"She pulled a gun. Look, you pull a gun. Hold your hand like that. Right. Well, I said 'Ha, ha,'—like that, very sinister. I switched out the lights! I leapt upon her! I grabbed her wrist! We fell on the bunk—"

"Steady on, sir, yer 'urting!"

"You shut up. She was crushed against me. Her lips were an inch from mine. For heaven's sake stop whiffling your moustache like that. I felt her breath on my face. I was on fire with passion. I seized her in my arms . . . and . . ." Simon planted a smacking kiss on his crew's horrified brow. "I said 'Don't you think Strindberg is too sweet?' Now go and drown yourself."

He picked himself up and erupted out of the cabin, slinging the towel round his neck, while Orace gaped goggle-eyed after him. In a few minutes he was back, tightening the belt of a pair of swimming trunks, and stuffing cigarettes into a waterproof metal case.

"By the way," he said, "we aren't full up on juice for the auxiliary. As soon as you've cleared up, you'd better take the dinghy and fetch a couple of dozen *bidons*. Get some oil, too, and see that there's plenty of food and drink. There's another bird mixed up in this who's less beautiful—a guy named Kurt Vogel—and we ought to be ready for travelling."

He went up on deck and looked around. The sun was flooding down on stucco villas and the rise of green behind, and cutting innumerable diamonds from the surface of the water. It was going to be a hot brilliant day. People were well awake on the other yachts nearby. A gramophone opened up cheerfully on one, and a loud splash and a shout heralded another of the morning's bathers. The *Falkenberg* was too far away for him to be able to distinguish its signs of life: a couple of seamen were swabbing down the paint forward, but nothing that resembled the hook nosed man was visible. Simon noticed that besides the outboard dinghy there was now a small speed tender also tied up alongside which had not been there when he made his first survey—it had the air of being part of the *Falkenberg*'s equipment, and probably it had been away on a trip to the shore and returned while he was below.

After a while he dived off the side and swam round the Pointe du Moulinet to the beach. He strolled the length of the plage while the sun dried him, and then chose a clear space to stretch himself out opposite the Casino.

He had not seen Loretta Page during his walk, but he knew she would come. He lay basking in the voluptuous warmth, and knew with an exquisite certainty that the kind gods of adventure would take care of that. The story she had told him went through his memory, not in an exuberant riot of comprehension as it had when he first heard it, but in a steady flow, fact by fact, a sequence of fragments of accepted knowledge which strung logically together to make a tale that was breath-taking in its colossal implications. If it was something on a more grandiose scale than anything he had ever dreamed of even in his wildest flights of buccaneering, he was still ready to give it a run. He blew smoke into the sparkling air and considered the profile of Kurt Vogel. Properly worked on by an octet of bunched knuckles . . .

"Hullo, old timer."

He dropped his gaze and saw her. She wore the same elementary swim suit, with a bathrobe that fitted her better than his had done, swept back by her hands on her hips and leaving her long satiny legs to the sun. The grey eyes were dark with devilment.

He rolled up on one elbow. "Hullo, pardner."

"Did you sleep well?"

"I saw ghosts," he said sepulchrally. "Ghosts of the dead past that can never be undone. They rose up and wiggled their bony fingers at me, and said 'You are not worthy of her!' I woke up and burst into tears."

She slipped out of the striped gown and sat down beside him. "Wasn't there any hope?"

"Not unless you stretched out your little hand and lifted me out of the abyss. Couldn't you take on the job of saving a lost soul? Of course you might always get lost yourself, but that wouldn't matter. We could always console each other."

"I wonder why Ingerbeck's didn't think of signing you up years ago." He smiled.

"They might have tried, but I'm afraid I haven't got any sort of affinity for dotted lines. Besides, I'm not naturally honest. You try to recover stolen property for the insurance companies, don't you?"

"That's part of the job."

"Well, I do the same thing, but not for any insurance company."

"Not even on a ten per cent commission?"

"I have worked on that basis, but it was a long time ago. My tastes were a lot more innocent and simple in those days."

"It's not a bad reward, when there are millions to look for," she said temptingly.

He sighed.

"It's so dull to be honest. Nobody else but you could make it even bearable. But I know what you mean. I'm on a holiday, and I can always pick up a few millions some other time. It was your picnic originally, and you let me in on it—"

"I needn't have done that."

There was a cool and rather sad finality in her voice, so much in contrast to the wavering dance of her eyes that he looked at her keenly for a moment before replying. In that vivid and carefree surround of laughing swimmers and brightly-clad sunbathers he felt a shadow round them, cutting them off in a dynamic isolation of their own from all these thoughtless and ordinary things.

"It was my charm," he explained at length. "My father-confessor touch. You just couldn't resist me."

She shook her head. The gold flashed in her hair, and her lips smiled, but the light mockery of her eyes was subdued to an elfin seriousness.

"I mean I needn't have given up hope and gone in for such desperate measures so soon."

"What's happened?" he asked, and the brown smooth-muscled arm on which he was propped up turned so that his hand closed over hers.

She looked down at him steadily, and the shadow around them failed to touch her enchanting face.

"I had a note this morning," she said. "It was delivered at the hotel before I woke up.

I've got an invitation to have dinner with Vogel on the *Falkenberg*."

CHAPTER TWO:

HOW SIMON TEMPLAR ALSO RECEIVED AN INVITATION AND A PAIR OF PINK SOCKS HOVE UP ON THE HORIZON

1

A stout gentleman ambled by, with a green eyeshade on his brow and a diminutive slip clinging by some miracle of adhesion to the re-entrant curve of his abdomen, looking like a debauched Roman emperor on his way to the bath; a Parisian sylph in a startling lace costume that left nothing except her birthday to the imagination arranged her white limbs artistically under a gaudy sunshade and waited for the rush of art students to gather round; two children disputing the ownership of a bucket opened up on a line of personalities that would have left a couple of bootleggers listening in awe; but these were events that might have been happening on another planet.

He remembered the speedboat tied up alongside the *Falkenberg*, which had not been there before.

"You hadn't got some crazy idea of accepting, had you?" he said mechanically. "It's what I've been waiting for."

"I know, but—what do you think happened last night?" She took one of his cigarettes.

"I don't think I could have been seen. I didn't see the man who caught me—he came up behind. And it was pretty dark where I was.

He caught me round the neck with his arm; then I fired the shot, he let go, and I dived."

"He'd know it was a woman."

"Not necessarily. Don't you remember that Vogel said he was looking for a man?"

"An obvious lie."

"A very stupid one—if it was. But what could it gain him? If you'd already seen a woman, it'd make you think there was something queer going on. If you hadn't, what did it matter?"

"He might have been trying to tempt me to keep up the lie—which would have given me away."

She shrugged her intoxicating shoulders. "Aren't you rather looking for trouble?" she said.

"That's my job," answered the Saint evenly. "And incidentally, it happens to be one of the reasons why I didn't come to a sticky end many years ago. I'll give you something else. Suppose Vogel wasn't quite happy about me last night?"

"Well?"

"It was rather an unusual hour for anyone to be up and about—messing around with fenders. Not impossible, but unusual. And if Vogel's the kind of man we think he is, he keeps alive by sorting out unusual things—like I do. He couldn't make any fuss, because that'd be letting himself in if he was wrong. But he could puff away in that outboard, stop the engine, and paddle back quietly on the oars. He couldn't have seen you—probably he couldn't even have heard what you said—but he could hear that there was a girl on board."

"Which isn't impossible either," she said demurely. Simon frowned.

"You forget my Saintly reputation. But still, maybe to Vogel, with his low criminal mind, it isn't impossible either. But it's still unusual enough to be worth looking at. And then there's you."

"Without a reputation."

"And not deserving one. You've been making a clear set at him for several days— weeks—whatever it is. That again may not be impossible. It might be his money, or his beauty, or because he sings so nicely in his bath. But if it isn't even unusual, if I were in his place I'd think it was—interesting. Interesting enough, maybe, to try and find out some more about you."

She pressed his hand—she had been letting it rest in his all that time, as if she hadn't noticed.

"Dear man," she said, "don't you think I know all this?"

"And if he only wants to see exactly where you stand in the game?"

"I can pack a gun."

"Like any other ordinary innocent woman."

"Then I'll go without it."

"You wouldn't be much worse off."

"All the same, I'll go."

"Three," he quoted her, "didn't come back."

She nodded. The impish humour still played on her lips and the surface of her eyes, but the depths behind it were clear and still.

"When you join Ingerbeck's, you don't sign on for a cocktail party. You join an army. You take an oath—to do your job, to keep your mouth shut, and to take the consequences. Wouldn't you go?"

"Yes. But there are special risks."

"For a poor defenceless girl?"

"They call it Worse than Death."

"I've never believed it."

He sat up and stared thoughtfully over the water. There was a quality of lightness in her decision that ended argument more finally than any dramatic protestations. She would go; because whatever the risk might be, it was not fact. It was her job to find out, not to guess.

"I take it you've already accepted," he said wryly.

"The messenger was going to call back for my answer. I left a letter when I came out. I said I'd be delighted. Maybe Kurt Vogel isn't so bad as he's painted," she said dreamily. "He left some lovely flowers with the invitation."

"I shouldn't be surprised if you fell for him."

"I might."

"But now and then your conscience would prick you. When you were riding around in your Rolls, half strangled with diamonds, the memory of lost love would haunt you. I can see you stifling a sob, and pressing a penny into a poor beggar's hand before you hurry on, because he reminds you of me."

"Don't say it," she pleaded tremulously. "I can't bear it. How was I to know you cared like that?"

The Saint scratched his head.

"I must have forgotten to tell you," he admitted. "Never mind." He turned to her with cavalier blue eyes sobered to a thoughtful directness that she had seen before. "But does it leave me out?"

"I don't know," she said steadily. "Have you decided to break off your holiday?"

"Let's have a drink and talk about it."

She shook her head.

"I can't risk it. Vogel may be ashore now—he may be anywhere. I've risked enough to talk to you at all. If you've changed your mind since last night, we'll fight over it."

"Did I tell you I'd made up my mind?" Simon inquired mildly.

"You let me think you had. I took a chance when I told you the story. I wanted you to know. I still do." She was facing him without banter now, cool and possessed and momentarily unpossessable, and yet with a shadow of wistfulness deepening in her gaze. "I think Ingerbeck himself would have done the same. We might get a long way together, and if we came through there'd be plenty of commission to split. Just once, it might be fun for you to look at a dotted line."

His eyebrows slanted quizzically.

"Otherwise?"

"I suppose we can still be hung out to dry."

She stood up, dusting the sand from her robe. Simon picked himself up after her, and the grey eyes came back to his face.

"Where should we meet on this—dotted line?" he asked resignedly.

"I'll be here tomorrow. No, not here—we can't take this risk again. Suppose I swam out and met you, off the Pointe du Moulinet. Halfway house. At eleven." She smiled, as he had seen her smile once before. "Are you looking for your pen?"

"I can't write, Loretta."

"You can make a cross."

"You know what that stands for?"

"If it does," she said, "you signed last night."

He watched her walking up towards the white spires of the Casino Balnéum, with all the maddening delight of movement in the swing of her brown body, and searched his vocabulary for words to describe the capaciousness of fortune. Admitted that all the gifts of that immoral goddess had strings harnessed to them—there were strings and strings. There was no real need in adventure for quite such a disturbing complication. And the Saint smiled in spite of that. The beach was empty after she had left it; that is to say, there were about a thousand other people on the Plage de l'Ecluse, but he found all of them sickeningly bovine. Including the Parisian vamp, who by this time was enjoying the devotion of three muscle- conscious young men, the debauched Roman emperor, and a hungry-looking tourist from Egg Harbor, New Jersey, who should have been old enough to know better.

Simon turned away from the repulsive spectacle, and was rewarded by the almost equally unwelcome vision of Orace's moustache, through which something more than the sea air was filtering.

"You do break out at the most unromantic moments, Orace," he complained, and then he saw that Orace's eyes were still fixed glassily on the middle distance.

"Is that the lidy, sir?"

Orace's martial voice was hushed with a sort of awe, and the Saint frowned.

"She isn't a lady," he said firmly. "No lady would use such shameless eyes to try and seduce a self-respecting buccaneer from his duty. No lady would take such a mean advantage of a human being." He perceived that his audience was still scarcely following him, and looked round. "Nor is that the wench I'm talking about, anyway. Come on away— you'll be getting off in a minute."

They walked over the sand towards the bend by the swimming pool, where the Promenade des Alliés curves out towards the sea.

"If you arsk me," Orace remarked, recalling the grievance which had been temporarily smoothed over by his anatomical studies, "these Frogs are all barmy. First thing I arsks for petrol, an' they give me paraffin. Then when I says that ain't what I want, they tell me they've got some stuff called essence, wot's just as good. I 'as a smell of this stuff, an' blimey if it ain't petrol. 'Ow the thunderinell can they 'elp goin' barmy wiv a langwidge like that?"

"I don't suppose they can help it," said the Saint gravely. "Did you buy some of this essence?"

"Yessir. Then I tried to get some ice. They 'adn't got no ice, but they tried to sell me some *glass*. I gave it up an' brought the dinghy rahnd in case yer didn't wanter swim back. *Barmy?*" said Orace sizzlingly.

It was nearly one o'clock when the fuel tanks had been replenished from the cans which Orace had acquired at the cost of so much righteous indignation, and the Saint had cleaned himself up and put a comb through his hair. Orace produced a drink—freshened, in spite of gloomy prophecies, with ice—and required to know whether he should get lunch.

"I don't know," said the Saint, with unusual brusqueness.

He had no idea what he wanted to do. He felt suddenly restless and dissatisfied. The day had gone flat in prospect. They might have lazed through the long afternoon, steeping themselves in sunlight and romping through the light play of words. They might have plunged together through the cool rapture of the sea, or drifted out under spread sails to explore the Ile de Cézembre and picnic under the cliffs of St Lunaire. They might have enjoyed any of a dozen trivial things which he had half planned in his imagination, secure in a communion of pagan understanding that made no demands and asked no promises. Instead of which . . .

Because gold rippled in a girl's hair, and an imp of sophisticated humour lurked Pan- like in the shadows of her eyes, because the same gaze could sometimes hold a serenity of purpose beyond measure— Simon Templar, at thirty-four, with odysseys of adventure behind him that would have made Ulysses look like a small boy playing in a back yard—found himself in the beginning of that halcyon afternoon at a loose end.

It wasn't exactly the amount of money involved. Four million, if that was a minimum estimate of the total submerged wealth which Vogel had plundered from the sea bottoms, was certainly a lot of pounds. So was ten per cent of it. Or even half that. The Saint wasn't greedy, and he had come out of each of his past sorties into the hazardous hinterlands of adventure with a lengthening line of figures in his bank account which raised their own monument to his flair for boodle. He had no need to be avaricious. There were limits—lofty, vertiginous limits, but limits nevertheless—to how much money one could spend, and he had a sublime faith that the same extravagant providence which had held him up all his life so far would keep him near enough to those limits to save him from feeling depressed. It wasn't exactly that. It was a matter of principle.

"You're getting old," he reproached himself solemnly. "At this very moment, you're trying to persuade yourself to work for an insurance company. Just because she has a body like an old man's dream, and you kissed her. An insurance company!"

He shuddered.

And then he turned his eyes to study a speck of movement on the borders of his field of vision. The speed tender was moving away from the side of the *Falkenberg*, heading towards the Bec de la Vallée. For a moment he watched it idly, calculating that its course would take it within a few yards of the *Corsair*; as it came nearer he recognised Kurt Vogel, and with him a stout grey-bearded man in a Norfolk jacket and a shapeless yellow Panama hat.

Simon began to get up from his chair. He began slowly and almost uncertainly, but he finished in a sudden rush of decision. Any action, however vague its object, was better than no action at all. He skated down the companion with something like his earlier exuberance, and shouted for Orace.

"Never mind about lunch," he said, scattering silk shirts and white duck trousers out of a locker. "I'm going on shore to take up ornithology."

2

One of the vedettes from St Malo was coming in to the jetty when the Saint scrambled back on deck, and the *Falkenberg's* tender was still manoeuvring for a landing. Simon dropped into his dinghy and wound up the outboard.

Fortunately the *Corsair* had swung round on the tide so that she screened his movements from any chance backward glances from the quay, and he started off up-river and came round in a wide circle to avoid identifying himself by his point of departure. Not that it mattered much, but he wanted to avoid giving any immediate impression that he was deliberately setting off in pursuit.

He cruised along, keeping his head down and judging time and distance as the *Falkenberg's* tender squeezed in to the steps and Vogel and his companion went ashore. Looking back, he judged that with any luck no curious watcher on the *Falkenberg* had observed his hurried departure, and by this time he was too far away to be recognised. Then, as Vogel and the grey-bearded man started up the causeway towards the Grande Rue, the Saint opened up his engine and scooted after them. He shot in to the quay under the very nose of another boat that was making for the same objective, spun his motor round into reverse under a cloudburst of Gallic expostulation and profanity, hitched the painter deftly through a ring-bolt, and was up on land and away before the running commentary he had provoked had really reached its choicest descriptive adjectives.

The passengers who were disembarking from the ferry effectively screened his arrival and shielded his advance as he hustled after his quarry. The other two were not walking quickly, and the grey-bearded man's shabby yellow Panama was as good as a beacon. Simon spaced himself as far behind them as he dared when they reached the Digue, and slackened the speed of his pursuit. He ambled along with his hands in his pockets, submerging himself among the other promenaders with the same happy-go-lucky air of debating the best place to take an aperitif before lunch.

Presently the yellow Panama bobbed across the stream in the direction of the Casino terrace, and Simon Templar followed. At that hour the place was packed with a chattering sun-soaked throng of thirsty socialites, and the Saint was able to squeeze himself about among the tables in the most natural manner of a lone man looking for a place—preferably with company. His route led him quite casually past Vogel's table, and at the precise moment when the hook-nosed man looked up and caught his eye, Simon returned the recognition with a perfect rendering of polite interest.

They were so close together that Vogel could scarcely have avoided a greeting, even if he had wished to—which the Saint quietly doubted. For a moment the man's black expressionless stare drilled right through him, and then the thin lips spread in a smile that had all the artless geniality of a snake's.

"I hope you didn't think I was too unceremonious about disturbing you last night," he said.

"Not at all," said the Saint cheerfully. "I didn't leave the baccarat rooms till pretty late, so I was only just settling in."

His glance passed unostentatiously over the grey-bearded man. Something about the mud pink youthful-looking face struck him as dimly familiar, but he couldn't place it.

"This is Professor Yule," said the other, "and my name is Vogel. Won't you join us, Mr . . ."

"Tombs," said the Saint, without batting an eyelid, and sat down.

Vogel extended a cigarette-case.

"You are interested in gambling, Mr Tombs?" he suggested.

His tone was courteous and detached, the tone of a man who was merely accepting the obvious cue for the opening of a conventional exchange of small talk, but the Saint's hand hovered over the proffered case for an imperceptible second's pause before he slid out a smoke and settled back.

"I don't mind an occasional flutter to pass the time," he murmured deprecatingly. "Ah, yes—an occasional flutter." Vogel's eyes, like two beads of impenetrable jet, remained fixed on his face, but the cold lipless smile remained also. "You can't come to much harm that way. It's the people who play beyond their means who come to grief."

Simon Templar let a trickle of smoke drift down his nostrils, and that instantaneous instinctive tension within him relaxed into a pervasive chortle of pure glee which spread around his inside like a sip of old brandy. Kurt Vogel, he reflected, must have been taking a diet of the kind of mystery story in which the villain always introduces himself with some lines of sinister innuendo like that—and thereby convinces the perhaps otherwise unsuspecting hero that something villainous is going on. In the same type of story, however, the hero can never resist the temptation to respond in kind—thereby establishing the fact that he is the hero. But the Saint had been treading the fickle tight-ropes of piracy when those same romantic juveniles were cooing in their cradles, and he had his own severely practical ideas of heroism.

"There's not much chance of that," he said lightly, "with my overdraft in its present state."

They sat eye to eye like two duellists baffled for an opening, and the Saint's smile was wholly innocent. If Kurt Vogel had hoped to get him to betray himself by any theatrical insinuations of that sort, there were going to be some disappointed hearts in Dinard that fine day. But Vogel's outward cordiality never wavered an iota. He gave away nothing either—the innuendo was only there if the Saint chose to force it out.

"Are you staying long?"

"I haven't made any plans," said the Saint nebulously. "I might dart off at any moment, or I might hang around until they make me a local monument. It just depends on how soon I get tired of the place."

"It doesn't agree with everybody," Vogel assented purringly. "In fact, I have heard that some people find it definitely unhealthy." Simon nodded.

"A bit relaxing, perhaps," he admitted. "But I don't mind that. Up to the present, though, I've found it rather dull."

Vogel sat back and stroked the edge of the table with his fingertips. If he was disconcerted, the fact never registered on his face. His features were a flat mask of impassively regulated scenery behind that sullen promontory of a nose.

A waiter equilibrating under a dizzy tray of glasses swayed by and snatched their order as he passed. At the same time an adjoining table became vacant, and another party of thirst-quenchers took possession. The glance of one of them, sweeping round as he wriggled his legs in, passed over the Saint and then became faintly fixed. For a brief second it stayed set, then he leaned sideways to whisper. His companions turned their heads furtively. The name of Yule reached the Saint clearly, but after that the surrounding buzz of conversation and the glutinous strains of the Casino band swallowed up the conversation for a moment. And then, above all interfering undertones, the electric sotto voce of a resplendently peroxided matron in the party stung his eardrums like a saw shearing through tin: "I'm sure it must be! . . . You know, my dear—the bathy-something man . . ."

Simon Templar's ribs lifted under his shirt with the deep breath that he drew into his lungs, and the twirtle of bliss within him rose to a sweet celestial singing. He knew now why the name of Professor Yule had seemed familiar, and why he had tried to place that fresh apple-cheeked face over the trim grey beard. Only a few months ago the newspapers had run their stories and the illustrated weeklies had carried special pictures: the *National Geographic Magazine* had brought out a Yule Expedition number. For Wesley Yule had done something that no man on earth had ever done before. He had been down five thousand feet into the Pacific Ocean, beyond any depth ever seen before by human eyes—not in any sort of glorified diving bell, but in a fantastic bulbous armour built to withstand the terrific pressure that would have crushed an unprotected man like a midge on a window-pane, in which he was able to move and walk about on the ocean floor nearly a mile below the ship from which he was lowered. He was the man who had perfected and proved a deep-sea costume compared with which the "iron men" of previous diving experiments were mere amateurish makeshifts, a combination of metallic alloys and scientific construction that promised to revolutionise the exploring of the last secrets of the sea . . . And now he was in Dinard, the guest of Kurt Vogel, arch hijacker of Davy Jones!

That long pregnant breath floated back through the Saint's lips and carried a feather of cigarette-smoke with it—the pause during which he had held it in his lungs was the only physical index of his emotion. He became aware that the Professor was joining in with some affable commonplace, and that Vogel's black eyes were riveted on him un-winkingly. With a perfectly steady hand he tilted the ash off his cigarette, and schooled every scrap of tension out of his face as he turned his head.

"Of course you've heard about Professor Yule?" said Vogel urbanely.

"Of course . . ." Simon's rendering of slight apologetic confusion was attained with an effort that no one could have felt but himself. "Now I know who he is . . . But I hadn't placed him until that lady said something just now." He looked at Yule with a smile of open admiration. "It must have been an amazing experience, Professor."

Yule shrugged, with a pleasant diffidence.

"Naturally it was interesting," he replied frankly. "And rather frightening. Not to say uncomfortable . . . Perhaps you know that the temperature of the water falls rapidly when you reach really great depths. As a matter of fact, at five thousand feet it is only a few degrees above freezing point. Well, I had been so taken up with the other mechanical details of pressure and lighting and air supply that I actually forgot that one. I was damned cold!" He chuckled engagingly. "I'm putting an electrical heating arrangement in my improved bathystol, and I shan't suffer that way next time."

"You've decided to go down again, then?"

"Oh, yes. I've only just started. That first trip of mine was only a trial. With my new bathystol I hope to get down twice as far—and that's nothing. If some of the latest alloys turn out all right, we may be able to have a look at the Cape Verde Basin—over three thousand fathoms—or even the Tuscarora Trough, more than five miles down."

"What do you hope to find?"

"A lot of dull facts about depth currents and globigerina ooze. Possibly some new forms of marine life. There may be some astounding monsters living and dying down there, and never seeing the light of day. We might even track down our old friend the sea serpent."

"There are some marvellous possibilities," said the Saint thoughtfully.

"And some expensive ones," confessed Yule, with attractive candour. "In fact, if it hadn't been for Mr Vogel they might not have been possibilities at all—my first descent just about ruined me. But with his help I hope to go a lot further."

The Saint did not smile, although a sudden vision of Kurt Vogel as a connoisseur of globigerina ooze and new species of fish tempted him almost irresistibly. He saw beyond that to other infinitely richer possibilities—possibilities which had probably never occurred to the Professor.

He knew that Vogel was watching him, observing every microscopic detail of his reactions with coldly analytical precision. To show a poker-faced lack of interest would be almost as suspicious as breaking loose with a hungry stream of questions. He had to judge the warmth of his response to the exactest hundredth of a degree, if he was to preserve any hope of clinging to the bluff of complete unsuspecting innocence which he had adopted. In the next twenty minutes of ordinary conversation he worked harder than he had done for half his life.

". . . so the next big descent will show whether there's any chance of supporting Wegener's theory of continental drift," concluded the Professor.

"I see," said the Saint intelligently.

A man wandering about the terrace with a large camera pushed his way to their table and presented a card with the inscription of the Agence Française Journalistique.

"*Vous permettez, messieurs?*"

Yule grinned ruefully, like a schoolboy, and submitted blushingly to the ordeal. The photographer took two snapshots of the group, thanked them, and passed on with a vacuous air of waiting for further celebrities to impinge on his autocratic ken. A twice-divorced countess whom he ignored glared after him indignantly, and Kurt Vogel beckoned a waiter for the addition.

"Won't you have another?" suggested the Saint.

"I'm afraid we have an engagement. Next time, perhaps." Vogel discarded two ten-franc notes on the assiette and stood up with a flash of his bloodless smile. "If you're interested, you might like to come out with us on a trial trip. It won't be very sensational, unfortunately. Just a test for the new apparatus in moderately deep water."

"I should love to," said the Saint slowly. Vogel inclined his head pleasantly.

"It won't be just here," he said, "the water's too shallow. We thought of trying it in the Hurd Deep, north of Alderney. There are only about ninety fathoms there, but it'll be enough for our object. If you think it's worth changing your plans, we're leaving for St Peter Port in the morning."

"Well—that sort of invitation doesn't come every day," said the Saint, with a certain well-timed embarrassment. "It's certainly worth thinking about—if you're sure I shouldn't be in the way . . ."

"Then we may look forward to seeing you." Vogel held out his hand. He had a firm muscular grip, but there was a curious reptilian coldness in the touch of his skin that prickled the Saint's scalp. "I'll give you a shout in the morning as we go by, and see if you've made up your mind."

Simon shook hands with the Professor, and watched them until they turned the corner by the Petit Casino. His blue eyes were set in a lambent glint, like polished sapphires. He had got what he wanted. He had made actual contact with Kurt Vogel, talked with him, touched him physically and experienced the cold-blooded fighting presence of the man, crossed swords with him in a breathless finesse of nerves that was sharper than any bludgeoning battle. He had gained more than that. He had received a gratuitous invitation to call again. Which meant that he was as good as on the prize list.

Or in the coffin.

3

A highly conclusive and illuminating deduction, reflected the Saint grimly. And then all the old reckless humour flickered back into his eyes, and he lighted another cigarette and ordered himself a second drink. So be it. As Loretta Page had said, there were no dividends in guessing. In the fullness of time all uncertainty would doubtless be removed—one way or the other. And when that happened, Simon Templar proposed to be among those present.

Meanwhile he had something else to think about. A man came filtering through the tables on the terrace with a sheaf of English and American papers fanned out in his hand. Simon bought an *Express*, and he had only turned the first page when a single-column headline caught his eye.

TO SALVE CHALFONT CASTLE
£5,000,000 Expedition Fits Out

A ship will leave Falmouth early in August with a contract for the greatest treasure-hunt ever attempted in

British waters.

She is the Restorer, *crack steamer of the Liverpool &*
Glasgow Salvage Association—

Simon skimmed through the story with narrowing eyes. So that
was it! If Kurt Vogel was cruising in the vicinity of the Channel Islands
on active business, and not merely on a holiday, the *Chalfont Castle*
was his most obvious target. And it seemed likely—otherwise why not
take Professor Yule and his bathystol down to some place like Madeira,
where there was really deep water close at hand for any number of
experiments? The *Chalfont Castle* could not wait. If an authorised
expedition was being organised so quickly, there was not much time for
a free-lance to step in and forestall it. Perhaps the underwriters, taught
by past experience, had thought of that. But for a man of Vogel's nerve
there might still be a chance . . .

Simon Templar lunched at the Gallic, and enjoyed his meal. The
sting of the encounter from which he had just emerged had driven out
every trace of the rather exasperated lassitude which had struck him
an hour or two before; this providential hint of new movement swept
new inspiration in like a sea breeze. The spice of certain danger laced
his wine and sparkled through his veins. His brain was functioning like
an awakened machine, turning over the urgencies of the moment with
smooth and effortless ease.

When he had finished, he went out into the main foyer and
collected a reception clerk.

"You have a telephone?"

"*Oui, m'sieu. A gauche—*"

"No, thanks," said the Saint. "This isn't local—I want to talk to
England. Let me have a private room. I'll pay for it."

Ten minutes later he was settled comfortably in an armchair with
his feet on a polished walnut table.

"Hullo, Peter." The object of his first call was located after the London exchange had tried three other possible numbers which he gave them. "This is your Uncle Simon. Listen— didn't you tell me that you once had a respectable family?"

"It still is respectable," Peter Quentin's voice answered indignantly. "I'm the only one who's had anything to do with you."

Simon grinned gently and slid a cigarette out of the package in front of him. "Do any of them know anything about Lloyd's?"

"I've got a sort of cousin, or something, who works there," said Peter, after a pause for reflection.

"That's great. Well, I want you to go and dig out this sort of cousin, or something, and stage a reunion. Be nice to him—remind him of the old family tree—and find out something for me about the *Chalfont Castle*."

"Like a shot, old boy. But are you sure you don't want an estate agent?"

"No, I don't want an estate agent, you fathead. It's a wreck, not a ruin. She sank somewhere near Alderney about the beginning of March. I want you to find out exactly where she went down. They're sure to have a record at Lloyd's. Get a chart from Potter's, in the Minories, and get the exact spot marked. And send it to me at the Poste Restante, St Peter Port, Guernsey—tonight. Name of Tombs. Or get a bearing and wire it. But get something. All clear?"

"Clear as mud," There was a suspicious hiatus at the other end of the line. "But if this means you're on the war path again—"

"If I want you, I'll let you know, Peter," said the Saint contentedly, and rang off.

That was that . . . But even if one knew the exact spot where things were likely to happen, one couldn't hang about there and wait for them. Not in a stretch of open water where a floating bottle would be visible for miles on a calm day. The Saint's next call was to another erstwhile companion in crime.

"Do you think you could buy me a nice diving suit, Roger?" he suggested sweetly. "One of the latest self-contained contraptions with oxygen tanks. Say you're representing a movie company and you want it for an undersea epic."

"What's the racket?" inquired Roger Conway firmly.

"No racket at all, Roger. I've just taken up submarine geology, and I want to have a look at some globigerina ooze. Now, if you bought that outfit this afternoon and shipped it off to me in a trunk—"

"Why not let me bring it?"

The Saint hesitated. After all, why not? It was the second time in a few minutes that the suggestion had been held out, and each time by a man whom he had tried and proved in more than one tight corner. They were old campaigners, men with his own cynical contempt of legal technicalities, and his own cool disregard of danger, men who had followed him before, without a qualm, into whatever precarious paths of breathless filibustering he had led them, and who were always accusing him of hogging all the fun when he tried to dissuade them from taking the same risks again. He liked working alone, but some aspects of Vogel's crew of modern pirates might turn out to be more than one man's meat.

"Okay." The Saint drew at his cigarette, and his slow smile floated over the wire in the undertones of his voice. "Get hold of Peter, and any other of the boys who are looking for a sticky end. But the other instructions stand. Ship that outfit to me personally, care of the Southern Railway—you might even make it two outfits, if you feel like looking at some fish— and Peter's to do his stuff exactly as I've already told him. You toughs can put up at the Royal; but you're not to recognise me unless I recognise you first. It may be worth a point or two if the ungodly don't know we're connected. Sold?"

"Cash," said Roger happily.

Simon walked on air to the stairs. As he stepped down into the foyer, he became aware of a pair of socks. The socks were particularly noticeable because they were of a pale brick-red hue, and intervened between a pair of blue trousers and a pair of brown and yellow co-respondent shoes. It was a combination of colours which, once seen, could not be easily forgotten, and the Saint's glance voyaged idly up to the face of the man who wore it. He had already seen it once before, and his glance at the physiognomy of the wearer confirmed his suspicion that there could not be two men simultaneously inhabiting Dinard with the identically horrible taste in colour schemes. The sock stylist was no stranger. He had sat at a table close to the Saint's at lunch-time, arriving a few moments later and calling for his bill in unison— exactly as he was sitting in the foyer now, with an aloof air of having nothing important to do and being ready to do it at a minute's notice.

The Saint paid for his calls and the use of the room, and sauntered out. He took a roundabout route to his destination, turned three or four corners, without once looking back, and paused to look in a shop window in the Rue du Casino. In an angle of the plate glass he caught a reflection—of pale brick-red socks.

Item Two . . . So Vogel's affability had not been entirely unpremeditated. Perhaps it had been carefully planned from the start. It would have been simplicity itself for the sleuth to pick him up when he was identified by sitting with Vogel and Yule at the café.

Not that the situation was immediately serious. The pink-hosed spy might have discovered that Simon Templar had rented a room and made some telephone calls, but he wasn't likely to have discovered much more. And that activity was not fundamentally suspicious. But with Vogel already on his guard, it would register in the score as a fact definitely to be accounted for. And the presence of the man who had observed it added its own testimony to the thoroughness with which the fact would doubtless be scrutinised.

The Saint's estimation of Kurt Vogel went up another grim notch. In that dispassionate efficiency, that methodical examination of every loophole, that ruthless elimination of every factor of chance or guesswork, he recognised some of the qualities that must have given Vogel his unique position in the hierarchy of racketeers—the qualities that must have been fatally underestimated by those three nameless scouts of Ingerbeck's, who had not come home . . .

And which might have been underestimated by the fourth.

The thought checked him in his stride for an almost imperceptible instant. He knew that Loretta Page was ready to be told that she was suspected, but was she ready for quite such an inquisitorial surveillance as this?

He turned into the next tobacconist's and gained a breathing space while he purchased a pack of cigarettes. To find out, he had to shake off his own shadow. And it had to be done in such a way that the shadow did not know he was being intentionally shaken off, because an entirely innocent young man in the role Simon had set himself would never discover that he was being shadowed anyway.

He came out and walked more quickly to the corner of the Rue Levasseur. A disengaged taxi met him there, almost as if it had been timed for the purpose, and he stopped it and swung on board without any appearance of undue haste, but with a movement as swift and sure as an acrobat's on the flying trapeze.

"*À la gare,*" he said, and the taxi was off again without having actually reached a standstill.

Looking back through the rear window, he saw the pink socks piling into another cab a whole block behind. He leaned forward as they rushed into the Place de la République.

"*Un moment,*" he said in the driver's ear. "*Il faut que j'aille premièrement à la Banque Boutin.*"

The driver muttered something uncomplimentary under his breath, trod on the brakes, and spun the wheel. By his limited lights, he was not without reason, for the Banque de Bretagne and Travel Agency of M. Jules Boutin are at the eastern end of the Rue Levasseur—in exactly the opposite direction from the station.

They reeled dizzily round the corner of the Rue de la Plage, with that sublime abandon of which only French chauffeurs and suicidal maniacs are capable, gathered speed, and hurtled around another right-hand hairpin into the Boulevard Féart, Simon looked back again, and saw no sign of the pursuit. There were three other possible turnings from the hairpin junction which they had just circumnavigated, and the Saint had no doubt that his pink-socked epilogue, having lost them completely on that sudden swerve out of the Place de la République, and not expecting any such treacherous manoeuvre, was by that tune frantically exploring routes in the opposite direction.

They turned back into the Rue Levasseur, and to make absolutely certain the Saint changed his mind again and ordered another twist north to the post office. He paid off the driver and plunged into a telephone booth.

She was in. She said she had been writing some letters.

"Don't post 'em till I see you," said the Saint. "What's the number of your room?" "Twenty-eight. But—"

"I'll walk up as if I owned it. Can you bear to wait?"

4

She was wearing a green silk robe with a great silver dragon crawling round it and bursting into fire-spitting life on her shoulders. Heaven knew what she wore under it, if anything, but the curve of her thigh sprang up in a sheer sweep of breath-taking line to her knee as she turned. The physical spell of her wove a definite hiatus in between his entrance and his first line.

"I hope I intrude," he said.

The man who was with her scowled. He was a hard-faced, hard-eyed individual, rather stout, rather bald, yet with a solid atmosphere of competence and courage about him.

"Loretta—how d'ya know this guy's on the rise?"

"I don't," she said calmly. "But he has such a nice clean smile."

"Just a home girl's husband," murmured the Saint lightly. He tapped a cigarette on his thumb-nail, and slanted his brows sidelong at the objector. "Who's the young heart's delight?"

She shrugged.

"Name of Steve Murdoch."

"Of Ingerbeck's?"

"Yes."

"Simon to you," said the Saint, holding out his hand.

Murdoch accepted it sullenly. Their grips clashed, battled in a sudden straining of iron wrists, but neither of them flinched. The Saint's smile twitched at his lips, and some of the sullenness went out of the other's stare.

"Okay, Saint," Murdoch said dourly. "I know you're tough. But I don't like fresh guys."

"I hate them, myself," said the Saint unblushingly. He sat on the arm of a chair, making patterns in the atmosphere with cigarette-smoke. "Been here long?"

"Landed at Cherbourg this morning."

"Did you ask for Loretta downstairs?"

"Yeah."

"Notice anyone prick up his ears?" Murdoch shook his head.

"I didn't look."

"You should have," said the Saint reprovingly. "I didn't ask, but I looked. There was a bloke kicking his heels in a corner when I arrived, and he had watchdog written across his chest in letters a foot high. He didn't see me, because I walked through with my face buried inside a newspaper; but he must have seen you. He'd've seen anyone who wasn't expecting him, and he was placed just right to hear who was asked for at the desk."

There was a short silence. Loretta leaned back against a table with her hands on the edge and her long legs crossed.

"Did you know Steve was here?" she asked.

"No. He only makes it more difficult. But I discovered that a ferret-faced bird with the most beautiful line in gent's half-hose was sitting on my tail, and that made me think. I slipped him and came round to warn you." Simon looked at her steadily. "There's only a trace of suspicion attached to me at the moment, but Vogel's taking no chances. He wants to make sure. There's probably a hell of a lot of suspicion about you, so you weren't likely to be forgotten. And apparently you haven't been. Now Steve has rolled up to lend a hand—he's branded himself by asking for you, and he'll be a marked man from this moment."

"That's okay," said Murdoch phlegmatically. "I can look after myself without a nurse."

"I'm sure you can, dear old skunk," said the Saint amiably. "But that's not the point. Loretta, at least, isn't supposed to be looking after herself. She's the undercover ingénue. She isn't supposed to have anything to look after except her honour. Once she starts any Mata Hari business, that boat is sunk."

"Well?"

Simon flicked ash on to the carpet.

"The only tune is the one I'm playing. Complete and childlike innocence. With a pan like yours, Steve, you'll have a job to get your mouth round the flute, but you've got to try it. Because any sucker play you make is going to hit Loretta. The first thing is to clean yourself up. If you've got a star or anything like that of Ingerbeck's, flush it down the lavatory. If you've got anything in writing that could link you up, memorise it and burn it. Strip yourself of every mortal thing that might tie you on to this party. That goes for you too, Loretta, because sooner or later the ungodly are going to try and get a line on you from your luggage, if they haven't placed you before that. And then, Steve, you blow."

"What?"

"Fade. Waft. Pass out into the night. Loretta can go downstairs with you, and you can take a fond farewell in the foyer, with a few well-chosen lines of dialogue from which any listeners can gather that you're an old friend of her father's taking a holiday in Guernsey, and hearing she was in Dinard you hopped an excursion and came over for the day. And then you beetle down to the pier, catch the next ferry to St Malo, and shoot on to the return steamer to St Peter Port like a cork out of a bottle. Vogel will be there tomorrow."

"How do you know that?" asked Loretta quickly.

"He told me. We got into conversation before lunch." Simon's gaze lifted to hers with azure lights of scapegrace solemnity playing in it. "He was trying to draw me out, and I was just devilling him, but neither of us got very far. I think he was telling me the truth, though. If I chase him to St Peter Port, he'll be able to put my innocence through some more tests. So when you're saying goodbye to Steve, he might ask you if you're likely to take a trip to Guernsey, and you can say you don't think you'll be able to—that may make them think that you haven't heard anything from me."

Murdoch took out a cigar and bit the end from it with a bulldog clamp of his jaws. His eyes were dark again with distrust.

"It's a stall, Loretta," he said sourly. "How d'ya know Vogel isn't capable of having an undercover man, the same as us! All he wants to do is get me out of the way, so he can take you alone."

"You flatter yourself, brother," said the Saint coldly. "If I wanted to take her, you wouldn't stop me. Nor would you stop Vogel."

"No?"

"No."

"Well, I'm not running."

Loretta glanced from one man to the other. The animosity between them was creeping up again, hardening the square obstinacy of Murdoch's jaw, glittering like chips of elusive steel in the Saint's eyes. They were like two jungle animals, each superb in his own way and conscious of his strength, but of two different species whose feud dated back too far into the grey dawns of history for any quick forgetting.

"Yes, you are, Steve," said the girl.

"When I start taking orders from that—"

"You aren't." Her voice was quiet and soothing, but there was a thread of calm decision under the silky texture. "You're taking orders from me. The Saint's right. We'd better break off again, and hope we can alibi this meeting."

Murdoch was staring at her half incredulously.

"Orders?" he repeated.

"That's right, Steve. At present I'm running this end of it. Until Martin Ingerbeck takes me off the assignment, you do what I tell you."

"I think you're crazy."

She didn't answer. She took a cigarette from a box on the table and walked to the window, standing there with her arms lifted and her hands on either side of the frame. The silver dragon lifted on her waist.

Murdoch's lips flattened the butt of his cigar. His hands clutched the arms of his chair, and he started to get up slowly. With a sudden burst of vicious energy he grabbed for his hat and thumped it on his head.

"If you put it that way, I can't argue," he growled. "But you're going to wish I had!" He transferred his glare from her unconscious back to the Saint's face. "As for you—if anything happens to Loretta through my not being here—"

"We'll be sure to let you know about it," said the Saint, and opened the door for him. Murdoch stumped through with his fists clenched, and the Saint half closed it as Loretta turned from the window and came across the room. He took her hands.

"I shall be gone while you're seeing Steve off," he said. "I can't risk the foyer again, but I spotted a fire escape."

"Must you?" The faint irony of her voice was baffled by the enigma of her smiling mouth.

He nodded.

"Not because I want to. But they ought to see me going back to the *Corsair* before there's too much excitement about my shadow having lost me. You're still sure you mean to go tonight?"

"Quite sure."

"Did I dream the rest of it, after you'd gone last night?"

"I don't know, dear. What did you have for dinner?"

"Lobster mayonnaise. I dreamt that you came back from the *Falkenberg*. Safe. And always beautiful. To me."

"And then the danger really started."

"I dreamt that you didn't think it was too dangerous."

Her eyes searched his face, with the laughter stilled in them for a moment. The tip of the dragon's tongue stirred on her shoulder as she drew breath. One hand released itself to trace the half-mocking line of his mouth.

"But I am afraid," she said.

Suddenly he felt her lips crushed and melting against his, and her body pressed against him, for one soundless instant, and then, before he could move, she had brushed past him and gone.

Orace was waiting for him anxiously when he got back. "Yer bin a long time," Orace remarked shatteringly.

"Thousands of years," said the Saint.

He sat out on deck again after he had taken his last daylight swim, and sipped a glass of sherry, and dined on one of Orace's superlative meals. The speed tender had set out again from the *Falkenberg* and returned about half-past seven with Vogel, in evening dress, sitting beside Loretta. Through the binoculars, from one of the saloon portholes, he had seen Vogel smiling and talking, his great nose profiled against the water.

He sat out, with a cigarette clipped and half-forgotten between his lips and his eyes creased against the smoke, as motionless as a bronze Indian, while the water turned to dark glass and then to burnished steel. There was no fog that night. The river ran blue-black under the wooded rocks of the Vicomté and the ramparts and granite headland of St Malo. Lights sprang up, multiplying, on the island, and were mirrored in St Servan and Dinard, and spread luminous rapiers across the river. The hulls of the craft anchored in the Rance sank back into the gloom until the night swallowed them, and only their winking lights remained on the water. The lighthouses of the inlet were awake, green and red flashes stabbing irregularly across the bay and twinkling down from Grand Larron. A drift of music from one of the Casinos lingered across the estuary, and the anchorage where the *Falkenberg* should be was a constellation of lights.

Loretta was there, but Simon saw no need for her to be alone.

The idea grew with him as the dark deepened and his imagination worked through it. In his own way he was afraid, impatient with his enforced helplessness . . . Presently he sent another cigarette spinning like a glow-worm through the blackness, and went below to take off his clothes. He tested the working of his automatic, brought a greased cartridge into the breech, secured the safety-catch, and fastened the gun to the belt of his trunks. The dark water received him without a sound.

Curiously enough, it was during that stealthy swim that he had a sudden electric remembrance of a news photographer who had been so unusually blind to the presence of all celebrities save one. Perhaps it was because his mind had been unconsciously revolving the subject of Vogel's amazing thoroughness. But he had a startlingly vivid picture of a camera aiming towards him—fully as much towards him as towards Professor Yule—and a sudden reckless smile moved his lips as he slid through the water.

If that news photographer was not a real news photographer, and the picture had been developed and printed and rushed across to England by air that evening, a correspondent could show it around in certain circles in London with the virtual certainty of having it identified within forty-eight hours . . . And if the result of that investigation was cabled to Kurt Vogel at St Peter Port, a good many interrogation marks might be wiped out with deadly speed.

CHAPTER THREE:

HOW KURT VOGEL WAS NOT SO CALM AND OTTO ARNHEIM ACQUIRED A HEADACHE

1

A ceiling of cloud had formed over the sky, curtaining off the moon and leaving no natural light to relieve the blackness. Out in the river it was practically pitch dark, except where the riding lights of anchored craft sprang their small fragments of scattered luminance out of the gloom.

The Saint slid through the water without sound, without leaving so much as a ripple behind him. All of the rhythmic swing of his arms and legs was beneath the surface, and only his head broke the oily film of the still water; so that not even as much as the pit-pat of two drops of water could have betrayed his passing to anyone a yard away. He was as inconspicuous and unassertive as a clump of sea-weed drifting up swiftly and silently with the tide.

He was concentrating so much on silence that he nearly allowed himself to be run down by some nocturnal sportsman who came skimming by in a canoe when he was only a stone's throw from the *Falkenberg*. The boat leapt at him out of the darkness so unexpectedly that he almost shouted the warning that came instinctively to his lips; the prow brushed his hair, and he submerged himself a fraction of a second before the paddle speared down at him. When he came up again the canoe had vanished as silently as it had come. He caught a glimpse of it again as it arrowed across the reflected lights of the Casino de la Vicomté, and sent a string of inaudible profanities sizzling across the water at the unknown pilot, apparently without causing him to drop dead by remote control.

Then the hull of the *Falkenberg* loomed up for undivided attention. At the very edge of the circle of visibility shed by its lights, he paused to draw a deep breath, and then even his head disappeared under the water, and his hands touched the side before he let himself float gently up again and open his lungs.

He rose under the stern, and trod water while he listened for any sound that would betray the presence of a watcher on the deck. Above the undertones of the harbour he heard the murmur of voices coming through open portholes in two different directions, the dull creak of metal and the seep of the tide making under the hull, but there was no trace of the sharper sound that would have been made by a man out in the open, the rustle of cloth or the incautious easing of a cramped limb. For a full three minutes the Saint stayed there, waiting for the least faint disturbance of the ether that would indicate the wakefulness of a reception committee prepared to welcome any such unauthorised prowler as himself. And he didn't hear any such thing.

The Saint dipped a hand to his belt and brought it carefully out of the water with a mask which he had tucked in there before he left the *Corsair*. It was made of black rubber, as thin and supple as the material of a toy balloon, and when he pulled it on over his head it covered every inch of his face from the end of his nose upwards, and held itself in place by its own gentle elasticity. If by any miscalculation he was to be seen by any member of the crew, there was no need for him to be recognised.

Then he set off again to work himself round the boat. There were three lighted portholes aft, and he stopped by the first of them to find a finger-hold. When he had got it he hauled himself up out of the water, inch by inch, till he could bend one modest eye over the rim.

He looked into a large cabin running the whole width of the vessel. A treble tier of bunks lined two of the three sides which he could see, and seemed to be repeated on the side from which he was looking in. On two of them half-dressed men were stretched out, reading and smoking. At a table in the centre four others, miscellaneously attired in shirtsleeves, jerseys, and singlets, were playing a game of cards, while a fifth was trying to poach enough space out of one side to write a letter. Simon absorbed their faces in a travelling glance that dwelt on each one in turn, and mentally ranked them for as tough a harvest of hard-case sea stiffs as anyone could hope to glean from the scouring of the seven seas. They came up to his expectations in every single respect, and two thin fighting lines creased themselves into the corners of his mouth as he lowered himself back into the river as stealthily as he had pulled himself out of it.

The third porthole lighted a separate smaller cabin with only four bunks, and when he looked in he had to peer between the legs of a man who was reclining on the upper berth across the porthole. By the light brick-red hosiery at the ends of the legs he identified the sleuth who had trailed him that afternoon, and on the opposite side of the cabin the man who had been busily doing nothing in the foyer of the Hotel de la Mer, with one shoe off and the other un-laced, was intent on filling his pipe.

He couldn't look into any of the principal rooms without actually climbing out on to the deck, but from the scraps of conversation that floated out through the windows he gathered that that was where the entertainment of Loretta Page was still proceeding. Professor

Yule appeared to be concluding some anecdote about his submarine experiences.

". . . and when he squashed his nose against the glass, he just stayed there and stared. I never imagined a fish could get so much indignation into its face."

There was a general laugh, out of which rose Vogel's smooth toneless suavity: "Wouldn't even that tempt you to go down, Otto?"

"Not me," affirmed a fat fruity voice which the Saint had not heard before. "I'd rather stay on top of the water. Wouldn't you, Miss Page?"

"It must be awfully interesting," said Loretta—and Simon could picture her, sitting straight and slim, with the light lifting the glints of gold from her brown head. "But I couldn't do it. I should be frightened to death . . ."

The Saint passed on, swimming slowly and leisurely up to the bows. He eeled himself round the stem and drifted down again, close up in the shadow of the other side. As he paddled under the saloon windows on the return journey, Vogel was offering more liqueurs. The man in the pink socks was snoring, and his companion had lighted his pipe. The card game in the crew's quarters finished a deal with a burst of raucous chaff, the letter-writer licked his envelope, and the men who had been reading still read.

Simon Templar edged one hand out of the water to scratch the back of his ear. During the whole of that round tour of inspection he hadn't collected one glimpse or decibel of any sight or sound that didn't stand for complete relaxation and goodwill towards men. Except the faces of some of the crew, which may not have been their faults. But as for any watch on deck, he was ready to swear that it simply didn't exist.

Meaning . . . perhaps that Loretta had been caught the night before by accident, through some sleepless mariner happening to arable up for a breath of fresh air. But even if that was the explanation, a watch would surely have been posted afterwards to frustrate any second attempt.

Unless . . . and he could only see that one reason for the moment . . . unless Loretta had been promoted from a suspect to a certainty—in which case, since she was there on board, the watch could take an evening off.

The Saint gave it up. By every ordinary test, anyhow, he could find nothing in his way, and the only thing to do was to push on and search further.

He hooked his fingers over the counter and drew himself up until he could hitch one set of toes on to the deck. Only for an instant he might have been seen there, upright against the dark water, and then he had flitted noiselessly across the dangerous open space and merged himself into the deep shadow of the superstructure.

Again he waited. If any petrified watcher had escaped detection on his first tour, and had seen his arrival on board, no alarm had been raised. Either the man would be deliberating whether to fetch help, or he would be waiting to catch him when he moved forward. And if the Saint stayed where he was, either the man would go for help or he would come on to investigate. In either of which events he would announce his presence unmistakably to the Saint's tingling ears.

But nothing happened. Simon stood there like a statue while the seconds ticked into minutes on his drumming pulses, and the wetness drained down his legs and formed a pool around his feet, hardly breathing, but only the drone of conversation in the saloon, and a muffled guffaw from the crew's quarters under his feet, reached him out of the stillness.

At last he relaxed, and allowed himself to glance curiously at his surroundings. Over his head, the odd canvas-shrouded contrivance which he had observed from a distance reached out aft like an oversized boom—but there was no mast at the near end to account for it. The *Falkenberg* carried no sail. He stretched up and wriggled his fingers through a gap in the lacing, and felt something like a square steel girder with wire cables stretched inside it; and suddenly the square protuberance, likewise covered with tarpaulin, on which the after end of the boom rested took on a concrete significance. At the end up against the deckhouse he found wheels, and the wire cables turned over the wheels, and ran down close beside the bulkhead to vanish through plated eyes in the deck at his feet . . . He was exploring a nifty, well-oiled, and up-to-date ten-ton grab!

"Well, well, well," murmured the Saint admiringly, to his guardian angel.

And that curiously low flattened stern . . . It all fitted in. Divers could be dropped over that counter with the minimum of difficulty; and the grab could telescope out or swing round, and run its claw round to be steered on to whatever the divers offered it. While, forward of all those gadgets, there were a pair of high-speed engines and a super-streamlined hull to facilitate a lightning getaway if an emergency emerged . . . Which, however priceless a conglomeration of assets, is not among the amenities usually advertised with luxurious pleasure cruisers.

A slow smile tugged at the Saint's lips, and he restrained himself with a certain effort from performing an impromptu hornpipe. The last lingering speck of doubt in his mind had been catastrophically obliterated in those few seconds. Loretta Page hadn't been pulling his leg, or raving, or leading him up the garden. He wasn't kidding himself to make the book read according to the blurb. That preposterous, princely, pluperfect racket did exist, and Kurt Vogel was in it. In it right up to the blue cornice of his neck.

If Simon had been wearing a hat, he would have raised it in solemn salute to the benign deities of outlawry that had poured him into such a truly splendiferous tureen of soup.

And then a door opened further up the deck, and footsteps began to move down towards him. Where he was standing, there wasn't cover for a cat, except what was provided by the shadow of the deckhouse. In another second even that was taken from him, as a switch was clicked over somewhere and a pair of bulkhead lights behind frosted panels suddenly wiped out the darkness in a glow of yellowish radiance.

The Saint's heart arrived in his mouth, as if it had soared up there in an express elevator, and for a moment his hand dropped to the gun in his belt.

And then he realised that the lights which had destroyed his hiding-place hadn't been switched on with that intention. They were simply a part of the general system of exterior illumination of the boat, and their kindling had doubtless been paralleled by the lighting up of other similar bulbs all around the deck. But the footsteps were drawing close to the corner where they would find him in full view, and he could hear Vogel discoursing proprietorially on the details of beam and draught.

Simon looked up speculatively, and his hands reached for the deckhouse roof. In another second he was up there, spread out flat on his stomach, peeping warily down over the edge.

2

All the evening Kurt Vogel had been studiously affable. The dinner had been perfectly cooked and perfectly served; the wine, presented with a charming suggestion of apology, just dulcet enough to flatter a feminine palate, without being too sweet for any taste. Vogel had set himself out to play the polished cosmopolitan host, and he filled the part brilliantly. The other guest, whom he called Otto and who had been introduced to Loretta as Mr Arnheim, a fat broad-faced man with small brown eyes and a moist red pursed-up mouth, fitted into the play with equal correctness. And yet the naive joviality of Professor Yule, with his boyish laugh and his anecdotes and his ridiculously premature grey beard, was the only thing that had eased the strain on her nerves.

She knew that from the moment when she set foot on board she was being watched like a mouse cornered by two patient cats. She knew it, even without one single article of fact which she could have pointed out in support of her belief. There was nothing in the entertainment, not the slightest scintilla of a hint of an innuendo, to give her any material grounds for discomfort. The behaviour of Vogel and Arnheim was so punctilious that without their unfailing geniality it would have been almost embarrassingly formal.

The menace was not in anything they said or did. It was in their silences. Their smiles never reached their eyes. Their laughter went no deeper than their throats. All the time they were watching, waiting, analysing. Every movement she made, every turn of a glance, every inflection of her voice, came under their mental microscope—was watered down, dissected, scrutinised in all its component parts until it had given up its last particle of meaning. And the fiendish cleverness of it was that a perfectly innocent woman in the role she had adopted wouldn't have been bothered at all.

She had realised halfway through the meal that that was the game they were playing. They were merely letting her own imagination work against her, while they looked on. Steadily, skilfully, remorselessly, they were goading her own brain against her, keying her millimetre by millimetre to the tension of self-consciousness where she would make one false step that would be sufficient for their purpose. And all the time they were smiling, talking flatteringly to her, respecting her with their words, so cunningly that an outside observer like Professor Yule could have seen nothing to give her the slightest offence.

She had clung to the Professor as the one infallible lodestar on the tricky course she had to steer, even while she had realised completely what Vogel's patronage of scientific exploration meant. Yule's spontaneous innocence was the one pattern which she had been able to hold to, and when he remained behind in the saloon she felt a cold emptiness that was not exactly fear.

Arnheim had engineered it, with a single sentence of irreproachable and unarguable tact, when Vogel suggested showing her over the ship.

"We'll stay and look after the port," he said, and there was not even the suspicion of a smirk in his eyes when he spoke.

She looked at staterooms, bathrooms, galleys, engines, and refrigerators, listening to his explanations and interjecting the right expressions of admiration and delight, steeling herself against the hypnotic monotone of his voice. She wondered whether he would kiss her in one of the rooms, and felt as if she had been let out of prison when they came out on deck under the open sky.

His hand slid through her arm. It was the first time he had touched her, and even then the touch had no more than an avuncular familiarity.

". . . This open piece of deck is rather pleasant for sitting out when it's hot. We rig an awning over that boom if the sun's too strong."

"It must be marvellous to own a boat like this," she said.

They stood at the rail, looking down the river. Somewhere among the lights in the broadening of the estuary was the *Corsair*, but there was nothing by which she could pick it out.

"To be able to have you here—this is pleasant," he said. "At other times it can be a very lonely ownership."

"That must be your own choice."

"It is. I am a rich man. If I told you how rich I was you might think I was exaggerating. I could fill this boat hundreds of times over with—delectable company. A generous millionaire is always attractive. But I've never done so. Do you know that you're the first woman who has set foot on this deck?"

"I'm sorry if you regret it," she said carelessly.

"I do."

His black eyes sought her face with a burning intensity. She realised with a thrill of fantastic horror that he was absolutely sincere. In that cold passionless iron-toned voice he was making Love to her, as if the performance was dragged out of him against his will. He was still watching her, but within that inflexible vigilance there was a grotesque hunger for illusion that was an added terror.

"I regret it because when you give a woman even the smallest corner of your mind, you give her the power to take more. You are no longer in supreme command of your destiny. The building of a lifetime can be betrayed and broken for a moment's foolishness."

She smiled.

"You're too cynical—you sound as if you'd been disappointed in love."

"I have never been in love—"

The last word was bitten off, as if it had not been intended to be the last. It gave the sentence a curiously persistent quality, so that it seemed to reverberate in the air, repeating itself in ghostly echoes after the actual sound was gone.

She half turned towards him, in a natural quest for the conclusion of that unfinished utterance. Instead she found his hands pinning her to the rail on either side, his great predatory nose thrust down towards her face, his wide lipless mouth working under a torrent of low-pitched quivering words.

"You have tempted me to be foolish. For years I shut all women out of my life, so that none of them could hurt me. And yet what does wealth give without women? I knew that you wanted to come and see my boat. For you it might only have been a nice boat to look at, part of your holiday's amusement; for me it was a beginning. I broke the rule of a lifetime to bring you here. Now I don't want you to go back."

"You'll change your mind again in the morning." Somehow she tore her gaze away, and broke through his arms. "Besides, you wouldn't forget a poor girl's honour—"

She was walking along the deck, swinging her wrap with an affectation of sophisticated composure, finding a moment's escape in movement. He walked beside her, speaking of emotion in that terrifying unemotional voice.

"Honour is the virtue of inferior people who can't afford to dispense with it. I have enough money to ignore whatever anyone may think or anyone may say. If you shared it with me, nothing need hurt you."

"Only myself."

"No, no. Don't be conventional. That isn't worthy of you. It's my business to understand people. You are the kind of woman who can stand aside and look at facts, without being deluded by any fogs of sentimentality. We speak the same language. That's why I talk to you like this."

His hand went across and gripped her shoulder, so that she had to stop and turn.

"You are the kind of woman with whom I could forget to be cold."

He drew her towards him, and she closed her eyes before he kissed her. His mouth was hard, with a kind of rubbery smoothness that chilled her so that she shivered. After a long time he released her. His eyes burned on her like hot coals.

"You'll stay, Loretta?" he said hoarsely.

"No." She swayed away from him. She felt queerly sick, and the air had become heavy and oppressive. "I don't know. You're too quick . . . Ask me again tomorrow. Please."

"I'm leaving tomorrow."

"You are?"

"We're going to St Peter Port. I hoped you would come with us."

"Give me a cigarette."

He felt in his pockets. The commonplace distraction, thrust at him like that, blunted the edge of his attack.

"I'm afraid I left my case inside. Shall we go in?"

He opened the door, and her hand rested on his arm for a moment as she passed him into the wheelhouse. He passed her a lacquer box and offered her a light.

"You didn't show me this," she said, glancing round the room.

Besides being the wheelhouse, it also contrived to be one of the most attractive living- rooms on the ship. At the after end there were shelves of books, half a dozen deep long armchairs invited idleness, a rich carpet covered the floor. Long straight windows ran the length of the beam sides, and the forward end was one curved panel of plate glass in the streamlined shape of the structure. There were flowers in chromium wall brackets, and concealed lights built into the ceiling. The wheel and instrument panel up in one corner, the binnacle in front of it and the littered chart table filling the forward bay, looked almost like property fittings, as if a millionaire's whim had played with the idea of decorating a den in an ordinary house to look like the interior of a yacht.

"We were coming here," said Vogel.

He did not smoke, and he had an actor's mastery over his unoccupied hands which in him seemed to be only the index of an inhuman restraint. She thought he was gathering himself to recover the mood of a moment ago, but before he spoke again there was a knock on the door.

"What is it?" he demanded sharply—it was the first time she had seen a crack in the glassy veneer of his self-possession.

"Excuse me, sir."

The steward who had served dinner stood at the door, his saturnine face mask-like and yet obsequiously expressive. He stood there and waited, and Vogel turned to Loretta with an apologetic shrug.

"I'm so sorry—will you wait for me a moment?"

The door closed on the two men, and she relaxed against the back of a chair. The cigarette between her fingers was held quite steadily— there wasn't a crease or an indentation in the white oval paper to level a mute accusation at the mauling of unsteadied fingers. She regarded it with an odd detached interest. There was even a full half-inch of ash built out unbroken from the end of it—a visible reassurance that she hadn't once exposed the nervous strain that had keyed up inside her almost to breaking pitch.

She dragged herself off the chair-back and moved across the room. This was the first time she had been left alone since she came on board. It was the chance which had forced her through the ordeal of dinner, the one faint hope of finding a shred of evidence to mark progress on the job, without which anything she suffered would have been wasted—and would have to be gone through again.

She didn't know exactly what she was looking for. There was no definite thing to find. She could only search around with an almost frantic expectancy for any scrap of something that might be added to the slowly mounting compilation of what was known about Kurt Vogel—for something that might perhaps miraculously prove to be the last pointer in the long paper-chase. Others had worked like that before, teasing out fragments of knowledge with infinite patience and at infinite risk. Fragments that had been built up over many months into the single clue that had brought her there.

She ran her eyes over the titles of the books in the cases. There were books on philosophy, books on engineering and navigation, books on national and international law in various languages. There were works on criminology, memoirs of espionage, a very few novels of the highly mathematical detective type. They didn't look like dummies. She pulled out a couple at random and flicked the pages. They were real, but it would have taken twenty minutes to try them all.

Her fingers curled up and tightened. Nothing in the books. The littered chart table, perhaps . . . She crossed the room quickly, startled by the loud swish of her dress as she moved, her heart throbbing at a speed which surprised her even more. Funny, she thought. Three weeks ago she would have sworn she didn't possess a heart—or nerves. A week ago. A day ago. Or a century.

She was staring down at the table, at a general chart of the Channel Islands and the adjacent coast of France, spread out on the polished teak. But what was there in a chart? A course had been ruled out from Dinard to St Peter Port, with a dog's-leg bend in it to clear the western end of the Minquiers. There was a jotted note of bearings and distances by the angle of the thin pencilled lines. Nothing in that . . . Her glance wandered helplessly over the scattered smudges of red which stood for lighthouses and buoys.

And then she was looking at a red mark that wasn't quite the same as the other red marks. It was a distinct circle drawn in red ink around a dot of black marked to the east of Sark. Beside it, also in red ink, neat tiny figures recorded the exact bearing.

The figures jumbled themselves before her eyes. She gripped on her bag, trying to stifle the absurd pulse of excitement that was beginning to work under her ribs. Just like that. So easy, so plain. Perhaps the last due, the fabulous open sesame that had been tormenting her imagination. Whatever those red marks meant—and others would soon find that out.

There was a pencil lying on the table, and she had opened her bag before she remembered that she had nothing in it to write on. Lipstick on a handkerchief, then . . . but there were a dozen scraps of torn-up paper in an ashtray beside the pencil, and a square inch of paper would be enough.

Her hand moved out.

Suddenly she felt cold all over. There was a feeling of nightmare limpness in her knees, and when she breathed again it was in a queer little shuddering sigh. But she put her hand into her bag quite steadily and took out a powder box. Quite steadily she dabbed at her nose, and quite steadily she walked away to another table and stood there turning the pages of a magazine—with the thrum of a hundred demented dynamos pounding through her body and roaring sickeningly in her brain.

Those scraps of inviting paper. The pencil ready to be picked up at the first dawn of an idea. The chart left out, with the red bearing marked on it. The excuse for Vogel to leave the room. The ordeal on the deck, before that, which had sabotaged her self-control to the point where the finest edge of her vigilance was dulled . . . to the point where her own aching nerves had tempted her on to the very brink of a trap from which only the shrieked protest of some indefinable sixth sense had held her back . . .

She stood there shivering inside, although her hand was quite steady—scanning a meaningless succession of pictures which printed themselves on her retinas without ever reaching her brain. For several seconds she hadn't the strength to move again.

She fought back towards mastery of herself. After an eternity that could scarcely have lasted a quarter of a minute, she let the magazine fall shut on the table and strolled idly back to the chair from which she had started. She sat down. She could feel that her movements were smooth and unhurried, her face calm and untroubled in spite of the tumult within her. Before that, her face and hands might have betrayed her—it only depended on the angle from which she must have been watched. But when Vogel came back, the smile with which she looked up to greet him was serene and artless.

He nodded.

"Please excuse me."

The smile with which he answered her was perfunctory and preoccupied—he didn't even make the mistake of looking closely at her. He went straight across to a folding bureau built into the panelling on one side of the room, and pulled out a drawer.

"I don't want you to be alarmed," he said in his cold even voice, "but I should like you to stay here a few minutes longer."

She felt the creep of her skin up towards the nape of her neck, and searched for the voice that had once been her own.

"I'm quite comfortable," she said.

"I think you'd better stay," he said, and turned round as he slipped the jacket of a big blued automatic in his hand. "The stewards have seen someone prowling about the ship again, just like that mysterious person I told you about who was here last night. But this time he isn't going to get away so easily."

3

Something as intangible as air and as vicious as a machine-gun began hammering at the pit of Loretta's stomach. The cohort of ghostly dynamos sang in her ears again, blotting out her precarious instant of hard-won peace in a din that was twice as bad as anything before it. She felt the blood draining down from her head until only a dab of powder and the sea-tan on her skin were left to save her from ultimate disaster.

"Not really?" she said.

Her voice seemed to come from four or five miles away, a mere hollow echo of itself. She knew that by some miracle of will-power she had kept the smile steady on her face, but even that wasn't enough. The disaster was not dispelled—it was barely checked.

A queer glimpse of desperate humour was the only thing she could ding to. She, who had met case-hardened men on their own ground, who had faced death as often as dishonour, and with the same poised contempt and unfaltering alertness—she, Loretta Page, who was ranked at Ingerbeck's as the coolest head on a roster of frost-bitten intellects which operated in the perpetual bleakness of temperatures below zero—was being slowly and inevitably broken up. The rasps of a third degree more subtle and deadly than anything she had ever dreamed of were achieving what mere violence and crude terrorism could never have achieved. They were working away as implacably and untiringly as fate, turning her own self into her bitterest enemy.

Vogel's jet-black eyes were fixed on her now. They had moved on to her face like the poles of a magnet from which she would have had to struggle transparently to get away, and yet his aquiline features were still without positive expression.

"You've nothing to worry about," he said, in a purr of caressing reassurance.

"But I'm thrilled." She met his gaze unflinchingly, with the same smile of friendly innocence. "What is it that makes you so popular?"

He shrugged.

"They're probably just some common harbour thieves who think the boat looks as if she might have some valuables on board. We shall find out."

"Let me come with you."

"My dear—"

"I'm not a bit frightened. Not while you've got that gun. And I'll be awfully quiet. But I couldn't bear to miss anything so exciting. Please—would you mind?"

He hesitated for a moment only, and then opened the door on the starboard side.

"All right. Will you keep behind me?"

He switched out the lights, and she followed him out on to the deck. Under the dim glow of the masthead light she caught sight of his broad back moving forward, and stepped after him. In the first shock of transition from the bright illumination of the wheelhouse there was no difference in quality between the blackness of the air and the sea, so that the night seemed to lie all around them, above and below, as if the *Falkenberg* was suspended in a vast bowl of darkness sprinkled with tiny twinkling lights. Vogel was almost invisible in his black evening clothes as he tiptoed round in the half-solid shadow to the other side of the deck, and when he halted she could hardly have been a pace behind him—his shape swam up before her eyes so suddenly that she touched him as she stopped.

"He's still there."

His voice touched her eardrums as a mere bass vibration in the stillness. From where she stood she could look down the whole length of the deck, a grey pathway stencilled with the yellow windows of the saloon where Yule and Arnheim were still presumably discussing the port. The deckhouse profiled itself in black and slanted black banks of shadow across the open space. Away aft there was another shadow merging into the rest, a thing that distinguished itself only by its shorter and sharper carves from the long cubist lines of the others—something that her eyes found and froze on.

Vogel lifted his automatic.

Her left hand gripped the weather-rail. She was trembling, although her mind was working with a clarity that seemed outside herself. That psychological third degree had accomplished its purpose.

Vogel had got her. Even if she had bluffed him all the evening, even if she had betrayed nothing in that paralysed moment of realisation at the chart table, even if she had kept the mask unmoved on her face when he came back—he had got her now. The story of a man prowling on the ship might be a lie. She might be imagining the shadow out of her own guilty fear; or it might only be a member of the crew put out to play the part and build up the deception—to be aimed at and perhaps shot at by Vogel with a blank cartridge. But she didn't know. There was no way for her to know. She had to choose between letting the Saint be shot down without warning, or—

A dozen crazy thoughts crashed through her head. She might throw a noisy fit of maidenly hysterics. She might sneeze, or cough, or faint on his shoulder. But she knew that that was just what he was waiting for her to do. The first hint of interference that she gave would brand her for all time. He would have no more doubts.

She stared at him in a kind of chilled hopeless agony. She could see his arm extended against the lighter grey of the deck, the dull gleam of the automatic held rigidly at the end of it, his black deep-set eyes lined unwinkingly along the sights. Something in the nerveless immobility of his position shouted at her that he was a man to whom the thought of missing had never occurred. She saw the great hungry crook of his nose, the ends of his mouth drawn back so that the thin lips rolled under and vanished into two parallel lines that were as vicious and pitiless as the smile of a cobra would have been. Her own words thundered through her head in a strident mocking chorus: "When you join Ingerbeck's, you don't sign on for a cocktail party . . . You take an oath . . . to do your job . . . keep your mouth shut . . . take the consequences . . ." She had to choose.

So had the Saint.

Moving along the deckhouse roof as silently as a ghost, he had followed everything that happened outside; lying spread-eagled over the wheelhouse, he had leaned out at a perilous angle until he could peer down through one of the windows and see what was happening inside. He had bunched his muscles in a spasm of impotent exasperation when he saw Loretta's hand going out to touch the pencil and spring the trap, and had breathed again when she drew back. Everything that she had endured he had felt sympathetically within himself, and when Vogel came back and took out his automatic, Simon had heard what was said and had understood that also.

Now, gathering his limbs stealthily under him, so close above Loretta's head that he could almost have reached down and touched her, he understood much more. The first mention of a man prowling about the deck had prickled a row of nerve centres all along his spine;

then he had disbelieved; then he had seen the shadow that Loretta
was staring at, and had remembered the dark speeding canoe which
had nearly run him down on his way there. But Loretta hadn't seen
that, and he knew what she must be thinking. He could read what was
in her mind, could suffer everything she was suffering, as if by some
clairvoyant affinity that transcended reason he was identified with her
in the stress of that satanically conceived ordeal, and there was a queer
exaltation in his heart as he stepped off the wheelhouse roof, out into
space over her head.

She saw him as if he had fallen miraculously out of the sky, which
was more or less what he did—with one foot knocking down the
automatic and the other striking flat-soled at the side of Vogel's head.
The gun went off with a crash that echoed back and forth across the
estuary, and Vogel staggered against the rail and fell to his knees.

Simon fell across the rail, caught it with his hands, and hung on
for a moment. Down at the after end of the deck, the shape that had
been lurking there detached itself from the shadows and scurried across
the narrow strip of light to clamber over the rail and drop hectically
downwards.

Loretta Page stared across six feet of Breton twilight at the
miracle—half incredulously, with the breathlessness of indescribable
relief choking in her throat. She saw the flash of white teeth in a
familiar smile, saw him put his fingers to his lips and kiss them out to
her with a debonair flourish that defied comparison, and then, as Vogel
began to drag himself up and around with the gun still clutched in his
right hand, she saw the Saint launch himself up with a ripple of brown
muscles to curve over with hardly a splash into the sea.

He went down in a long shallow dive, and swam out of the
Falkenberg's circle of light before he rose. He had judged his timing
and his angle so well that the canoe flashed past his eyes as he broke
the surface. He put up one hand and caught the gunnel as it went by,

nearly upsetting the craft until the man in it leaned out to the other side and balanced it.

"I thought I told you to say goodbye to France," said the Saint.

"I thought I told you I didn't take your orders," said the other grimly.

"They were Loretta's orders, Steve."

Murdoch dug in the paddle and dragged the canoe round the stern of another yacht moored in the river.

"She's crazy, too," he snarled. "Because you've got around her with your gigolo line doesn't mean I don't know what she'll say when she comes to her senses. I'm staying where I like."

"And getting shot where you like, I hope," murmured Simon. "I won't interfere in the next bonehead play you make. I only butted in this time to save Loretta. Next time, you can take your own curtain."

"I will," said Murdoch prophetically. "Let go this boat." Simon let go rather slowly, resisting the temptation to release his hold with a deft jerk that would have capsized the canoe and damped the pugnaciousness of its ungrateful occupant. He wondered whether Murdoch's aggressiveness was founded on sheer blind ignorance of what might have been the result of his clumsy intrusion, or whether it was put up to bluff away the knowledge of having made an egregious mistake, and most of all he wondered what else would come of the insubordinations of that tough inflexible personality.

One of those questions was partly answered for him very quickly.

He sculled back with his hands, under the side of the yacht near which they had parted company, listening to the low sonorous purr of a powerful engine that had awoken in the darkness. There were no lights visible through any of the portholes, and he concluded that the crew were all on shore. He was on the side away from the *Falkenberg*, temporarily screened even from the most lynx-eyed searcher. The purr of the engine grew louder, and with a quick decision he grasped a stanchion, drew himself up, and rolled over into the tiny after cockpit.

He reached it only a second before the beam of a young searchlight swept over the ship, wiping a bar of brilliant illumination across the deck in its passing. The throb of the engine droned right up to him, and he hitched a very cautious eye over the edge of the cockpit, and saw the *Falkenberg*'s speed tender churning around his refuge, so close that he could have touched it with a boathook. A seaman crouched up on the foredeck, swinging the powerful spotlight that was mounted there; two other men stood up beside the wheel, following the path of the beam with their eyes. Its long finger danced on the water, touched luminously on the hulls of other craft at their anchorages, stretched faintly out to the more distant banks of the estuary . . . fastened suddenly on the shape of a canoe that sprang up out of the dark as if from nowhere, skimming towards the bathing pool at the end of the Plage du Prieuré. The canoe veered like a startled gull, shooting up parallel with the rocky foreshore, but the beam clung to it like a magnetised bar of light, linking it with the tender as if it were held by intangible cables. At the same time the murmur of the tender's engine deepened its note: the bows lifted a little, and a white streamer of foam lengthened away from the stern as the link-bar of light between the two craft shortened.

The canoe turned once more, and headed south again, the man in it paddling with unhurried strokes again, as if he was trying to undo the first impression he had given of taking flight. The *Falkenberg*'s tender turned and drifted up alongside him as the engine was shut off, and at that moment the spotlight was switched out.

Simon heard the voices clearly across the water. "Have you seen anyone swimming around here?"

And Murdoch's sullen answer: "I did see someone—it was over that way."

"Thanks."

The voice of the tender's spokesman was the last one Simon heard. And then, after the very briefest pause, the engine was cut in again, and the tender began to slide smoothly back towards the *Falkenberg*, while the canoe went on its way to the shore. In that insignificant pause the only sound was a faint thud such as a man might have made in dumping a heavy weight on a hard floor. But Simon Templar knew, with absolute certainty, that the man who paddled the canoe on towards the shore was not the man who had been caught by the spotlight, and that the man who had been in the canoe was riding unconsciously in the speedboat as it turned back.

4

The tender slid in under the side of the *Falkenberg*, and the man on the foredeck who had been working the spotlight stood up and threw in the painter. Vogel himself caught the rope and made it fast. Under the natural pallor of his skin there was a curious rigidity, and the harsh black line of his brows over that great scythe of a nose was accentuated by the shadows that fell across his face as he leaned over the rail.

"Did you find anything?"

"No." The man at the wheel answered, standing up in the cockpit. He looked up at Vogel intently as he spoke, and his right hand fingered a rug that seemed to have been thrown down in a rather large bundle on the seat beside him. His phlegmatic voice, with a thick guttural accent, boomed on very slowly and deliberately: "We asked a man in a boat, but he had seen nobody."

"I see," answered Vogel quietly.

He straightened up with a slight shrug, and Professor Yule and Arnheim, on his right, turned away from the rail with him.

"That's a pity," said Yule enthusiastically. "But they can't have searched very far. Shall we go out and have another look?"

"I'm afraid we shouldn't be likely to have any more success, my dear Professor," replied Vogel. "There is plenty of room in the river for anyone to disappear quite quickly, and we were slow enough in starting after them." He turned to Loretta. "I'm very sorry—you must have had rather a shock, and you're more important than catching a couple of harbour thieves."

In some way the quality of his voice had altered—she could feel the change without being able to define it. She felt like somebody who has been watching a fuse smouldering away into a stack of lethal explosives under her feet, and who has seen the fuse miraculously flicker and go out. The sensation of limpness in her muscles was no longer the paralysis of nightmare; it was the relaxation of pure relief. She knew that for that night at least the ordeal was over. Vogel had shot his bolt. In a few hours he would be as balanced and dangerous as ever, his brain would be working with the same ruthless insistence and ice-cold detachment, but for the moment he himself was suffering from a shock, intrinsically slight, and yet actual enough to have jarred the delicately calculated precision of his attack. Something told her that he realised what he had lost, and that he was too clever to waste any more effort on a spoiled opportunity.

"I'm perfectly all right," she said, and her nerves were so steady again that she had to call on acting for the vestiges of trepidation which she felt were demanded. "All the same, I expect you would like a drink."

"That wouldn't do any of us any harm," agreed Arnheim.

In his own way he had altered, although his broad flat face was as bland as ever, and his wet little red mouth was pursed up to the same enigmatic sensual bud that it had been all the evening. He took it on himself to officiate with the decanter, and swallowed half a tumbler of neat whisky in two methodical gulps. Vogel took a very modest allowance with a liberal splash of soda, and sipped it with impenetrable restraint.

But even the artificial film of lightness had gone murky. Vogel's unshaken suavity, with Arnheim's solid co-operation, eliminated any embarrassing silences, but a curious heavy tenseness like the threat of thunder had crept into the atmosphere, a tenseness so subtle and well concealed that at any other time she might have been persuaded that it was purely subjective to her own fatigue. When at last she said that she had had too many late nights already that week, and asked if they would excuse her, she detected a tenuous undercurrent of relief in their protestations.

"I'm sorry all this should have happened to upset the evening," said Vogel, as they left the saloon.

She laid her hand on his arm.

"Honestly, it hasn't upset me," she said. "It's been quite an adventure. I'm just rather tired. Do you understand?"

In that at least she was perfectly truthful. A reaction had set in that had made her feel mentally and physically bruised, as if her mind and body had been crushed together through machine rollers. Sitting beside him again in the cockpit of the speed tender, with a light sea breeze stirring refreshingly through her hair, it seemed as if a whole week of ceaseless effort had gone by since she set out to keep that dangerous appointment.

She felt his arm behind her shoulders and his hand on her knee, and steeled herself to be still.

"Will you come with us tomorrow?"

She shook her head, with a little despairing breath.

"I've been through too much tonight . . . You don't give a girl a chance to think, do you?"

"But there is so little time. We go tomorrow—"

"I know. But does that make it any easier for me? It's my life you want to buy. It mayn't seem very much to you, but it's the only one I've got."

"But you will come."

"I don't know. You take so much for granted—"

"You will come."

His hand on her shoulder was weighting into her flesh. The deep toneless hypnotic command of his voice reverberated into her ears like an iron bell tolling in a resonant abyss, but it was not his command which scarred itself into her awareness and told her that she would have to go. There had been danger, ordeal, respite, but nothing accomplished. She would still have to go.

"Oh, yes . . . I'll come." She turned her face in to his shoulder, and then she broke away. "No, don't touch me again now."

He left her alone, and she sat in the far corner of the cockpit and stared out over the dark water while the tender came in alongside the quay. He walked up to her hotel with her in the same silence, and she wondered what kind of superhumanly immobilised exaltation was pent up in his obedience. She turned at the door, and held out her hand.

"Goodnight."

"Will half-past ten be too early? I could send a steward down before that to do your packing."

"No. I can be ready."

He put her fingers to his lips, and went back to the jetty. On the return journey he took the wheel himself, and sent the speedboat creaming through the dark with her graceful bows lifting and the searchlight blazing a clear pathway over the water. The man who had been in charge of the hunt a little while before stood beside him.

"Where did you put him, Ivaloff?" Vogel asked quietly.

"In No. 9 cabin," answered the man in his sullen throaty voice. "He is tied up and gagged, but I think he will sleep for a little while."

"Do you know who he is?"

"I have not seen him before. Perhaps one of the men who has been watching on shore will know him."

Vogel said nothing. Even if the captive was a stranger, it would be possible to find out who he was. If he carried no papers that would identify him, he would be made to talk. It never occurred to him that the prisoner might be innocent: Ivaloff made no mistakes, and Vogel himself had seen the canoe's significant swerve and first instinctive attempt to dodge the searchlight. He threw the engine into neutral and then into reverse, bringing the tender neatly up to the companion, and went across the deck to the wheelhouse.

Professor Yule was there. He glanced up from a newspaper.

"I wish I knew what these gold mining shares were going to do," he remarked casually. "I could sell now and take a profit, but I'd like to see another rise first."

"You should ask Otto about it—he is an expert," said Vogel. "By the way, where is he?"

"I don't know. He went out to look for part of a broken cuff-link. Didn't you see him on deck?"

Vogel shook his head.

"Probably he was on the other side of the ship. Do you hold very many of these shares?"

He selected a cigar from a cedar wood cabinet and pierced it carefully while Yule talked. So Arnheim hadn't been able to wait more than a few minutes before he tried to find out something about the man they had captured. Otto had always been impatient—his brain lacked that last infinitesimal milligram of poise which gave a man the power to possess himself indefinitely and imperturbably. He should have waited until Yule went to bed.

Not that it was vitally important. The Professor was as unsuspecting as a child, and No. 9 cabin was the dungeon of the ship—a room so scientifically soundproofed that a gun fired in it would have been inaudible where they were. Vogel drew steadily at his cigar and discussed the gold market with unruffled composure for a quarter of an hour, until Yule picked himself up and decided to retire.

Vogel stood at the chart table and gave the Professor time to reach his stateroom. In front of him was the chart with that lone position marked in red ink, the scraps of torn paper in the ashtray, the pencil lying beside it . . . untouched. Loretta Page had stood over those things for a full minute, but from where he was watching he could not see her face. When she turned away she had seemed unconcerned. And yet . . . there were more things than that to be explained. Kurt Vogel was not worried—his passionlessly efficient brain had no room for such a futile emotion—but there had been other moments in his career, like that, when he knew that he was fighting for his life.

He left the chart table without a shrug, and left the wheel-house by the door at the after end. Between him and the saloon a companion ran down to the lower deck. He went aft along the alleyway at the bottom—the door of the Professor's cabin was close to the foot of the companion, and he paused outside it for a couple of seconds and heard the thud of a dropped shoe before he went on. His cigar glowed evenly, gripped with the barest necessary pressure between his teeth, and his feet moved with a curious soundlessness on the thick carpet.

No. 9 cabin was the last door in the passenger section. Just beyond it another companion sloped steeply up to the after deck, and abaft the companion a watertight door shut off the continuation of the alleyway on to which the crew's quarters opened. Vogel stopped and turned the handle, and a faint frown creased in between his eyebrows when the door did not move.

He raised his hand to knock, and then for some reason he glanced downwards and saw that the key was in the lock on the outside. At the same time he became conscious of a cool dampness on his hand. He opened it under the light, and saw a glisten of moisture in the palm and on the inside of his fingers.

For an instant he did not move. And then his hand went down slowly and touched the door-handle again. He felt the wetness of it under the light slide of his fingertips, and bent down to touch the carpet. That also was damp; so were the treads of the companion.

Without hesitation he turned the key silently in the lock, slipped an automatic out of his pocket, and thrust open the door. The cabin was in darkness, but his fingers found the switch instantaneously and clicked it down. Otto Arnheim lay at his feet in the middle of the floor, with his face turned whitely up to the light and his round pink mouth hanging vacuously open. There were a couple of lengths of rope carelessly thrown down beside him— and that was all.

CHAPTER FOUR:
HOW STEVE MURDOCH REMAINED OBSTINATE AND SIMON TEMPLAR RENDERED FIRST AID

1

If the quality of surprise had ever been a part of Orace's emotional make-up, the years in which he had worked for Simon Templar had long since exhausted any trace of its existence. Probably from sheer instinctive motives of self-preservation he had acquired the majestically immutable sang-froid of a jellied eel, and he helped Simon to haul his prize out on to the deck of the *Corsair* as unconcernedly as he would have lent a hand with embarking a barrel of beer.

"How d'you like it?" asked the Saint, with a certain pardonable smugness.

He was breathing a little deeply from the effort of life-saving Steve Murdoch's unconscious body through the odd half-mile of intervening water, and the shifting muscles glistened over his torso as he filled his chest. Murdoch, lying in a heap with the water oozing out of his sodden clothes, was conspicuously less vital, and Orace inspected him with perceptible distaste.

"Wot is it?" he inquired disparagingly.

"A sort of detective," said the Saint. "I believe he's a good fellow at heart, but he doesn't like me and he's damned stubborn. He's tried to die once before tonight, and he didn't thank me when I stopped him."

Orace sucked his moustache ghoulishly over the body. "Is 'e dead now?"

"Not yet—at least I don't think so. But he's got a lump on the back of his head the size of an apple, and I don't expect he'll feel too happy when he wakes up. Let's try him and see."

They undressed Murdoch out on the deck, and Simon wrung out his clothes as best he could and tied them in a rough bundle which he chucked into the galley oven when they took the still unconscious man below. He left Orace to apply the usual restoratives, and went back into the saloon to towel himself vigorously and brush his hair. He heard various groans and thumps and other sounds of painful resuscitation while he was doing this, and he had just settled into a clean shirt and a pair of comfortable old flannel trousers when the communicating door opened and the fruit of Orace's labours shot blearily in.

It was quite obvious that the Saint's prophecy was correct. Mr Murdoch was not feeling happy. The tender imprint of a skilfully wielded blackjack had established at the base of his skull a high-powered broadcasting station of ache from which messages of hate and ill-will were radiating in all directions with throbbing intensity, while the grinding machinery of transmission was setting up a roaring din that threatened to split his head. Taking these profound disadvantages into consideration, Mr Murdoch entered, comparatively speaking, singing and dancing, which is to say that he only looked as if he would like to beat somebody on the head with a mallet until they sank into the ground.

"What the hell is this?" he demanded truculently.

"Just another boat," answered the Saint kindly. "On your left, the port side. On your right, the starboard. Up there is the forward or sharp end, which goes through the water first—"

Murdoch glowered at him speechlessly for a moment, and then the team of pneumatic drills started work again under the roof of his skull, and he sank on to a bunk.

"I thought it would be you," he said morosely.

Orace came in like a baronial butler, put down a tray of whisky and glasses, sniffed loudly, and departed. Murdoch stared at the door which closed behind him with the penumbras of homicide darkening again on his square features.

"I could kill that guy twice, and then drown him." Murdoch grabbed the whisky- bottle, poured three fingers into a glass, and swallowed it straight. He compressed his lips in a grimace, and looked up at the Saint again. "Well, here I am—and who the hell asked you to bring me here?"

"You didn't," Simon admitted.

"Didn't you tell me you'd keep out of the way next time?"

"That was the idea."

"Well, what d'ya think I'm going to do—fall on your neck and kiss you?"

"Not in those trousers, I hope," said the Saint.

The trousers belonged to Orace, who was taller but not so bulky. As a result, they were stretched dangerously across the seat, and hung in a graceful concertina over the ankles. Murdoch glared down at them venomously, and they responded with an ominous rending squeak as he moved to get hold of the whisky again.

"I didn't ask you to pull me out, and I'm not going to thank you. If you thought I'd fall for you, you're wrong. Was that the idea, too? Did you think you might be able to get under my skin that way—make the same sort of monkey outa me that you've made outa Loretta? Because you won't. I'm not so soft. You can slug me again and take me back to the *Falkenberg*, and we'll start again where we left off, and that's as far as you'll get."

Simon sauntered over to the table and helped himself to a measured drink.

"Well, of course that's certainly a suggestion," he remarked. He sat down opposite Murdoch and put up his feet along the settee. "I've always heard that Ingerbeck's was about the ace firm in the business."

"It is."

"Been with them long?" asked the Saint caressingly.

"About ten years."

"Mmm."

Murdoch's eyes narrowed suspiciously. "What the hell d'you mean?"

"I mean they can't be so hot if they've kept you on the overhead for ten years."

"Yeah?"

"Yeah—as we used to say in the movies. Stay where you are, Steve. If you try to start any rough stuff with me I shall hit your face so hard that you'll have to be fed from behind. Besides which, those pants will split."

"Go on."

Simon flicked open the cigarette-box and helped himself to a smoke. He slipped a match out of the ash stand and sprung it into flame with his thumb-nail.

"Now and for the last time," he said, with the caress in his voice smoothed out until it was as soothing as a sheet of ice, "will you try to understand that I don't give a good God- damn how soon you have your funeral. Your mother may miss you, and even Ingerbeck's may send a wreath, but personally I shall be as miserable as a dog with a new tree. The only reason I interfered on the *Falkenberg* was because Vogel wasn't half so interested in shooting you as in seeing how Loretta would like it. The only reason I pulled you out again—"

"Was what?"

"Because if you'd stayed there they'd have found out more about you. You're known. Thanks to your brilliant strategy in tearing into the Hotel de la Mer and shouting for Loretta at the top of your voice, the bloke who was sleuthing her this afternoon knows your face. And if he'd seen you tonight on an identification parade—that would have been that. For Loretta, anyway. And that's all I'm interested in. As it is, you may have been recognised already. I had to take a chance on that. I could only lug you out as quickly as possible, and hope for the best. Apart from that, you could have stayed there and been massaged with hot irons, and I shouldn't have lost any sleep. Is that plain enough or do you still think I've got a fatherly interest in your future?"

Murdoch held himself down on the berth as gingerly as if it had been red hot, and his chin jutted out as if his fists were itching to follow it.

"I get it. But you feel like a father to Loretta—huh?"

"That's my business."

"I'll say it is. There are plenty of greasy-haired dagoes making big money at it."

"My dear Steve!"

"I know you, Saint," Murdoch said raspingly. His big hands rolled his glass between them as if they were playing with the idea of crushing it to fragments with a single savage contraction, and the hard implacable lights were smouldering under the surface of his eyes. "You're crook. I've heard all about you. Maybe there aren't any warrants out for you at the moment. Maybe you kid some people with that front of yours about being some kind of fairy-tale Robin Hood trying to put the world right in his own way. That stuff don't cut any ice with me. You're crook—and you're in the racket for what you can get out of it."

Simon raised his eyebrows. "Aren't you?"

"Yeah, I get one hundred bucks a week out of it, and the man who says I don't earn 'em is a liar. But that's the last cent I take."

"Of course, that's very enterprising of you," murmured the Saint, in the same drawl of gentle mockery. "But we can't all be boy scouts. I gather that you think I wouldn't be content with one hundred bucks a week?"

"You?" Murdoch was viciously derisive. "If I thought that, I'd buy you out right now." "Where's your money?"

"What for?"

"To buy me out. One hundred dollars a week—and that's more than I thought I was going to get out of it."

The other stared at him.

"Are you telling me you'll take a hundred a week to get out?"

"Oh, no. But I'll take a hundred a week to get in. You'll have the benefit of all my brains, which you obviously need pretty badly, and I shall get lots of quiet respectable fun and a beautiful glow of virtue to keep me warm for the winter. I'm trying to convince you that I'm a reformed character. Your loving sympathy has made me see the light," said the Saint brokenly, "and from now on my only object will be to live down my evil past—"

"And I'm trying to convince you that I'm not so dumb that a twister like you can sell me a gold brick!" Murdoch snarled violently. "You came into this by accident, and you saw your chance. You greased around Loretta till she told you what it was about, and you've made her so crazy she's ready to eat outa your hand. If I hadn't come along you'd of played her for a sap as long as it helped you, and ditched her when you thought you had a chance to get away with something. Well, you bet you're going to get out. I'm going to find a way to put you out—but it ain't going to be with a hundred dollars!"

The Saint rounded his lips and blew out a smoke-ring. For a moment he did actually consider the possibilities of trying to convince

Murdoch of his sincerity, but he gave up the idea. The American's suspicions were rooted in too stubborn an antagonism for any amount of argument to shake them, and Simon had to admit that Murdoch had some logical justification. He looked at Murdoch thoughtfully for a while, and read the blunt facts of the situation on every line of the other's grim hard-boiled face. Oh, well . . . perhaps it was all for the best. And that incorrigible imp of buffoonery in his make-up would have made it difficult to carry the argument to conviction, anyway . . .

The Saint sighed.

"I suppose you're entitled to your point of view, Steve," he conceded mildly. "But of course that makes quite a difference. Now we shall have to decide what we're going to do with you."

"Don't worry about me," retorted Murdoch. "You worry about yourself. Give me my clothes back, and I'll be on my way."

He dumped his glass on the table and stood up, but Simon Templar did not move. "The question is—will you?" said the Saint.

His voice was pleasant and conversational, coloured only with the merest echo of that serene and gentle mockery which had got under Murdoch's toughened hide at their first encounter, and yet something behind it made the other stand momentarily very still.

Murdoch's chunky fists knotted up slowly at his sides, and he scowled down at the slim languid figure stretched out on the settee with his eyes slotting down to glittering crevices in the rough-hewn crag of his face.

"Meaning what?" he demanded grittily.

"I'm not so thrilled with your promise to put me out," said the Saint. "And I don't know that we can let you go on getting into trouble indefinitely. Twice is all right, but the third time might be unlucky. I may be a boy scout, but I'm not a nursemaid. One way and another, Steve, it looks as if we may have to shut you up where you won't be able to get into mischief for a while."

2

Murdoch hunched over him as if he couldn't believe his ears. There was stark pugnacious incredulity oozing out of every pore of him, and his jaw was levered up till his under lip jutted out in a bellicose ridge under his nose. His complexion had gone as red as a turkeycock's.

"Say that again?"

"I said we may have to keep you where you won't get in the way," answered the Saint calmly. "Don't look so unhappy—there's another bottle of whisky on board, and Orace will bring you your bread and milk and tuck you up at night."

"That's what you think, is it?" grated Murdoch. "Well, you try to keep me here!"

The Saint nodded. His right hand, with the half-smoked cigarette still clipped between the first two fingers, slid lazily into the shelf beside the settee, under the porthole. It came out with the automatic which he had put down there when he began to dress.

"I'm trying," he said, almost apologetically.

Murdoch shied at the gun like a startled horse. His screwed-up eyes opened out in two slow dilations of rabid unbelief.

"Do you mean you're trying to hold me up?" he barked.

"That was the rough idea, brother," said the Saint amiably, "I'm not very well up in these things, but I believe this is the approved procedure. I point a rod at you, like this, and then you either do what I tell you or try to jump on me and get shot in the dinner. Correct me if I'm wrong."

The bantering serenity of his voice lingered on in the air while Murdoch stared at him. The Saint was smiling faintly, and the sheen of sapphire in his eyes was alive with irrepressible humour, but the automatic in his hand was levelled with a perfectly sober precision that denied the existence of any joke.

Murdoch blinked at it as if it had been the first specimen of its kind which he had ever seen. His gaze travelled lingeringly up from it to the Saint's face, and the incredulity faded out of his features before a spreading hardness of cold calculating wrath. He swallowed once, and his chin settled down on his chest.

"You think you can get away with that, do you?"

"I'm betting on it."

Simon met the other's reddened glare as if he hadn't a shadow on his horizon, and wondered what the odds ought to be if it were a betting proposition. And he became reluctantly aware that any prudent layer would consider them distinctly hazardous. There was something consolidating itself on Murdoch's thinned-out lips which stood for the kind of raging foolhardy fearlessness that produces heroes and tombstones in cynically unequal proportions.

And at the same time something quite different was thrusting itself towards the front of the Saint's consciousness. It had started like the burn of a cruising bee away out in the far reaches of the night, a mere stir of sound too trivial to attract attention. While they were talking it had grown steadily nearer, until the drone of it quivered through the saloon as a definite pulse of disturbance in the universe. And now, in the silence while he and Murdoch watched each other, it suddenly roared up and stopped, leaving a sharp void in the auditory scale through which came the clear swish and chatter of settling waters.

Simon felt the settee dip gently under him, and Murdoch's glass tinkled on the table as the wash slapped against the side. And then an almost imperceptible jar of contact ran through the boat and a voice spoke somewhere outside.

"Ahoy, *Corsair!*"

The Saint felt as if a starshell had burst inside his head. Understanding dawned upon him in a blinding light that showed him the meaning of that sequence of sounds, the owner of the voice that had hailed them, and everything that had led up to what lay outside, as clearly as if they had been focused under a batten of sun arcs. If he had not been so taken up with the immediate problem that had been laid in front of him, he might have guessed it and waited for it all down to the last detail, but now it came to him as a shock that electrified all his faculties as if he had taken a shot of liquid dynamite.

It could hardly have taken a second to develop, that galvanic awakening of every nerve, but in the latter half of that scorching instant the Saint reviewed the circumstances and realised everything that had to be done. Murdoch was still half arrested in the stillness which the interruption had brought upon him: his head was turned a little to the left, his mouth a little open, his gaze fractionally diverted. At that moment his train of thought was written across him in luminous letters a yard high. He also was considering the interruption, working over its bearing on his own predicament, while the simmer of fighting obstinacy in him was boiling up to outright defiance. The Saint knew it. That chance event was wiping out the last jot of hesitation in the American's mind. In another split second he would let out a yell or try to jump the gun—or both. But his powers of comprehension were functioning a shade less rapidly than the Saint's, and that split second made as much difference as twenty years.

Simon let go the automatic and unfolded himself from the settee. He came up like the backlash of a cracked whip, and his fist hit Murdoch under the jaw with a clean crisp smack that actually forestalled the slight thud of the gun hitting the carpet. Murdoch's eyes glazed mutely over, and Simon caught him expertly as he straightened up on his feet.

"Ahoy, *Corsair!*"

"Ahoy to you," answered the Saint.

The communicating door at the end of the saloon was opening, and Orace's globular eyes peered over his moustache through the gap. There was no need of words. Simon heaved Murdoch's inanimate body towards him like a stuffed dummy, with a dozen urgent commands sizzling voicelessly on his gaze, and followed it with the glass from which Murdoch had been drinking. And then, without waiting to assure himself that Orace had grasped the situation to the full, he snatched up his gun and leapt for the companion in one continuous movement, slipping the automatic into his hip pocket as he went.

He started with lightning speed, but he emerged into the after cockpit quite leisurely, and everything else had been packed into such a dizzy scintilla of time that there was no undue hiatus between the first hail and his appearance. He turned unhurriedly to the side, and Kurt Vogel, standing up in the speedboat, looked up at him with his sallow face white in the dim light.

"Hullo," said the Saint genially.

"May I come aboard for a moment?"

"Surely."

Simon reached out an arm and helped him up. Again he experienced the peculiar revulsion of the other's strong clammy grip.

"I'm afraid this is a most unseemly hour to pay a visit," said Vogel, in his suave flat voice. "But I happened to be coming by, and I hoped you hadn't gone to bed."

"I'm never very early," said the Saint cheerfully. "Come on below and have a drink."

He led the way down to the saloon, and pushed the cigarette-box across the table. "D'you smoke?" Vogel accepted, and Simon raised his voice. "Orace!"

"As a matter of fact, I only called in in case you'd made up your mind about tomorrow," said Vogel, taking a light. "Perhaps you didn't take my invitation seriously, but I assure you we'll be glad to see you if you care to come."

"It's very good of you." Simon looked up as Orace came in. "Bring another glass, will you, Orace?"

He put the match to his own cigarette and lounged back on the opposite berth while Orace brought the glass. He rested his fingertips on the edge of the table and turned his hand over with a perfectly natural movement that brought his thumb downwards. With his back turned to Vogel, Orace set down the glass. His face was always inscrutable, and the fringe of his luxuriant moustache concealed any expression that might ever have touched his mouth, but without moving another muscle of his features he drooped one eyelid deliberately before he retired, and the Saint felt comforted.

"I would rather like to come," said the Saint frankly, as he poured out the whisky.

"Then we'll expect you definitely. Loretta is coming, too."

"Who's coming?"

"You know—Miss Page—"

Simon eased a drop of liquid from the neck of the bottle on to the rim of the glass with a hand as steady as a rock, and looked up with a smile.

"I'm afraid I don't," he murmured. "Who is the lady?"

"She was with us—I beg your pardon," Vogel said quickly. "My memory is playing me tricks—I had an idea she was with us when we met this morning. Perhaps you will meet her in Guernsey."

"If she's as pretty as her name, I hope I do," said the Saint lightly.

He passed the glass over and sat down again, feeling as if his stomach had been suddenly emptied with a vacuum pump.

"We shall be sailing about eleven," proceeded Vogel urbanely. "But we shan't take long on the trip—we marine motorists have rather an advantage in speed," he added deprecatingly. "I don't wonder you thorough-going yachtsmen despise us, but I'm afraid I'm too old to learn your art." Simon nodded vaguely. But there was nothing vague in his mind. Every fibre of his being seemed to have been dissected into an individual sentience of its own: he was conscious of the vitality of every cell and corpuscle of his body, as though each separate atom of him was pressed into the service of that supercharged aliveness. His whole intellect was waiting, cat-like, for Vogel to show his hand.

Vogel gave him no sign. His smooth aggressively profiled face might have been moulded out of wax, with its appearance of hard and uniform opacity under the thin glaze of skin. The Saint's keenest scrutiny could find no flaw in it. He had watched Vogel working up through a conspiracy of intricate and marvellously juggled tensions towards a climax of cunning that had been exploded like a soap-bubble at the very instant of crisis; he knew that even after that Vogel must have taken, a re-staggering shock when he discovered the vanishment of their prisoner and the slumber of Otto Arnheim; he could guess that even Vogel's impregnable placidity must have felt the effect of a cumulation of reverses that would have shaken any other man to the beginnings of fear; and yet there was not a microscopical fissure in the sleek veneer of that vulturine face. Simon admitted afterwards that the realisation of all that was implied by that immovable self-command gave him a queer momentary superstitious feeling of utter helplessness, like nothing else that he had ever experienced in the presence of another human being.

He took hold of the feeling with a conscious effort and trod it ruthlessly down. Vogel was holding his drink up in one steady hand, imperturbably surveying the details of the saloon, with the eyelids drooping under the shadow of his black overhanging brows, and Simon watched him without a tremor in the careless good humour of his gaze.

"But this is a charming boat," Vogel, remarked idly. "What is her tonnage?"

"About twenty-five."

"Delightful . . ." Vogel got up and began to wander around, studying the panelling, touching the fittings, investigating the ingenious economy of space with all the quiet pleasure of an enthusiast. "I envy you, really—to be able to have something like this all to yourself, without bothering about crews and formalities. If I were twenty years younger . . . Did you have her fitted out yourself?"

"Yes."

"Of course. And are all the other rooms as attractive as this one?"

So that was how it was coming. The Saint felt a tiny pulse beginning to beat way back in the depths of his brain, like the frantic ticking of a distant clock racing with time.

"They're pretty comfortable," he said modestly, and Vogel caught him up without a second's hesitation.

"I wish I could see them. I'm tremendously interested—I had no idea a small boat could be so luxurious. You might even convert me!"

Simon brought the tip of his cigarette to a red glow, and feathered a fading cloud of smoke through his lips.

He was for it. The fuse was lighted. There was no excuse, however plausible, no tactful way of changing the subject, however fluent, from which Vogel would not draw his own conclusions. Vogel had got him, exactly as he had got Loretta a few hours before. He had paid that belated call, transparently, with the one object of discovering whether the *Corsair* would yield any connecting link with the night's disturbances, and he would not be prepared to go home satisfied after one brief confined session in the saloon. Simon could see the man's black unswerving eyes fixed on him intently, outwardly with no more than the ingenuous eagerness which made the granting of his request a favour that it would be difficult in any circumstances to refuse— inwardly with a merciless insistence of which no one without the Saint's knowledge would have been conscious. The fuse was lighted, and how soon the mine would go up depended only on Orace's perception of the secondary uses of keyholes.

Now that the die was cast, Simon felt a curious contented relaxation.

"By all manner of means," he said amicably. "Let me show you the works."

3

He stood up, lighting a second cigarette from the stub of the first. The movement gave a few seconds' grace in which Orace, if he had been listening, might prepare for the emergency as best he could. But it could not be prolonged a moment beyond the requirements of the bare physical facts, and with an inaudible prayer to the hard worked gods of all good buccaneers, the Saint flattened his discarded butt in the ashtray and opened the communicating door.

Simon Templar could rake over his memory at any time and comb out an impressive crop of moments which he had no desire to live over again. In spite of the ultimate balance of success that showed on the books of his meteoric career, his life had contained its full quota of occasions that definitely looked their best in distant retrospect. But of all that collection of unenjoyable contingencies there were very few to which he would so fervently have refused an encore as those hectic instants during which the vista beyond the saloon unrolled itself before the opening door. The spectacle of Orace sitting curled up in the diminutive galley, alone, with a paper-covered detective story on his knee, was such a dizzy anti-climax that it made the Saint feel somewhat light-headed. He could have raised the protective curtain of Orace's moustache and kissed him.

Fortunately the presence of Kurt Vogel precluded any such regrettable demonstration. Simon cleared his throat and spoke almost hesitatingly through the ecstatic glow which enveloped him.

"This is the kitchen, where we heat the tins and open the bottles. On the right, the refrigerator, where we keep the beer warm . . ."

He exhibited all the features of the galley with feverish pride, and Vogel, as flatteringly impressed as any proud owner could want a guest to be, admired them all in turn—the cunningly fitted glass and crockery racks, the planned compartments for all kinds of provisions, the paraffin geyser that provided hot water at the turn of a tap, the emergency stove slung in gimbals for use when the weather was too rough for a kettle to stand on the ordinary gas cooker, and all the other gadgets which had been installed to reduce discomfort to the vanishing point. All the time Simon was casting hopeful glances at Orace, searching for a hint of what his staff had done to meet the situation, but the staff had returned phlegmatically to its volume of blood, and its battle-scarred race offered as many clues as a boiled pudding.

Eventually they had to move on. Beyond the galley there was a short alleyway, and Simon led the way briskly down it.

"That's the bathroom and toilet," he explained casually, indicating the first door on the left as he went by, and he would have gone quickly on, but Vogel stopped.

"A bathroom—really? That's even more remarkable on a boat this size. May I look at it?"

Simon turned, with the glow of relief on him dying down again to a cold resignation.

Of all the places where Orace might have been expected to dump his charge in a hurry, the bathroom seemed the most probable. Simon looked innocently at Vogel, and the edge of his gaze, overlapping his guest, sought frantically for inspiration over Vogel's shoulder. But Orace was deep in his sanguinary literature; only the back of his head could be seen, and he had not moved.

"There's nothing much to see," began the Saint diffidently, but Vogel had already turned the handle.

Simon leaned sidelong against the bulkhead and very deliberately estimated the chances of a shot going unheard by the seaman whom Vogel had left outside in charge of his speedboat. He also gave some consideration to the exact spot on Vogel's anatomy where a bullet could be made to do a regulated amount of damage without leaving any margin for an outcry to add itself to the noise. His left thumb was tucked loosely into his belt; his right hand was a little behind his hip, the fingers hovering on the opening of the pocket into which he had slipped his gun. The cigarette between his lips slanted out at a rakish angle that would have made certain people who knew him well stand very still while they decided what scrap of cover they were going to dive for when the storm broke loose. And yet there was the ghost of a smile lingering on his mouth, and a shifting twinkle in his blue eyes, which might have misled those who were not so well informed.

"But that's almost luxurious!" came Vogel's bland ingratiating accents. "And a shower, too . . . I certainly am learning a lesson—I almost wish I could find something that you've forgotten."

Simon prised himself off the bulkhead and let his right hand fall to his side. He didn't take out a handkerchief and mop his brow, but he wished he could have indulged in that sedative gesture. His shirt felt damp in the small of his back.

"I hope you won't do that," he said earnestly. "Now, this is just a small single cabin—" The tour went on. Vogel praised the small single cabin.

He studied the berth, the lockers under it, and peeped inside the wardrobe.

The Saint began to wonder if he was simply undergoing one of Vogel's diabolically clever psychological third degrees. There was something as nightmarish as a slow-motion avalanche about Vogel's patient thoroughness, a suggestion of feline cruelty in his velvety smoothness that burred the edges of Simon's nervous system into crystals of jagged steel. He felt an almost irresistible temptation to throw guile to the winds—to say, "Okay, brother. I have got Steve Murdoch here, and he is the bird who paid you a call earlier this evening, and so what?"—to do any foolish thing that would wipe that self-assured smirk off the other's face and bring the fencing match to a soul-satisfying showdown. Only the knowledge that that might very well be what Vogel was playing for eased the strain of holding himself in check.

On the starboard side there was one double cabin. Vogel admired this also. There were two fitted wardrobes for him to peer into, and also a large recessed cupboard for storing blankets and other dry gear, besides the usual lockers under the berths. As Vogel methodically opened each door in turn, to the accompaniment of a tireless flow of approbation, the Saint felt himself growing so much older that it wouldn't have surprised him to look down and see a long white beard spreading over his shirt.

"This is the most perfect thing I've ever seen." Vogel was positively purring by then: his waxen skin shone with a queer gloss, as if it had been polished. "You should have made this your profession—I should have been one of your first clients . . . And that door at the end?"

Simon glanced up the alleyway.

"The fo'c'sle? That's only Orace's quarters—"

And at the same time he knew that he might just as well save his breath. Vogel had already declared himself, at the bathroom door and since then, as a sightseer who intended to see every sight there was, and it would have been asking a miracle for him to have allowed himself to be headed off on the threshold of the last door of all.

The Saint shrugged.

At any rate, the gloves would be off. The nibbling and niggling would be finished, and the issue would be joined in open battle, and the Saint liked to fight best that way. Behind that door lay the showdown. He knew it, as surely as if he could have seen through the partition, and he faced it without illusion. Even at that transcendental moment the irrepressible devil in him came to his aid, and he was capable of feeling a deep and unholy glee of anticipation at the thought of the conflicting emotions that would shortly be chasing each other across Vogel's up-ended universe.

He opened the door and stood aside, with a sense of peace in the present and a sublime faith in the exciting future.

Vogel went in.

Perhaps after all, Simon reflected, his gun could stay where it was. A clean sharp blow with the edge of his hand across the back of the other's neck might achieve the same immediate effect with less commotion, and with less risk of letting him in for the expenses of a high-class funeral later. Of course, that would still leave the loyal mariner outside, but he would have had to be dealt with anyhow . . . And then what? The Saint's brain raced through a hectic sequence of results and possibilities . . .

And then he heard Vogel's voice again, through a kind of giddy haze that swept over him at the sound of it.

"Excellent . . . excellent . . . Why, I've seen a good many boats in which the owner's accommodation was not half so good. And this is all, is it?"

If a choir of angels had suddenly materialised in front of him and started to sing a syncopated version of *Christmas Day in the Workhouse*, Simon Templar could hardly have had a more devastating reason to mistrust his ears. If the *Corsair* had suddenly started to spin round and round like a top, his insides couldn't have suffered a more cataclysmic bouncing on their moorings. With a resolute effort he swallowed his stomach, which was trying to cake-walk up into his mouth, and looked into the fo'c'sle.

Vogel was coming out, and his cordial smile was unchanged. If he had just suffered the crowning disappointment of his unfortunate evening, there was no sign of it on his face. And behind him, quite plainly visible to every corner, Orace's modest cabin was as naked of any other human occupancy as the ice-bound fastnesses of the North Pole.

The Saint steadied his reeling brain, and took the cigarette from between his lips. "Yes, that's all," he answered mechanically. "You can't get much more into a fifty- footer."

"And that?" Vogel pointed upwards.

"Oh, just a hatchway on to the deck."

Forestalling any persuasion, he caught the ladder rungs screwed to the bulkhead, drew himself up, and opened it. After all he had been through already, his heart was too exhausted to turn any more somersaults, but the daze deepened round him as he hoisted himself out on to the deck and found no unconscious body laid neatly out in the lee of the coaming. They had been through the ship from stern to stem, and that hatchway was the last most desperate door through which Murdoch's not inconsiderable bulk could have been pushed away. If Orace hadn't dumped the man out there, he must have melted him and poured him down the sink, or ordered a fiery chariot from Heaven to take him away: the Saint was reaching a stage of blissful delirium in which any miracle would have seemed less fantastic than the facts.

He stretched down a hand and helped Vogel to follow him out. They stood together under the dimly luminous canopy of the masthead light, and Vogel extended his cigarette- case. There were only the ordinary shadows on the deck, and the one seaman sat patiently smoking his pipe in the cockpit of the speed tender tied up astern.

"I'm afraid my enthusiasm ran away with me," said Vogel. "I should never have asked you to show me round at this hour. But I assure you it's been worth it to me—in every way."

He laid the faintest and most innocent emphasis on the last three words.

Simon leaned on the mast, with one arm curled round it, as if it had been a giant's lance. The stub of his old cigarette fizzed into the water.

"It's been no trouble at all," he murmured courteously. "What about one for the road?"

"Many thanks. But I've kept you up too late already."

"You haven't."

"Then I'll leave before I do." Vogel waved a hand to his marine chauffeur. "Ivaloff!" He smiled, and held out his hand. "We'll look out for you, then, at St Peter Port?"

"I'll be there by tea-time, if we have any wind." The Saint sauntered aft beside his guest. Beyond all doubt, the stars in their courses fought for him. If he could have given vent to his feelings, he would have serenaded them with crazy carols. He thought about the munificent rewards which might suitably be heaped on the inspired head of Orace, when that incomparable henchman could be made to reveal the secrets of his wizardry.

His right hand trailed idly along the boom. And suddenly his whole body prickled with an almost hysterical effervescence, as if the two halves of some supernal seidlitz powder had been incontinently fused under his belt.

"Goodnight," said Vogel. "And many thanks."

"Au 'voir," responded the Saint dreamily.

He watched the other step down into the tender and touch the starter. The seaman cast off and the speedboat drew away, swung round in a wide arc, and went creaming away up the dark estuary.

Simon stood there until the blaze of its spotlight had faded into a brilliant blur, and then he put his hands on the companion rail and slid down below. First of all he poured himself out a large drink, and proceeded to absorb it with profound deliberation. Then he grasped Orace firmly by the front of his shirt and drew him forward.

"You god-damned old son of a walrus," he said, with his voice torn between wrath and laughter. "Men have been shot for less."

"I couldn't think of nothink else, sir, sudding like," said Orace humbly.

"But it makes the ship look so untidy."

Orace scratched his head.

"Yessir. But it was a bit untidy ter start wiv. J remernber the mains'l started to tear comin' dahn from St Helier?

Well, when yer went orf tonight I thought I might swell do somefink abaht it. I sewed a patch on it while yer was awy, but I 'adn't 'ad time ter furl it agyne when yer came back. So when yer chucked that detective bloke at me—"

"You took him along to the hatch—"

"An' dreckly I sore yer go below, I 'auled 'im aht an' laid 'im on the boom an' folded the mains'l over 'im. I couldn't think of nothink else, sir," said Orace, clinging to his original defence.

Words failed the Saint for a while. And then, with a slow helpless grin dragging at his mouth, he brought up his fist and pushed Orace's chin back.

"Go up and fetch him in again, you old humbug," he said. "And don't play any more tricks like that on me, or I'll wring your blessed neck."

He threw himself down on the settee and began to think again. Murdoch still remained to be dealt with, and the Saint feared that he might not have been made any more amenable to reason by the sock on the jaw which had unfortunately been obliged to interrupt their conversation. Not that Murdoch could have been called an unduly sympathetic listener before that . . . Probably it made very little difference, but the original problem remained. There was also the question arising in his mind of whether Orace's manoeuvres with the mainsail had passed unnoticed by the seaman who had stayed in the speedboat—which would be even more difficult to determine. And the Saint's attention was busily divided between these two salient queries when he looked up and discovered that Orace had returned to the saloon and was gaping at him with a peculiarly fish-like expression in his eyes.

Simon Templar regarded the spectacle thoughtfully for one or two palpitating seconds. Orace's rounded eyes goggled back at him with the same trout-like intensity. The fringes of Orace's moustache waved in the draught of his breathing like the ciliated epithelium of a rabbit's oviduct. It became increasingly apparent to the Saint that Orace had something on his mind.

"Are you laying an egg?" he inquired at length.

"E's—e's *gorn*, sir!" said Orace weakly.

4

Simon got up slowly. Of all the spectacular things he had done that evening, he was inclined to estimate that restrained and dignified uprising as the supreme achievement. It was a crowning triumph of mind over matter for which he felt justly entitled to take off his hat to himself, afterwards, and when wearing a hat.

"He's gorn, has he?" he repeated.

"Yessir," said Orace hollowly.

Simon moved him aside and went up on to the deck. The disordered mainsail, draped sloppily away from the boom, offered its own pregnant testimony to the truth of Orace's conjecture. Simon strolled round it and prodded it with his toe. There was no deception. The lump that had been Steve Murdoch, which he had felt under his hand as he walked by with Vogel, hadn't simply slipped off its insecure perch and buried itself under the folds of canvas. Murdoch had taken it on the hoof.

"'E must've woke up while yer was talkin' to me an' 'opped overboard," said Orace gloomily.

The Saint nodded. He scanned the surrounding circle of black shining water, his hands in his pockets, listening with abstracted concentration. He could hear dance music still coming from one of the casinos, a waif of melody riding over the liquid undertones of the harbour; that was all. There was no sight or sound to tell him where Murdoch had gone.

"You have the most penetrating inspirations, Orace," he murmured admiringly. "I suppose that's what must have happened. But we shan't get him back. It's nearly low tide, and he's had time to reach the shore by now. I hope he catches his death of cold."

He smoked his cigarette down with remarkable serenity, while Orace fidgeted uncomfortably round him. Certainly the problem of what to do with Steve Murdoch was effectively disposed of. The problem of what Steve Murdoch would now be doing with himself took its place, and the question marks round the problem were even more complicated and more disturbing. But the doubt of how much Kurt Vogel knew stayed where it was—intensified, perhaps, by the other complication.

"Do you think anyone saw you parking our friend up here?" he asked.

Orace sucked his teeth.

"I dunno, sir. I brought 'im aht soon's I sore yer go in an' lugged 'im along on me stummick. It didn't take arf a tick to lay 'im aht on the boom an' chuck the sile over 'im, an' the other bloke was lightin' 'is pipe an' lookin' the other way." Orace frowned puzzledly. "Yer don't think them thunderin' barstids came back an' took 'im orf, do yer?"

"No, I don't think that. I watched them most of the way home, and they wouldn't have had time to get back here and do it. If they saw you, they may come back later. Or something. The point is—were you seen?"

Simon's brow creased over the riddle. If the seaman had observed Orace's manoeuvres, he might have been clever enough to give no sign. He would have told Vogel on their way back. After which the sunshine would have come back into Vogel's ugly life, Simon reflected malevolently. And then . . .

Vogel would know that the Saint didn't know he knew. And the Saint wouldn't know whether Vogel knew, or whether Vogel was banking on the Saint knowing that Vogel didn't know he knew he knew. And Vogel would still have to wonder whether the Saint knew he knew he knew he didn't know. Or not. It was all somewhat involved. But the outstanding conclusion seemed to be that the Saint could still go to St Peter Port with the assurance that Vogel wouldn't know definitely whether the Saint knew he knew, and Vogel could issue walk-into-my-parlour Invitations with the certainty that the Saint couldn't refuse them without admitting that he knew Vogel knew he knew Vogel knew. Or vice versa. Simon felt his head beginning to ache, and decided to give it a rest.

"We'd better sleep on it," he said.

He left Orace slapping down the mainsail into a neat roll with a condensed viciousness which suggested that Orace's thoughts were concerned with the way he would have liked to manhandle Murdoch if that unfortunate warrior had been available for manhandling, and went below. As he got into his pyjamas he realised that there was at least one certainty about Murdoch's future movements, which was that he would try to reach Loretta Page either that night or early in the morning with his story. He would be able to do it, too. There might be many places on the continent of Europe where anyone clothed only in a pair of trousers couldn't hope to get far without being arrested, but Dinard in the summer was not one of them, and presumably the man had parked his luggage somewhere before he set out on his pig-headed expedition. The Saint only hoped that their encounter that afternoon had taught Murdoch the necessity of making his approach with a discreet eye for possible watchers, but he was inclined to doubt it.

He was awake at eight, a few moments before Orace brought in his orange juice, and by half-past nine he was dressed and breakfasted.

"Have everything ready to sail as soon as I get back," he called into the galley, where Orace was washing up.

He went out on deck, and as he stepped up into the brightening sunlight, he glanced automatically up-river to where the *Falkenberg* lay at anchor. Something about the ship caught his eye, and after leisurely picking up a towel, as if that was all he had come out for, he went back to the saloon and searched for his field-glasses.

His eyesight had served him well. There was a man sitting in the shade aft of the deckhouse with a pair of binoculars on his knee, and even while the Saint studied him he raised the glasses and seemed to be peering straight through the porthole from which the Saint was looking out.

Simon drew back, with the chips of sapphire hardening in his blue eyes. His first thought was that he was now out of the doubtful class into the privileged circle of known menaces, but then he realised that this intense interest in his morning activities need only be a part of Vogel's already proven thoroughness. But he also realised that if he set off hurriedly for the shore, the suspicion which already centred on him would rise to boiling point, and if somebody set off quickly to cover him at the Hotel de la Mer—that would be that.

The Saint lighted a cigarette and moved restlessly round the cabin. Something had to be done. Somehow he had to reach Loretta, tell her—what? That she was suspected? She knew that. That Murdoch was suspected? She might guess it. That she must not take that voyage with Vogel? She would go anyway. Simon's fist struck impatiently into the palm of his hand. It didn't matter. He had to reach her—even if the entire crew of the *Falkenberg* was lined up on the deck with binoculars trained on the *Corsair*, and even if the Hotel de la Mer was surrounded by a cordon of their-watchers.

With a sudden decision he opened the door of the galley again.

"Never mind the washing up, Orace," he said. "We're sailing now."

Orace came out without comment, wiping his hands on the legs of his trousers. While Simon started the auxiliary, he swung out the davits and brought the dinghy up under the falls. While the engine was warming up, the Saint helped him to haul up the dinghy, and then sent him forward at once to get up the anchor.

It was a quarter to ten when the nose of the *Corsair* turned down the estuary and began to push up the ripples towards the sea.

"Let it hang," said the Saint, when Orace was still working at the anchor. "We'll want it again in a minute."

Orace looked at him for a moment, and then straightened up and came aft, lowering himself into the cockpit.

"Get ready to drop the dinghy again, and swing her out as soon as we're round the point," said the Saint.

He turned and gazed back at the *Falkenberg*. There was a midget figure standing up on her deck which might have been Kurt Vogel. Simon waved his arm, and the speck waved back. Then the Saint turned to the chart and concentrated on the tricky shoals on either side of the main channel. He brought the *Corsair* round the Pointe du Moulinet as close as he dared, and yelled to Orace to get up into the bows. Then he brought the control lever back into reverse.

"Let go!"

The anchor splashed down into the shallow water and Simon left the wheel and sprang to the dinghy. With Orace helping him, it was lowered in a moment, and Simon dropped between the thwarts and reached for the oars. It was quicker than fitting the outboard, for a short pull like that, but the boat seemed to weigh a ton, and his shirt was already hot with sweat when the last fierce heave on the oars sent the dinghy grinding up on to the sands of the Plage de l'Ecluse. He jumped out and dragged it well up on the beach, and made his way quickly between the early sunbathers to the Digue.

It was five-past ten when he climbed up on to the pavement, and there was an uneasy emptiness moving vaguely about under his lower ribs. That watcher on the *Falkenberg* had made a difference of half an hour—half an hour in which, otherwise, he could have done all that he wanted to do. He realised that he had been incredibly careless not to have allowed for any obstacles such as the one which had delayed him, and it dawned on him that he only had Vogel's word for it that the *Falkenberg* would not sail before eleven. Loretta might be already on board, and they might be already preparing to follow him out to sea.

And then, straight in front of him, as if it had materialised out of empty air, he saw the square dour visage of Steve Murdoch coming towards him. It brought him back to the urgent practical present with a jar that checked him in his stride, but Murdoch came on without a pause.

"Not recognising me today, Saint?" Murdoch's grim harsh voice grated into his ears with a smug challenge that flexed the muscles of the Saint's wrists.

Simon looked him up and down. He was wearing a suit of his own clothes again, and every inch of him up to his glittering eyes told the story of what he had done in the intervening hours.

"I've only got one thing to say to you," said the Saint coldly. "And I can't say it here."

"That cramps your style, I bet. You talk pretty well with your fists, Saint. But you can't have it your own way all the time. Where you goin' now?"

"That's my business."

The other nodded—a curt jerk of his head that left his jaw set in a more unbroken square than it had been before.

"I bet it is. But it's my business too. Thought you'd get up early and pick up cards with Loretta again, did you? Well, you weren't early enough."

"No?"

"No. Take your eyes off my chin, Saint—it's ready for you this morning. Look at that gendarme down the road instead. Gazing in a shop window an' not takin' any notice of us now, ain't he? You're all right. But this ain't your boat now. You try to get tough with me again and he'll look at us quick enough. And when he comes up here, I'll have something to tell him about what you tried to do last night." Murdoch's own fists were quietly clubbed at his sides, and he was on his toes. There was vengeful unfriendliness and the bitter memory of another occasion gleaming out of his small unblinking eyes. "You turn round and go back the way you came from, Saint, unless you want to sit in a French precinct house and wait while they fetch over your dossier from Scotland Yard. And don't go near St Peter Port unless you want the same thing again. I said I was goin' to put you out, and you're out!"

Simon took a pack of cigarettes out of his pocket and tapped a smoke thoughtfully on the edge of the packet. He put the cigarette in his mouth and slipped the package into the side pocket of his coat.

"It's too bad you feel that way about it, Steve," he said slowly, and his right hand jolted forward from his side like a piston.

For the second time in that young day Steve Murdoch felt the impact of the Saint's fist. And once again he never saw it coming. The blow only travelled about six inches, and it covered the distance so swiftly that even a man who had been watching them closely might not have seen it. It leapt straight from the edge of the Saint's side pocket to Murdoch's solar plexus, with the power of a pile-driver behind it, and Murdoch's face went grey as he doubled up.

Simon caught him and lowered him tenderly to the ground. By the time the first interested spectator had formed the nucleus of a crowd, the Saint was fanning Murdoch with his handkerchief and feeling for his heart with every symptom of alarm. By the time the shop-gazing gendarme had joined the gathering, it was generally agreed among the spectators that the Breton sun must have been at least a contributory cause to Murdoch's sudden collapse. Somebody spoke about an ambulance. Somebody else thought he could improve on the system of first aid which was being practised, and Simon handed the case over to him and faded quietly through the swelling congregation.

He moved on towards the Hotel de la Mer, as quickly as he dared, but with anxiety tearing ahead of his footsteps. That chance encounter—if it was a chance encounter—had wasted more of his precious and dwindling margin of time.

And then he stopped again, and plunged down in a shop doorway to tie up an imaginary shoelace. He had seen Kurt Vogel, smooth and immaculate in a white suit and a white-topped cap, turning into the entrance of the hotel. He was too late. And something inside him turned cold as he realised that there was nothing more that he could do about it— nothing that would not risk making Loretta's danger ten times greater by linking her with him. Murdoch had won after all, and Loretta would have to make the voyage unwarned.

CHAPTER FIVE:

HOW SIMON TEMPLAR WALKED IN A GARDEN AND ORACE ALSO HAD HIS TURN

1

It was half-past four when the *Corsair* came skimming up over the blue swell past St Martin's Point, with her sails trimmed to coax the last ounce of power from the mild south-westerly breeze which had held steadily on her quarter all the way from the Pierres des Portes. In those five and a half hours since they had cleared the rocks and shoals that fringe the Côtes du Nord, Simon Templar had never taken his hands from the wheel; his eyes had been reduced to emotionless chips of blue stone, mechanical units of cooperation with his hands, ceaselessly watching the curves of the canvas overhead for the first hint of a flutter that would signify a single breath of the wind going by unused. During those hours he almost surrendered his loyalty to the artistic grace of sail, and yearned for the drumming engines of the *Falkenberg*, which had overtaken them in the first hour and left a white trail of foam hissing away to the horizon.

He hardly knew himself what was in his mind. With all the gallant thrust of the *Corsair* through the green seas under him, he was as helpless as if he had been marooned on an iceberg at the South Pole. Everything that might be meant to happen on the *Falkenberg* could still happen while he was out of reach. Vogel could say "She decided not to come," or "There was an accident"; with all the crew of the *Falkenberg* partnering in the racket, it would be almost impossible to prove.

The Saint stared at the slowly rising coastline with a darkening of satirical self-mockery in his gaze. Did he want proof? There had been many days when he was his own judge and jury: it was quicker, and it left fewer loopholes.

And yet . . .

It wasn't quite so simple as that. Revenge was an unthinkable triviality, a remote shadow of tragedy that cut grim lines between his lowered brows. More than any revenge he wanted to see Loretta again, to see the untiring mischief in her grey eyes and hear the smiling huskiness of her voice, to feel the touch of her hand again, or . . . More than any boodle that might lie at the end of the adventure . . . Why? He didn't know. Something had happened to him in the few hours that he had known her—something, he realised with a twist of devastating candour, that had happened more than once in his life before, and might well happen again.

The breeze slackened as they drew up the channel, and he started the auxiliary. As they chugged past the sombre ugliness of Castle Cornet and rounded the point of the Castle Breakwater, he had a glimpse of the white aero-foil lines of the *Falkenberg* already lying snug within the harbour, and felt an odd indefinable pressure inside his chest.

He sat side-saddle on the edge of the cockpit and lighted a cigarette while Orace finished the work of tidying up. The *Falkenberg* had probably been at her berth for three hours by then, and apart from a jerseyed seaman who was lethargically washing off the remains of salt spray from her varnish, and who had scarcely looked at the *Corsair* as she came past, there was nothing to be observed on board. Most likely Vogel and his party were on shore, but Loretta . . . He shrugged, with the steel brightening in his eyes. Presently he would know—many answers.

"Wot nex', sir?"

Orace stood beside him, as stoical as a whiskered gargoyle, and the Saint moved his cigarette in the faintest gesture of direction.

"You watch that boat. Don't let them know you're doing it—you'd better go below and fix yourself behind one of the portholes most of the time. But watch it. If a girl comes off it, or a box or a bundle or anything that might contain a girl, you get on your way and stick to her like a fly-paper. Otherwise—you stay watching that ship till I come back or your moustache grows down to your knees. Got it?"

"Yessir."

Orace went below, unquestioningly, to his vigil, and the Saint stood up and settled his belt. There was action and contact, still, to take his mind away from things on which it did not wish to dwell: he felt a kind of tense elation at the knowledge that the fight was on, one way or the other.

He went ashore with a spring in his step, and a gun in his pocket that helped him to a smile of dry self-derision when he remembered it. It seemed a ridiculously melodramatic precaution in that peaceful port, with the blue afternoon sky arching over the unrippled harbour and the gay colour-splashes of idle holiday-makers promenading on the breakwaters, but he couldn't laugh himself out of it. Before the end of the adventure he was to know how wise and necessary it was.

The cross-Channel steamer from Weymouth was standing out on the continuation of her voyage to Jersey, and Simon threaded his way to the New Jetty through the stream, of disembarked passengers and spectators, and eventually secured a porter. Inquiries were made. Yes, the steamer had landed some cargo consigned to him. Simon gazed with grim satisfaction at the two new and innocent-looking trunks labelled with his name, and spread a ten-shilling note into the porter's hand.

"Will you get 'em to that boat over there? The *Corsair*. There's a man on board to take delivery. And don't mistake him for a walrus and try to harpoon him, because he's touchy about that."

He went back down the pier to the esplanade, fitting a fresh cigarette into his mouth as he went. Those two trunks which he had collected and sent on equipped him for any submarine emergencies, and the promptness of their arrival attested the fact that Roger Conway's long retirement in the bonds of respectable if not holy matrimony had dulled none of his old gifts as the perfect lieutenant. There remained the matter of Peter Quentin's contribution, and the Saint moved on to the post office and found it already waiting for him, in the shape of a telegram:

> *Latitude forty-nine forty-one fifty-six north longitude two twenty-three forty-five west Roger and I will be at the Royal before you are others will catch first airplane when you give the word also Hoppy wants to know why he was left out if you've already made a corner in the heroine we are going home I have decided to charge you with the cost of this wire so have much pleasure in signing myself comma at your expense comma yours till Hitler dedicates a synagogue dash*

> *PETER*

Simon tucked the sheet away in his pocket, and the first wholly spontaneous smile of that day relaxed the iron set of his mouth as he ranged out into the street again. If he had been asked to offer odds on the tone of that telegram before he opened it, he would have laid a thousand to one to any takers that he could have made an accurate forecast, and at that moment he was very glad to have been right. It was a tribute to the spell which still bound the crew of hell-bent buccaneers which he had once commanded, a token of the spirit of their old brotherhood which no passage of time or outside associations could alter, which sent him on his way to the Royal Hotel with a quickened stride and a sudden feeling of invincible faith.

He found them in the bar, entertaining a couple of damsels in beach pyjamas who could be seen at a glance to be endowed with that certain something which proved that Peter and Roger had kept their speed and initiative unimpaired in more directions than one. Beyond the first casual inspection with which any newcomer would have been greeted, they took no notice of him, but as he approached the counter, Roger Conway decided that another round of drinks was due, and came up beside him.

"Four sherries, please," he said, and as the barmaid set up the glasses, he added: "And by the way—before I forget—would you get a bottle of Scotch and a siphon sent up to my room sometime this evening? Number fifteen."

Simon took a pull at the beer with which he had been served, and compared his watch with the clock.

"Is that clock right?" he inquired, and the barmaid looked up at it.

"Yes, I think so."

The Saint nodded, pretending to make an adjustment on his wrist.

"That's good—I've got an appointment at seven, and I thought I had half an hour to wait." He opened a packet of cigarettes while Roger teetered back to his party with the four glasses of sherry adroitly distributed between his fingers, and soon afterwards asked for a lavatory. He went out, leaving a freshly ordered glass of beer untouched on the bar, and the man who had taken the place next to him, who had been specifically warned against the dangers of letting his attentions become too conspicuous stood and gazed at that reassuring item of still life for a considerable time before being troubled with the first doubts of his own wisdom. And long before those qualms became really pressing, the Saint was reclining gracefully on Roger Conway's bed, blowing smoke-rings at the ceiling and waiting for the others to keep the appointment.

They came punctually at seven, and, having closed and locked the door, eyed him solemnly.

"He looks debauched," Peter said at length.

"And sickly," agreed Roger.

"Too many hectic moments with the heroine," theorised Peter.

"Do you think," suggested Roger, "that if we both jumped on him together—" They jumped, and there was a brief but hilarious tussle. At the end of which:

"Do your nurses know you're out?" Simon demanded sternly. "And who told you two clowns to start chasing innocent girls to their doom before you've hardly unpacked? Presently I shall want you in a hurry for some real work, and you'll be prancing over the hillsides, picking daisies and sticking primroses in your hair—Did you speak, Peter?"

"How the hell could he speak," gasped Roger, "while you're grinding your knee into his neck? You big bully . . . Ouch! That's my arm you're breaking."

The Saint picked himself off their panting bodies, sorted the smouldering remains of his cigarette out of the bedclothes, and lighted another.

"You're out of training," he remarked. "I can see that I've only just thought of you in time to save you from being put in a vase."

"I don't know whether we want to be thought of," said Peter, massaging his torso tenderly. "You always get so physical when you're thinking."

"It only means he's got into another mess and wants us to get him out of it," said Roger. "Or have you found a million pounds and are you looking for some deserving orphans?"

Simon grinned at them affectionately, and threw himself into a chair.

"Well, as a matter of fact there may be several millions in it," he answered.

There was a quiet dominance in his voice which carried them back to other times in their lives when the fun and horseplay had been just as easily set aside for the other things that had bound them together, and they sorted themselves out just as soberly and sat down, Roger on the bed and Peter in the other chair.

"Tell us," said Roger.

Simon told them.

2

"So that's the story. Now . . ."

He sat up and looked at them through a haze of smoke, in one of those supreme pauses when he knew most clearly that he would not, could not, have changed his life for any other. It was like old times. It was like coming home. It was the freebooter coming back to the outlaw campfire where he belonged. He saw their faces across the room, Peter's rugged young-pugilist vitality, Roger's lean and rather grim intentness, and under the turbulent thoughts that were clouding the background of his mind he knew an enduring and inexplicable contentment.

"As I see it, if all the evidence that's been collected since Ingerbeck's took on the case was worked up, there might be enough of it to put Vogel away. But that's not good enough for the underwriters, and it isn't good enough for Ingerbeck's. The underwriters can't show any dividends on gloating over Vogel sitting in prison for a few years. They want to recover some of the money they've lost on claims since he went into business. And Ingerbeck's want their commission on the same. And we want—"

"Both," said Peter Quentin bluntly.

The Saint gazed at him thoughtfully for a moment and did not answer directly. Presently he said, "The argument's fairly simple, isn't it? Boodle of that kind isn't exactly ready money. You can't take a sack of uncut diamonds or half a ton of bar gold into the nearest pawnshop and ask 'em how much they'll give you on it. It takes time and organisation to get rid of it. And it isn't so easy to cart around with you while your organisation's functioning— particularly the gold. You have to park it somewhere. And for similar reasons you can't use the ordinary safe deposit or keep it in a sock."

Roger nodded.

"Meaning if we could find this parking-place—" The Saint spread out his hands.

"Find it, or find out where it is. Join Vogel's crew and get the key. Follow him when he goes there to fetch some of the boodle out, or put some more in. Or something . . ." He smiled, and reached for his glass. "Anyway, you get the general idea."

They had got the general idea, and for a minute or two they digested it in efficient silence. The magnitude of the situation which had been unfolded to them provoked none of the conventional explosions of incredulity or excitement: it was only on the same plane with what they had come to expect from the shameless leader who sat there studying them with the old mocking light of irresistible dare-devilry on his dark reckless face. And it is doubtful whether the morality of their attitude ever troubled them at all.

"That seems quite clear," Peter said at last. "Except for the beautiful heroine."

"She's only trying to get at Vogel from his soft side—if he has one. That's why she had to make that trip today. I . . . wasn't in time to stop it. Don't know whether I could have stopped it anyway, but I might have tried. If she hasn't arrived here safely . . ." He left the thought in the air, but for an instant they saw a cold flame of steel in his eyes. And then there was only the glimmer of the scapegrace smile still on his lips. "But that's my own party," he said.

"It looks like it," Peter said gloomily. "I might have known we couldn't afford to give you a start like this. If you're staking a claim on the heroine, I think I *shall* go home."

"Is it a claim?" asked Roger seriously.

Simon drew the last smoke of his cigarette deep into his lungs, and shed the butt into an ashtray.

"I don't know," he said.

He stood up abruptly and prowled over to the window, almost unconsciously triangulating its exact position in the exterior geography of the hotel, in case he should ever wish to find it without using the ordinary entrances. Automatically his mind put aside Roger's question, and went working on along the sternly practical lines for which he had convened the meeting.

"Now—communications. We can't have a lot of these reunions. I had to ditch a shadow to make this one, and yesterday I did the same in Dinard. I think I was pretty smooth both times, but if I do it much more it'll stop looking so accidental. There's just a thin chance that Birdie is still wondering how smooth I am, and it's just possible I may be able to keep him guessing for another twenty-four hours, which might make a lot of difference. So we'll go back to splendid isolation for a while. Orace and I will get in touch with you here—one or the other of you must look in every hour, in case there's a message. If we can't send a message, we'll put a bucket on the deck of the *Corsair*, which means you look out for signals. Remember the old card code? We'll put the cards in one of the portholes. Those are general orders."

"Anything more particular?"

"Only for myself, at present. Tomorrow they're going out to try Yule's new bathystol—and I've got an invitation."

Peter sat up with a jerk. "You're not going?"

"Of course I am. Any normal and innocent bloke would jump at the chance, and until there's any evidence to the contrary I've got to work on the assumption that I'm still supposed to be a normal and innocent bloke. I've *got* to go. Besides, I might find out something."

"All about the After Life, for instance," said Peter.

The Saint shrugged.

"That's all in the kitty. But if it's coming to me, it'll come anyhow, whether I go or not. And if it happens tomorrow . . ." The Saintly smile was gay and unclouded as he buttoned his coat. "I looks to you gents to do your stuff."

Roger pulled himself off the bed.

"Okay, Horatius. Then for the time being we're off duty."

"Yes. Except for general communications. I just wanted to give you the lie of the land. And you've got it. So you can go back to your own heroines, if they haven't found something better by this time, and don't forget your powder-puffs."

He shifted nimbly through the door before the other two could prepare a suitable retaliation, and found his way back to the bar. His glass of beer was still on the counter, and the sleuth who had been watching it, who had been mopping his brow feverishly and running round in small agitated circles for some time past appeared to suffer a violent heart attack which called for a large dose of whisky to restore his shattered nerves.

Simon lowered his drink at leisure. It went down to join a deep and pervading glow that had come into being inside him, in curious contrast to an outward sensation of dry cold. That brief interview with Peter and Roger, the knowledge that they were there to find trouble with him as they had found it before, had given a solid foundation to a courage which had been sustained until then by sheer nervous energy. And yet, as the feeling of cold separateness in his limbs was there to testify, their presence had not altered the problem of Loretta or made her safe, and a part of him remained utterly detached and immune from the intoxicating scent of battle as he set out to find her.

To find her . . . if she was to be found. But he forced that fear ruthlessly out of his head. She would be found—he was becoming as imaginative as an overwrought boy. If Vogel had taken the risk of letting her sail on the *Falkenberg* at all, he must be interested, and if he was interested—there would be no point in murder until the interest had been satisfied. Vogel must be interested—the Saint had not watched that scene on the *Falkenberg's* deck last night with his eyes shut. And Vogel's mathematically dehumanised brain would work like that. To play with the attractive toy, guarding himself against its revealed dangers, until all its amusing resources had been explored, before he broke it . . . Surely, the Saint told himself with relentless insistence, Loretta would be found. The thing that troubled him most deeply was that he should be so afraid . . .

And he found her. As he walked by the harbour, looking over the paling blue of the water at the inscrutable curves of the *Falkenberg* as if his eyes were trying to pierce through her hull and superstructure to see what was left for him on board, he became aware of three figures walking towards him, and something made him turn. He saw the tall gaunt aquilinity of Kurt Vogel, the gross bulk of Arnheim, and another shape which was like neither of them, which suddenly melted the ice that had been creeping through his veins and turned the warmth in him to fire.

"Good evening," said Vogel.

3

Simon Templar nodded with matter-of-fact cheeriness. And he wanted
to shout and dance. "I was just going to look you up," he said.

"And we were wondering where you were. We inquired on the
Corsair, but your man told us you'd gone ashore. You had a good
crossing?"

"Perfect."

"We were thinking of dining on shore, for a change. By the way, I
must introduce you." Vogel turned to the others. "This is my friend Mr
Tombs—Miss Page . . ."

Simon took her hand. For the first time in that encounter he dared
to look her full in the face, and smile. But even that could only be for
the brief conventional moment.

". . . and Mr Arnheim."

"How do you do?"

There was a dark swollen bruise under Arnheim's fleshy chin, and
the Saint estimated its painfulness with invisible satisfaction as he
shook hands.

"Of course—you helped us to try and catch our robber, didn't you, Mr Tombs?"

"I don't think I did very much to help you," said the Saint deprecatingly.

"But you were very patient with our disturbing attempts," said Vogel genially. "We couldn't have met more fortunately—in every way. And now, naturally, you'll join us for dinner?"

The great hook of his nose curved at the Saint like a poised scimitar, the heavy black brows arched over it with the merest hint of challenge.

"I'd like to," said the Saint easily. And as they started to stroll on, "What about the Professor?"

"He refuses to be tempted. He will be working on the bathystol for half the night— you couldn't drag him away from it on the eve of a descent."

They had dinner at the Old Government House. To Simon Templar the evening became fantastic, almost frighteningly unreal. Not once did he catch Vogel or Arnheim watching him, not once did he catch the subtle edge of an innuendo thrust in to prick a guilty ear, and yet he knew, by pure reason, that they were watching. The brand of his fist on Arnheim's chin caught his eyes every time they turned that way. Did Arnheim guess—did he even know?—whose knuckles had hung that pocket earthquake on his jaw? Did Vogel know? There was no answer to be read in the smooth colourless face or the black unwinking eyes.

What did they know of Loretta, and what were their plans for her? If Murdoch had been identified while they had him on the *Falkenberg* she must have been condemned already, and it seemed too much to hope that Murdoch had not been seen by the sleuth who had observed his blatant arrival at the Hotel de la Mer the day before. How much had Loretta suffered already? . . . He could only guess at the answers.

It was an uncanny feeling to be eating and drinking on terms of almost saccharine cordiality with two men who might even then be plotting his funeral—and whose own funerals he himself would plot without compunction in certain circumstances—with every warning of antagonism utterly suppressed on both sides. If he had not had last night's experience of Vogel's methods to acclimatise him, he would have suffered the same sensation of nightmare futility again, doubled in intensity because Loretta was now with them, but his nerves had been through as much of that cat-and-mouse ordeal as they were capable of tolerating, and the normal reaction was setting in. Somehow he knew that that game could not be played much longer, and when the showdown came he would have his compensation.

But meanwhile Loretta was there, beside him—and he could give her no more than the polite interest called for by their recent introduction . . . when every desire in his mind was taking both her hands and laughing breathlessly with her and talking the quick sparkling nonsense which was the measure of their predestined understanding. He saw the shifting gold in her hair and the softness of her lips when she spoke, and was tormented with a hunger that was harder to fight than all Vogel's inhuman patience.

And then he was dancing with her.

They had discovered that there was a dance at the hotel, and after the coffee and liqueurs they had gone into the ballroom. Even so, he had waited while first Vogel and then Arnheim danced, before he had looked at her and stood up as if only to discharge his duty to a fellow-guest.

But he had her alone. He had her hand in his, and his arm round her, and they were moving quietly in their own world, like one person, to music that neither of them heard. "It's a long time since I've seen you all, Mary Jane," he said.

"Wasn't it before I put my hair up?"

"I think it was the Sunday School treat when you ate too many cream buns and had to give them up again in the rhododendrons."

"You would remember that. And now you're such a big man, doing such big and wonderful things. I'm so proud of you, Elmer."

"George," Simon corrected her, "is the name. By the way, did I ever give you the inside dope on that dragon business? This dragon, which was closely related to a female poet, a dowager duchess, and a prominent social reformer and purity hound, was actually a most mild and charitable beast, except when it felt that the morals of the community were being endangered. On those occasions it would become quite transformed, turning red in the face and breathing smoke and fire and uttering ferocious gobbling sounds like those of a turkey which has been wished a merry Christmas. The misguided inhabitants of the country, however, mistaking these symptoms for those of sadistic dyspepsia, endeavoured to appease the animal—whose name, by the way, was Angelica—by selecting their fairest damsels and leaving them as sacrifices, stripped naked and tied to trees and shrubbery in its path, Angelica, on the other hand, mistook these friendly offerings for further evidence of the depravity which had overtaken her friends, and was only raised to higher transports of indignation and gobbling. The misunderstanding was rapidly denuding the country in every sense, and in fact the dearth of beautiful damsels was become so acute that certain citizens were advocating that their grandmothers should be used instead, in the hope that Angelica might be moved by intellectual endowments where mere physical charm had only aggravated the gobbling, when I came along and . . . Why haven't I told you how beautiful you are, Loretta?"

"Because you haven't noticed?"

"Because it's too true, I think. And so many other ridiculous things have been happening all the time. And I've been so stupid . . . They'd have tied you to a tree for Angelica if they'd seen you, Loretta."

"With nothing on?"

"And everyone would have been asking 'Where's George?' He was a Saint, too."

There was a breath of cool night air on their faces, and as if there had been no voluntary movement they were outside. There must have been a window or a door, some steps perhaps, some mundane path by which they had walked out of the ballroom into the infinite evening, but it was as if mortar and stone and wood had melted away like shadows to leave them under the stars. Their feet moved on a soft carpet of grass, and the music whispered behind them.

Presently she sat down, and he sat behind her. He still kept her hand. "Well," he said.

She smiled slowly. "Well?"

"Apparently it wasn't death," he said, "So I suppose it must have been dishonour."

"It might be both."

He counted over her fingers and laid them against his cheek.

"You feel alive. You sound alive. Or are we both ghosts? We could go and haunt somebody."

"You knew something, Simon. When we met on the waterfront . . ."

"Was it as obvious as that?"

"No. I just felt it."

"So did I. My heart went pit-a-pat. Then it went pat-a-pit. Then it did a back somersault and broke its bloody neck. It still feels cracked."

Her other hand covered his mouth.

"Please. Simon. Every minute we stay here is dangerous. They may have missed us already. They may be talking. Tell me what you knew. What happened last night?"

"They caught Steve—slugged him, and hauled him out of his canoe. I went back to the *Falkenberg* and slugged Otto and brought home the blue-eyed boy. Otto never saw me, but I don't know how many other people had inspected the boyfriend before I butted in. If the same guy who heard him asking for you at the Hotel de la Mer yesterday had seen him, I knew you were in the book."

"What about you?"

"Vogel came over shortly afterwards and put on a great show of being shown over the *Corsair*, while I changed my nappies and did the honours. But he didn't find Steve. I'm still technically anonymous; Steve got away."

"Who from?"

"From me. In between Vogel going home and me congratulating Orace on the hiding-place, Steve saw the dawn and set a course for it. I saw him again in the morning, when I was trying to reach you before Vogel did and warn you what might be waiting—as a matter of fact, he held me up just long enough to let Vogel get in first. I missed seeing you by about thirty seconds. Where Steve is now I don't know, but if you bet your shirt he'll bob up here tomorrow you won't run much risk of being left uncovered." The Saint turned his face to her, and she saw the dim light shift on his eyes. "He saw you this morning, didn't he?"

"Yes."

"Telling you I tried to kidnap him."

"Yes."

"And speaking as follows: 'This guy Templar is just a tough crook from Toughville, Crook County, and if you think he's turned Horatio Alger because you gave him a pretty smile you're crazy.'"

"Were you listening?"

He shook his head.

"I'm a thought-reader. Besides, I did try to kidnap him, after a fashion. Anyway I tried to detain him. Obviously. He may be the hell of a good detective in some ways, but he doesn't fit into the game we're playing here. He'd done his best to break it up twice in one day, and I thought it'd be a good thing to keep him quiet for a bit. I still do."

"And the rest?" she said.

"What do you think?"

Her hand slipped down over his hair, came to rest on his shoulder. For once the dark mischievous eyes were quiet with a kind of surrendered sadness.

"I think Steve was right."

"And yet you're here."

"Yes. I'm a fool, aren't I? But I didn't tell you I was weak-minded. All Ingerbeck's people have to go through an intelligence test, and they tell me I've got the mentality of a child of five. They say I'll probably finish up in an asylum in another year or two."

"May I come and see you in the padded cell?"

"If you want to. But you won't When you've had all you want from me—"

He silenced her with his lips. And with her mouth he tried to silence the disbelief in his own mind that sat back and asked cold questions. There was a hunger in him, overriding reason, that turned against the weary emptiness of disbelief.

He was a man, and human. He kissed her, touched her, held her face in his hands, and found forgetfulness in the soft sweetness of her body. He was aware of her with every sense, and of his own desire. There was no other answer he could give. He should have been thinking of so many other things, but he had stopped thinking. He was tired—not with the painful fatigue of ordinary exhaustion, but with the peace of a man who has come home from a long journey. Presently he lay back with his head in her lap, looking up at the stars.

"Tell me something," she said.

"I'm happy."

"So am I. I've no reason to be, but I am. It doesn't seem to matter. You do love me, don't you?"

He was in a dream from which he didn't want to wake. Somewhere in his memory there was the cynical impress of a thought he had had so long ago, that if the need came she would use her fascination to tempt him as she had hoped to tempt Vogel. And there was his own thought that if that was her strategy he would meet her cheerfully with her own weapons.

But that was so faint and far away. Must he be always thinking, suspecting, fighting—when there was so much comfort in the present?

He said, "Yes."

"Say it all."

"I love you."

"Dear liar . . ."

She leaned over him. Her hair fell on his face. She kissed him.

"I don't care," she said. "Tomorrow I shall be wise—and sorry. You're going to hurt me, Saint. And I don't seem to mind. I'm happy. I've had tonight."

"Is there any tomorrow?"

She nodded.

"We must go in," she said.

Again they walked under the glittering sky, hand in hand, towards reality. There was so much that should have been said, so little that they could say. This was illusion, yet it was more real than life.

"What's your tomorrow?" he asked.

"The Professor's making his trial descent. I don't know what happens afterwards, but next week they're going down to Madeira. Vogel asked me to stay with them."

"And you said you would."

"Of course."

"Must you?"

"Yes." The word was quick, almost brutal in its curtness. And then, as if she had hurt herself also, she said, "You don't understand. This is my job. I took it on with my eyes open. I told you. I gave my word. Would you think the same of me if I broke it?"

Out of the sudden ache of madness in him he answered, "Yes. Just the same."

"You wouldn't. You think so now, because you want me, but you'd remember. You'd always remember that I ran away once—so why shouldn't I run away again? I know I'm right." He knew it, too. "You must let me finish the job. Help me to finish it."

"It's as good as finished," he said, with a flash of the old reckless bravado.

"Kiss me."

The lights of the ballroom struck them like a physical blow. The orchestra was still playing. How long had they been away? Ten minutes? Ten years? She slipped into his arms and he went on dancing with her, as if they had never stopped, mechanically. He let the lights and the noise drug his senses, deliberately sinking himself in a stupor into which emotion could not penetrate. He would not think.

They completed a circle of the floor, and rejoined the others. Vogel was just paying a waiter.

"We thought you would like another drink after your efforts, Mr Tombs. It's quite a good floor, isn't it?"

4

Simon forced himself back to reality, and it was like stepping under a cold shower. And exactly as if he had stepped under a cold shower he was left composed and alert again, a passionless fighting machine, perfectly tuned, taking up the threads of the adventure into which he had intruded. The madness of a few moments ago might never have lived in him: he was the man who had come out on to the deck of the *Corsair* at the sound of a cry in the night, the cynical cavalier of the crooked world, steady-handed and steady-eyed, playing the one game in which death was the unalterable stake.

"Not at all bad," he murmured. "If I'd been in the Professor's shoes I wouldn't have missed it."

"I suppose it must always be difficult for the layman to understand the single- mindedness of the scientist. And yet I can sympathise with him. If his experiments ended in failure, I'm sure I should be as disappointed as if a pet ambition of my own had been exploded."

"I'm sure you would."

Vogel's colourless lips smiled back with cadaverous suavity.

"But that's quite a remote possibility. Now, you'll be with us tomorrow, won't you? We are making a fairly early start, and the weather forecasts have promised us a fine day. Suppose you came on board about nine . . ."

They discussed the projected trip while they finished their drinks, and on the walk back to the harbour. Vogel's affability was at its most effusive; his stony black eyes gleamed with a curious inward lustre. In some subtle disturbing way he seemed more confident, more serenely devoid of every trace of impatience or anxiety.

"Well—goodnight."

"Till tomorrow."

Simon shook hands—touched the moist warm paw of Otto Arnheim. He saluted Loretta with a vague flourish and the outline of a smile.

"Goodnight."

No more. And he was left with an odd feeling of emptiness and surprise, like a man who has dozed for a moment and roused up with a start to wonder how long he has slept or if he has slept at all. Anything that had happened since they came in from that enchanted garden had gone by so quickly that that sudden awakening was his first real awareness of the lapse of time. He felt as if he had been whirled round in a giant sling and flung into an arctic sea, as if he had fought crazily to find his depth and then been hurled up by a chance wave high and dry on some lonely peak, all within a space of seconds. He remembered that he had been talking to Vogel, quietly, accurately, without the slightest danger of a slip, like a punch-drunk fighter who has remained master of his technique without conscious volition. *That* was illusion: only the garden was real.

He shook himself like a dog, half angrily, but in a way the sensation persisted. His thoughts went back slowly and deliberately, picking their footholds as if over slippery stepping-stones. Loretta Page. She had come out of the fog over Dinard and disturbed his sleep. He had been fascinated by the humour of her eyes and the vitality of her brown body. On an impulse he had kissed her. How long had he known her? A few hours. And she had been afraid. He also had been afraid, but he had found her. They had talked nothing except nonsense, and yet he had kissed her again, and found in that moment a completer peace than he had ever known. Then they had talked of love. Or hadn't they? So little had been said; so much seemed to have been understood. His last glimpse of her had been as she turned away, with Vogel tucking her hand into his arm; she had been gay and acquiescent. He had let her go. There was nothing else he could do. They were in the same legion, pledged to the same grim code. So he had let her go, with a smile and a flourish, for whatever might come of the fortunes of war, death or dishonour. And he had thought: "Illusion . . ."

Sssssh . . .

The Saint froze in the middle of a step, with his mind wiped clean like a slate and an eerie ballet of ice-cold pinpricks skittering up into the roots of his hair. Once again he had been dreaming, and once again he had been brought awake in a chilling flash. Only this time there was no feeling of unreality about the galvanic arresting of all his perceptions.

He stopped exactly as he was when the sound caught him, on his toes, with one foot on the deck of the *Corsair* and the other reaching down into the cockpit, one hand on a stanchion and the other steadying himself against the roof of the miniature wheelhouse, as if he had been turned into stone. All around him was the quiet dimness of the harbour, and the lights of the port spread up the slope from the waterfront in scintillating terraces of winking brilliance in front of him; somewhere on one of the esplanades a couple of girls were giggling shrilly at the inaudible witticisms of their escorts. But for that long-drawn moment the Saint was marooned as far from those outposts of the untroubled commonplace as if he had been left on the last outlaw island of the

Spanish Main. And in that space of incalculable separation he stayed like the inanimate imprint of a moving man on a photographic plate, listening for a confirmation of that weird tortured hiss that had transfixed him as he began to let himself down over the coaming.

He knew that it was no ordinary sound such as Orace might have made in moving about his duties; otherwise it would never have sent that unearthly titillation coursing over his spine. There was a strained intensity about it, a racking sibilance of frightful effort, that had crashed in upon his dormant vigilance as effectively as an explosion. His brain must have analysed it instinctively, in an instant, with the lightning intuition bred of all the dangerous years behind him: now, he had to make a laborious effort to recollect the features of the sound and work out exactly why it had stopped him, when subconscious reaction had achieved the same result in a microscopical fraction of the time.

A few inches in front of his left foot, the open door of the saloon stencilled an elongated panel of light across the cockpit. The ache eased out of his cramped leg muscles as he gently completed his interrupted movements and finished the transfer of his weight down on to his extended toes. And as both his feet arrived on the same deck he heard a low gasping moan.

He touched the gun on his hip, but that might be too noisy. His left hand was still grasping the stanchion by which he had been letting himself down, and with a silent twist he slipped it out of its socket. Then he took a long breath and stepped out across the door of the saloon, squarely into the light.

He looked down the companion into a room through which a young cyclone seemed to have passed. The bunks had been opened and the bedding taken apart; lockers had been forced open and their contents scattered on the floor; books had been taken from their shelves and thrown down anywhere. The carpet had been ripped up and rolled back, and a section of panelling had been torn bodily away from the bulkhead. The Saint saw all this at once, as he would have taken in the broad features of any background, but his gaze was fixed on the crumpled shape of a man who lay on the floor—who was trying, with set teeth and pain- wrinkled face, to drag himself up on to his hands and knees. The man whose hiss of convulsive breathing had shocked him out of his sleep-walking a minute ago. Orace.

Simon put a hand on the rail of the companion and dropped into the saloon. He left his stanchion on the floor and hoisted Orace up on to one of the disordered couches.

"What's the matter?"

Orace's fierce eyes stared at him brightly, while he clutched his chest with one rough hand, and Simon saw that the breast of his shirt was red with blood. The man's voice came with a hoarse effort.

"Ain't nothink. Look out . . ."

"Well, let's have a look at you, old son—"

The other pushed him away with a sudden access of strength. Orace's head was turned towards the half-closed door at the forward end of the saloon, and his jaw was clamped up under the pelmet of his moustache with the same savage doggedness that had been carved into it when Simon had seen him making that heroic fight to get himself up from the floor. And at the same moment, beyond the communicating door, Simon heard the faint click of a latch and the creak of a board under a stealthy foot . . .

A slight dreamy smile edged itself on to the Saint's mouth as he stooped in swift silence to recover his stanchion. Clubbed in his left hand, an eighteen-inch length of slender iron, it formed a weapon that was capable of impressing the toughest skull with a sense of painful inferiority, and the thought that the sportsman who had turned his cabin upside down and done an unascertained amount of damage to Orace was still on board, and might come within reach of a shrewd smack on the side of the head, brought a comforting warmth of grim contentment into his veins.

"Steady, me lad. We must get this coat off to see what the trouble is . . . I never thought you'd go and hit the bottle directly I was out of sight, Orace. And I suppose the cap blew off the ginger ale when you weren't looking . . . There we are. Now if we just change the cut of this beautiful shin of yours . . ."

He burbled on, as if he were still attending to the patient, while he picked his way soundlessly over the littered floor. His eyes were fixed on the door into the galley, and they were not smiling.

And then he stopped.

He stopped because the half-open door had suddenly jerked wide open. Beyond it, the further end of the alleyway was in darkness, but in the shadowy space between the light of the saloon and the darkness beyond he could see the black configuration of a man, and the gun in the man's hand was held well forward so that the light of the saloon laid dull bluish gleams along the barrel.

"Don't come any closer," said the shadow.

The Saint relaxed slowly, rising from the slight crouch to which his cautious advance had unconsciously reduced him. The man facing him seemed to be of medium height, square and thickset; his voice had a throaty accent which was unfamiliar.

"Hullo, old cockroach." Simon greeted him in the gentlest of drawls, with the stanchion swinging loosely and rather speculatively in his hand. "Come in and make yourself at home. Oh, but you have. Never mind. There's still some of the bulkhead you haven't pulled to pieces—"

"I'll finish that in a minute. Turn round."

"You're sure you haven't any designs on me?"

"Turn round!"

The Saint turned with a shrug.

"I suppose you know what'll happen if your hand shakes with that gun of yours, brother," he remarked. "You might have an accident and hit me. There's something about your voice which makes me think you've been practising in a place where little things like that don't matter, but over here they're a bit fussy. Have you ever seen a man hanged, old dear? It does the most comic things to his face. Although probably your face is comic enough—"

"You can forget that stuff," said the man behind him, coldly. "Now just drop that thing you've got in your hand."

"What, my little umbrella?"

"Yeah—whatever it is."

The Saint bent down slowly and laid the stanchion on the floor, choosing the place for it carefully.

"Now take two steps forward."

Simon measured the two paces, and stood still. His body was braced for the bullet which might conclude the interlude within the next three seconds, and yet his one desperate hope was pinned to the temptation he had left two steps behind—the iron rod which he had put down so carefully, with one end on an upset ashtray from which it could not be moved without the slight grating sound for which his ears were straining. Out of the corner of his eye he saw Orace leaning rigidly forward on the couch, his scarecrow face set in a stare of indomitable wrath . . .

It came—the faint gritting scrape of metal which told him that the stanchion was being picked up. And the Saint flung himself back with an instantaneous release of his tensed muscles.

His right heel went kicking backwards like a mule's, straight as a gunshot for the place where the head of the man behind him should have been if he was bending to pick up the stanchion, with all the power of the Saint's vengeful thews packed into it, and a silent prayer to speed it on its way. And the head of the intruder was exactly where Simon had computed it should have been. He felt the ecstatic squelch of the leather sogging home into something hard and only superficially yielding, heard the *plop!* of a silencer and felt something tug at his sleeve, and spun round, half overbalancing with the violence of his own impetuous effort.

From the man behind had come one single shrill hiccough of agony, and the Saint twisted round in time to see him rocking back on his haunches with one hand clapped to his face and the blood spurting through his fingers. His other hand still clutched the silenced gun, weaving it round in a blind search for a target. It plopped again, chipping the corner from a mirror on the after bulkhead, and Simon laughed softly and fell on him with his knees. As he grabbed the man's gun wrist he saw Orace lurching forward to pick up the iron bar which had given him his chance, and the obvious justice of the team play appealed to him irresistibly. He rolled under his victim with a quick squirm and a heave, and the man's weight came dead on his hands as Orace struck.

The Saint wriggled out from underneath and sat up, feeling for a cigarette and leaning against the bunk.

"A shrewd swipe, Orace—very shrewd," he commented, eyeing the sleeping beauty with professional approval. "It must have made you feel a lot better. What's all the excitement been about?"

While he explored the extent of his crew's injuries, Orace told him, "'E came alongside abaht 'arf-parst nine, sir. Said 'e 'ad a messidge from yer. 'Ho, yus?' I ses, 'wot is this 'ere messidge?' 'Yer to go an' meet Mr Tombs at the Queen's right awy,' 'e ses. 'Ho, yus?' I ses, 'well, Mr Tombs's larst words to me was to sty 'ere till it snows,' I ses. So 'e ses, 'This is very urgent. Can I come aboard an' tell yer the rest of the messidge?'—and before I could say anythink 'e'd come aboard. 'Not aht 'ere' 'e ses, 'where we can be seen. Let's go below.' So 'e goes below, wivout so much as a by-your-leave, an' I follers 'im to tell 'im where 'e gets orf. 'I gotter whisper it,' 'e ses, an' then, bang, I got a biff on the 'ead that lide me right aht."

"What about this bullet?"

"That was afterwards. When I woke up 'e was still tearin' the saloon to pieces, an' 'e didn't notice me. I lay doggo fra bit, an' then I got 'old of one of the drawers wot 'e'd pulled out an' shied it at 'im. Mustve knocked 'im arf silly, becos I nearly got me 'ands on 'im, but I 'adn't got me legs back so much as I though I 'ad, an' 'e pulled out 'is gun an' shot me."

"And damned nearly killed you," said the Saint thoughtfully.

The bullet had struck one of Orace's left ribs, glanced off, and torn an ugly gash in the muscle of his arm. So far as the Saint could tell, there were no bones broken, and he busied himself with expertly dressing and bandaging the wound, while his mind probed for the origins of that riotous visit.

It wasn't homicide alone and primarily, at least—he was sure of that. From the story, the shot which had crippled Orace looked more like an accident of panic, the desperate impulse of any thug who had felt himself on the point of being cornered and captured. And if that had been the object, it would have been easy enough to finish the job—he himself could have been picked off without warning while he stood at the head of the companion. If not that, then what? The eruptive appearance of the saloon provided a ready answer. Vogel was still searching for information, and the legend of convenient harbour thieves had already been established in Dinard.

There was another suggestion which he remembered as he put the last touches to Orace's bandages.

"Did a porter bring a couple of trunks along for me?" he asked, and Orace nodded. "Yessir. They came abaht arf-parst seven. I put 'em in the starboard cabin."

Simon went forward as soon as he had finished, and found more or less what he had expected. The cords had been cut away from the trunks, and the locks had been ripped away by the scientific application of a jemmy. One of them was already open, and the lid of the other lifted at a touch. Clearly the visitor had just been completing his investigations when the sound of the Saint's arrival had disturbed him.

"Which is all very festive and neighbourly," reflected the Saint, as he surveyed the wreckage.

He strolled back to the saloon in a meditative frame of mind. There remained the problem of the investigator himself, who seemed destined to wake up with a sore head as well as a flattened face. The sore head might return to normal in twenty-four hours; even the flattened face might endear itself by a few years of devotion, and become as acceptable to its owner as the symmetrical dial which perhaps it had once been, but the information which had been acquired during the same visit might prove to be more recalcitrant. It must not be allowed to take itself back to Vogel, but on the other hand it was doubtless keeping company with some useful information from the Vogel camp which might form a basis of fair exchange.

Simon Templar found himself warming to that idea on his return journey. He closed the door of the galley behind him and folded a wet towel which he had collected on his way, grinning at Orace rather dreamily.

"We might see if your boyfriend feels talkative," he said. "And if he doesn't, you may be able to think of some way to thaw him out."

He cleared a space on one of the settees and yanked the intruder up on it. For a minute or so he applied the cold towel methodically. Then he felt the back of the man's head, looked closely into his face, and opened up his shin. After which he moved away and finished his cigarette with contemplative deliberation. For nothing was more certain than that the sleeping beauty had listened to the last lullaby of all.

CHAPTER SIX:
HOW PROFESSOR YULE TESTED
THE BATHYSTOL AND KURT VOGEL
MADE A PROPOSITION

1

Definitely an uninvited complication, thought the Saint, although he admitted that it was the sort of accident that was always liable to happen when a man had an iron bar in his hand and good reason to be annoyed. Orace had had no cause to feel tender-hearted, and perhaps the deceased's cranium had been more fragile than the average. The Saint's attitude was sympathetic and broadminded. He did not feel that Orace was to be blamed, but he did feel that that momentary lapse had altered the situation somewhat drastically. Considering the point again in the placid light of the morning after, he could find no encouragement to revise his opinion. What he had no way of foreseeing was how drastic that alteration was destined to turn out.

He folded his arms on the rail of the *Falkenberg*, and frowned ruminatively at a flight of gulls wheeling over the blue water. Somewhere back under that same blue water, out in the channel between Guernsey and Herm, the unfortunate visitor lay in his long sleep, moored down to the sea bed by a couple of pigs of ballast. The *Corsair* had been cleaned up and tidied, and every record of his intrusion effaced.

Simon Templar had done that alone, before he went to sleep, but his own plans had kept him awake for longer.

"The balloon's gone up, anyway," he had reasoned. "When the search party doesn't come home, Vogel will start thinking until his head gets hot. What'll he decide? That the fellow ratted? . . . One chance in fifty . . . That he's had an accident, then? That's the forty-nine to one certainty."

He had thought round it from every angle that he could see, trying to put himself into Vogel's place, but there was no other conclusion he could come to. What then?

"Vogel won't talk to the police. For one thing, that would give him a hell of a tall story to think up, explaining how he knew anyone would be burgling my boat tonight. And to go on with, he doesn't want to draw the attention of the police any more than I do. And to put a lid on it, for all he may know up to this moment, I might *be* the police."

There was still that thin and brittle straw of anonymity to clutch.

"What would I do? . . . I'd come right over and have a look. But Vogel won't. He's pulled that one already, and he'd have a job to find another excuse to get shown over the boat for the second time in twenty-four hours. Besides, he knows he wouldn't find anything. If I'm police or if I'm just one of the idle rich, the burglar's already lodged in jail, and there's nothing he can do about it except try to bail him out in the morning when he hears the story. And if there's a chance that I'm police, he'd have to be damn careful how he went about that. On the other hand, if I'm in the racket too, I'd be waiting for something like that, and he'd expect to be walking into a reception if he did come over."

That seemed the most unlikely chance of all. The Saint modestly reckoned himself to be something unique in his profession, and there was a sober possibility that Vogel would not think of his peculiar brand of interference at all—unless he had already been identified. Simon slept with his hand on his gun and this debatable chance in mind, but he woke for the first time in the early morning. Yet this uninterrupted sleep gave him nothing more definite to work on. It was still possible that Vogel had stayed away for fear of being expected.

Over breakfast he had had to make his own decision, and his crew glared at him incredulously.

"Yer must be barmy," was Orace's outspoken comment.

"Maybe I am," admitted the Saint. "But I've got to do it. If I don't keep that date this morning, I'm branded. An innocent man would keep it, even if he had caught a burglar during the night. Even a policeman would keep it—and that card may be worth holding for another few hours, though it won't last much longer."

"It's that perishin' girl," said Orace morosely.

Simon paused in the act of fastening a strap around his leg just below the knee—a strap which supported the sheath of the slim razor-sharp knife, Belle, which in his hands was almost as deadly as any firearm. He looked up at Orace sardonically, then ruefully, and he smiled.

"She's not perishing, Orace. Not while I'm still on my feet."

"Yer won't be on yer feet fer long, any'ow," said Orace, as if the thought gave him a certain gloomy satisfaction. "And wot the 'ell 'appens to my job when yer feedin' the shrimps like that bloke I 'it last night?" he added, practically.

"I expect you could always go back to your old job as an artist's model," said the Saint.

He straightened his sock and stood up, smiling that curiously aimless and lazy smile which only came to him when he was shaking the dice to throw double or quits with death. His hand dropped on Orace's shoulder.

"But it won't be so bad as that. I'll put the cards in the porthole for Mr Conway or Mr Quentin to look you up during the day, and they'll see you don't starve. And I'll be having the time of my life. I'll bet Birdie is just hoping and praying that I'll plant myself by not showing up. Instead of which, it'll take all the wind out of their sails when I step on board, bright and beautiful as a spring morning, as if I hadn't one little egg of a wicked thought on my mind. It ought to be a great moment."

In its way, it had been quite a great moment, but it had suffered from the inherent brevity of its description.

Simon watched the play of light on the water, the swiftly-changing lace of the foam patterns swirling and spawning along the side, and recalled the moment for what it was worth. It was the first time he had found any of the signs of human strain on Vogel's face. Even so, his practised eyes had to search for them, but they were there. A fractionally more than ordinary glaze of the waxen skin, as if it had been drawn a shade tighter over the high prominent cheekbones. An extra trace of shadow under the black deep-set eyes. Nothing else. Vogel was as spotlessly turned out as usual, his handshake was just as cold and firm, his geniality no less smooth-flowing and urbane.

"A perfect morning, Mr Tombs."

"A lovely morning after a gorgeous night before," murmured the Saint.

"Ah, yes! You enjoyed our little evening?"

"And the bed-time story."

Vogel lifted his dark eyebrows in tolerant puzzlement—and the Saint could just imagine how well that gesture of polite perplexity must have been rehearsed.

Simon smiled.

"There must be something catching about this harbour thief business," he explained, with the air of a man in the street who is simply bursting with his little adventure and is trying to appear blasé about it. "I had a caller myself last night."

"My dear Mr Tombs! Did you lose anything valuable?"

"Nothing at all," said the Saint smugly. "We caught him."

"Then you were luckier than we were," said Arnheim, with his round flabby face full of admiration and interest. "Did he put up a fight?"

"He didn't have a chance—"

Simon looked up as Loretta came towards them along the deck. He had felt the beat of his heart when he saw her, had seemed to discover an absurd lightening of the perfect morning as if a screen had been taken away from before the sun. Vogel took her arm.

"My dear, Mr Tombs has been telling us what happened after he left us last night. He had one of those harbour thieves on board his own boat—and caught him!"

"But how exciting." She was smiling coolly, but her eyes were steady with questions. "How did you do it?"

"He came along to my bloke, Orace, and said I wanted him—it must have been while we were at the hotel. Orace was a bit suspicious and wanted to know more about it, and then this fellow hit him over the head with something. Orace came to again before the burglar had gone, and he went on with the fight. They were still at it when I got back.

The burglar had a gun and everything, but it had misfired."

"What happened?"

Vogel had asked the question, with his face as calm as stone, and the Saint had known that his answer would mark the sharp pinnacle of the moment which he had deliberately courted. He had allowed himself time to light a cigarette before he replied.

"Well, we were wrestling all over the saloon trying to get his gun away from him, and Orace grabbed hold of a stanchion that he'd brought down to clean and hit him over the head. Then we tied him up and took him ashore and lugged him along to the police station. But when they tried to give him first aid, they found he was—sort of dead."

For a little while there was an absolute silence. Even in the most humdrum circumstances, a revelation like that would naturally have taken a few seconds to establish itself in the minds of the audience, but the Saint had been waiting for a more pregnant silence than that. It was while he was actually on his way over to the *Falkenberg* that he had finally decided to bring his story as close to the truth as possible. If he had said that the burglar was lodged alive in jail, and Vogel's ingenuity had been equal to devising a way of putting through an inquiry, the fiction could have been exposed in an hour or two. But the truth would offer an obvious inducement to wait for confirmation in a newspaper story which could not appear for another twenty-four hours, and it might well dispose of direct inquiries by making their prospects manifestly unprofitable, and, as Simon had told it, it had a ring of authenticity which an invention might not have had.

Simon had been waiting for a pregnant silence, and he was not disappointed. Yet even he did not know until later how much that silence had contained.

"Dead?" Arnheim repeated at last, in a strained voice.

The Saint nodded.

"Orace must have underestimated his strength, or something—I suppose it's quite understandable, as we were fighting all over the place. He'd bashed the devil's skull right in."

"But—but won't you be arrested?" faltered Loretta.

"Oh, no. They call it accidental death. It was the fellow's own fault for being a burglar. Still, it's rather a gruesome sort of thing to have on your conscience."

Vogel put up a hand and stroked the side of his chin. His passionless eyes, hard and unwinking as discs of jet, were fastened on the Saint with a terrible brightness of concentration. For the first time since they had been talking there seemed to be something frozen and mechanical about his tight-lipped smile.

"Of course it must be," he agreed. "But as you say, the man brought it on himself. You mustn't let it worry you too much."

"What's worrying him?"

The Professor came ambling along, with his rosy cheeks beaming and his premature grey beard fluttering in the breeze, and the story had to be started over again. While it was being repeated, a seaman came up and handed Vogel a telegram. Vogel opened it with a slow measured stroke of his thumb-nail; while he read it, and during the conclusion of the second telling of the adventure, he seemed to regain complete command of himself with a mental struggle that showed only in the almost imperceptibly whitened pallor of his face.

He buttoned his jacket and glanced along the deck as Yule added his hearty voice to the general vote of exoneration.

"We're ready to sail," he said. "Will you excuse me if I go and attend to it?"

And in that way the big moment had touched its climax and gone on its incalculable trajectory, leaving Simon Templar to consider where it left him.

2

The Saint lighted a cigarette in the shield of his cupped hands, and stared thoughtfully over the sun-sprinkled ripple of the sea towards the blue-pencilled line of the horizon. An impenitent ripple of the same sunlight glinted at the back of his eyes and fidgeted impudently with the fine-drawn corners of his mouth. He had always been mad, by the Grace of God. He still was. Obviously.

Roger, Peter, and Orace were back in St Peter Port, and though they knew where he had gone, they could do nothing to help him. And there he was, with Loretta, racing through the broad waters of the Channel on the *Falkenberg* while Vogel and Arnheim thought him over. In addition to whom, there was a crew of at least ten more of Vogel's deep-water gangsters, whom he personally had inspected, also on board, and presumably none of them would be afflicted with any more suburban scruples than their master. Out there on the unrecording water, as he had realised to the full when Loretta was the only passenger, anything could happen: a shot could be fired that no unsuspected witnesses would hear, a cry for help could waste itself in the vast emptiness of the air, an unfortunate accident could be registered in the log which no investigations on shore could disprove. There were no prying busybodies peeping from behind curtains of seaweed to come forward later and upset a well-constructed story. The sea kept its secrets—only a few hours ago he had availed himself of that inviolable silence . . . Verily, he was an accredited member of the company of divine lunatics.

Wherefore the Saint allowed that twinkle of sublime recklessness to play at the back of his eyes, and drew sea air and smoke into his lungs with the seraphic zest which he had always found in the fierce tang of danger.

The deep-voiced hum of the engines died away suddenly to a soft murmur, and the curling bow wave sank down and shortened to a feather of ripples along the side, Simon looked about him and turned to the Professor, who was puffing a stubby briar at his side.

"Is this where you take your dip?"

Yule nodded. Vogel was in the wheelhouse with Loretta, and Arnheim had moved out of the sun to spread his perspiring bulk in a deck chair.

"This should be it. We went over the chart last night, and the deepest sounding we could find was ninety-four fathoms. It isn't much, but it'll do for the preliminary test."

Simon gazed out to sea with his eyebrows drawn down against the glare. Under them his set blue eyes momentarily gave up their carefree twinkle. He realised that there was a third person in the same danger as himself, about whom he had forgotten to worry very much before.

"Have you known Vogel long?" he asked casually.

"About six months now. He came to me after my first descent and offered to help, and I was very glad to accept his offer. He's been a kind of fairy godmother to me. And all I've been able to do in return was to name a new deep-water fish that I discovered after him— *Bathyphasma vogeli!*" The Professor chuckled in his refreshingly boyish way.

"You haven't started to think about the commercial possibilities of your invention yet?"

"No. No. I'm afraid it's just a scientific toy." Yule's eyes widened a little.

"Are there any commercial possibilities?"

The Saint hesitated. In the face of that child-like unworldliness he didn't know where to begin. And he knew that to be caught in the middle of an argument, into which Vogel or Arnheim might be drawn, would be more surely fatal than to keep silence.

"I was only thinking . . ." he began slowly, and then he heard footsteps behind him, and turned his head to see Vogel and Loretta coming out on to the deck. He shrugged vaguely, and said goodbye to the lost chance with a grim question in his mind of whether it had ever really come within his reach. "For instance, could you take movies down there? They'd be something quite new in travelogues."

"I don't know," said Yule seriously, "What do you think, Mr Vogel?"

"We must ask someone with more technical knowledge." Vogel's bland glance touched on the Saint for a moment with a puzzling dryness, and returned to his protégée. "Would you like to check over the gear before lunch?"

The Professor knocked out his pipe, and they moved aft. Arnheim stayed in his chair in the shade, with his mouth half open and his hat tilted over his eyes.

Simon fell in beside Loretta and followed the procession. It was the first time that day that he had had a chance to speak to her alone—Vogel had kept her close beside him from the moment they left the harbour, and Arnheim had gone puffing after her with some conversational excuse or other if she had ever moved more than a couple of yards away. The Saint dropped his cigarette and glanced back as he picked it up. Arnheim had not moved, and his round stomach was distending and relaxing with peaceful regularity . . . Simon rejoined the girl, and slackened his stride.

"Perhaps you heard how I'd been thinking," he said.

His hand brushed hers as they walked, and he took her fingers and held her back. "Is this safe?" she asked, hardly moving her lips.

"As safe as anything on this suicides' picnic. It'd be more suspicious if I didn't try to speak to you at all." He pointed back towards the turreted fortress of the Casquet lighthouse rising from its plinth of rocks to the south, as if he were making some remark about it, and said quietly, "There's one person who may be sitting on the same volcano as we are, but he doesn't know it."

"Professor Yule?"

"Yes. Have you thought about him?"

"Quite a lot."

"It's more than I've done. Until just now. Where does he come in—or go out?"

"I'd like to know."

"I wish I could tell you. We know Birdie isn't interested in scientific toys. When this new bathystol is passed okay, he'll've had all he wants out of Yule. Then he'll get rid of him. But how? And how soon?"

He turned away from the lighthouse and they walked on again. Vogel was watching them. The Saint laughed as if at some trivial flippancy, and said in the same sober undertone: "I'm worried. You can't help liking the old boy. If anything sticky happened to him, I'd feel I had a share in it. If you got a chance you might manage to talk to him. God knows how."

"I'll try." She smiled back at him, and went on in her natural voice as they came within earshot of Vogel: "But it must be hard for the lighthouse-keeper's wife."

"I expect it is, if she's attractive."

Simon came to a lazy halt in front of the apparatus which three seamen were manoeuvring out on to the deck—a creation like some sort of weird Martian robot drawn by an imaginative artist. The upper part of it combined torso and head in one great sphere of shining metal, from the sides of which projected arms that looked like strings of huge gleaming beads socketing together and terminating in steel pincers. It balanced on two short bulbous legs of similar construction. The spherical trunk was studded with circular quartz windows like multiple eyes, and tubes of flexible metal coiled round it from various points and connected with a six-foot drum of insulated cable on the deck.

"Is this the new regulation swim suit?" asked the Saint interestedly. "But it doesn't look as if you could move about in it."

"It's fairly hard work," Yule admitted. "But it looks a great deal heavier than it is. Of course, the air inside helps to take off quite a lot of the weight when it's under water. And then, the whole value of the bathystol is its light construction. Dr Beebe went down more than three thousand feet in his bathysphere in 1934, but he was shut up in a steel ball that half a dozen men couldn't have lifted. I set out with the idea of achieving strength by internal bracing on scientific principles instead of solid bulk, and this new metal helped me by reducing the weight by nearly seventy-five per cent. You need something pretty strong for this job."

"I suppose you do," said the Saint mildly. "I don't know what sort of pressures you meet down there—"

"At three thousand feet it's more than half a ton to the square inch. If you lowered a man in an ordinary diving suit to that depth, he'd be crushed into a shapeless pulp by nothing more solid than this water we've been cruising on." The Professor grinned cheerfully. "But in the bathystol I'm nearly as comfortable as I am now. You can go down in it yourself if you like, and prove it."

The Saint shook his head.

"Thanks very much," he murmured hastily. "But nothing could make me feel less like a hero. I'll take your word for it."

He stood aside and watched the preparations for a shallow test dive. The ten-ton grab on the after deck, which he had discovered on his nocturnal exploration, had been stripped of its tarpaulin and telescoped out over the stern, but the claw mechanism had been dismantled and stowed away somewhere out of sight. All that was visible now was a sort of steel derrick with an ordinary hook dangling from its cable.

The hook was hitched into a length of chain welded to what might have been the shoulders of the bathystol, the nuts were tightened up on the circular door through which Yule would lower himself into the apparatus when he went down in it, one of the engineers touched the controls of the electric winch, and the cumbersome contrivance dragged along the deck and rose sluggishly towards the end of the boom. For a moment or two it hung there, turning slowly like a monstrous futuristic doll, and then it went down with the cable whirring and vanished under the water. Again the engineer checked it, while Yule fussed round like an excited urchin, and the telescopic boom shortened on its runners like the horn of a snail until the wire cable came within the grasp of a man stationed at the stern. Three other men picked up the insulated electric cable and passed it along as it unreeled from the drum, and the man at the stern fastened it to the supporting cable at intervals with a deft twist of rope as the bathystol descended.

"That's enough."

At last the Professor was satisfied. He stepped back, mopping his forehead like a temperamental impresario who has finally obtained a rehearsal to his satisfaction, with his hair and beard awry and his eyes gleaming happily. The engineer reversed the winch, and the cable spooled back on to the drum with a deepening purr until the bathystol pushed its outlandish head above the surface and rose clear to swing again at the nose of the derrick.

"Five hundred feet," muttered Yule proudly. "And I'd hardly even call that a trial run." He put his handkerchief away, and watched anxiously while the bathystol was lowered on to the deck and two men with wrenches and hammers stepped up to unfasten the door. As soon as it was open he pushed them away, climbed up on a chair, and hauled out the humidity recorder. He frowned at it for a moment, and looked up grinning. "Not a sign of a leak, either. Now if I can walk about in it better than I could in the old one—"

"I take it there is no serious doubt of that?" said Vogel, with latent solicitude.

"Bless you, no. I'm not in the least worried. But this new jointing system has got to be tested in practice. It ought to make walking much easier, unless the packing won't stand up to the job. But it will."

"Then we shall have to try and find something special for lunch."

Vogel took the Professor's arm, and Yule allowed himself to be torn reluctantly away from his toys. Simon caught Loretta's eye with a gaze of thoughtful consideration. It would have said all that he could find to say without the utterance of a single word, but as they strolled on he spoke without shaping his mouth.

"A smile on the face of the tiger."

She glanced over the turquoise spread of the water, and said, "After we've been to Madeira."

"I suppose so."

The sunlight slanting across his face deepened the twin wrinkles of cold contemplation above his nose. After the *Falkenberg* had been to Madeira . . . presumably. There was deep water there, within easy reach. The Monaco Deep, if Yule wanted a good preliminary canter. The Cape Verde Basin, which the Professor had already mentioned, if he felt ambitious and they cruised further south. Enough water, at any rate, to establish the potentialities of the bathystol beyond any shadow of doubt. Which was unquestionably what Vogel wanted . . . But long before then, if the photographer in Dinard hadn't fogged his plates, and Vogel's intelligence service was anything like as efficient as his other departments, the Saint's own alibi of apologetically intruding innocence would have been blown sky-high, and there would be nothing to stop the joyride terminating according to the old Nigerian precedent. Unless Vogel himself had been disposed of by that time, which would have been the Saint's own optimistic prophecy . . . And yet the indefensible apprehension stayed with him through the theatrically perfect service of luncheon, to sour the lobster cocktail and embitter the exquisitely melting perfection of the quails in aspic.

He put it aside—thrust it away into the remoter shelves of his mind. Just then there seemed to be more urgent dangers to be met halfway. It was one of those mental sideslips which taunt the fallibility of human concentration.

"You're very preoccupied, Mr Tombs."

Vogel's insinuating accents slurred into his reverie, with a hint of malicious irony, and Simon looked up with unruffled nonchalance.

"I was just thinking what a sensation it must be for the fish when the Professor goes wading about among them," he murmured. "It ought to make life seem pretty flat for the soles when he goes home."

3

·

There were two oxygen cylinders, of the same alloy as the bathystol, unpacked from their case and being passed out on to the deck as Yule wriggled into a moth-eaten grey sweater in preparation for his descent. He tested the automatic valves himself before he shook hands all round and climbed up on to the deckhouse roof to lower himself into his armour. The door in the top of the bathystol was only just large enough to let him through, but presently he was inside, peering out of one of the portholes, exactly like a small brat at a window with his nose flattened against the pane. Then the oxygen cylinders were passed in to him, and fitted into the clamps provided for them on the interior of the sphere. After which the door was lowered into place by two men, and the clang of hammer and wrench rattled over the sea as the bolts which secured it were tightened up. To the submarine pioneer imprisoned inside the echoing globe of metal, the terrific din must have been one of the worst ordeals he had to suffer: they could see his face, through one of the quartz lenses, wrinkled in a comical contortion of agony, while he squeezed his fingers ineffectually into his ears.

Then it was finished, and the hammerers climbed down.

The Professor fitted a pair of earphones over his head and adjusted the horn-shaped transmitter on his chest, and his voice, curiously shrill and metallic, clattered suddenly out of a small loud speaker standing on a table by the rail.

"Can you hear me?"

"Perfectly. Can you hear us?"

Vogel had settled the loop of a similar transmitter round his neck, and it was he who checked up the telephone communication. The Professor grinned through his window.

"Fine! But I shall have to get this thing soundproofed if I'm going to use it much. I wish you knew what the noise was like!"

His hands moved over the racks of curious instruments with which he was surrounded, testing them one by one. Under one of the windows, on his right, there was a block of paper on a small flat shelf, for notes and sketches, with a pencil dangling over it on a length of ridiculously commonplace string. On his left, mounted on a sort of lazy-tongs on which it could be pulled out from its bracket, was a small camera. He touched a switch, and the interior of the globe was illuminated by a dim light over his notebook; at the touch of another switch, a dazzlingly powerful shaft of luminance beamed out from a quartz lens set in the upper part of the sphere like the headlight of a streamlined car. Then he slipped his arms into the sleeves of the apparatus, moved them about, and opened and closed the pincer hands. He bent his knees, and lifted first one leg and then the other in their ponderous harness. At last his voice came through the loud speaker again.

"Right! Let her go!"

"Good luck," said Vogel, and the bathystol lifted and swung out over the side as the winch whined under the engineer's movement of the control lever.

Peering over the side into the blue water beneath which the bathystol had disappeared, Simon Templar found himself forgetting the implications of the experiment he was watching, the circumstances in which he was there, and the menace that hung over the whole expedition. There was a quiet potency of drama in the plunge of that human sounding-line to the bottom of the sea which neutralised all the cruder theatricalities of battle, murder, and sudden death. Granted that this, according to Yule, was hardly even a preliminary canter, and that enough water did not exist under their keel to provide the makings of any sort of record—there was still the breathtaking comprehension of what should follow from this trial descent. It was the opening of a field of scientific exploration which had baffled adventurers far longer than the conquest of the air, a victory over physical limitations more spellbindingly sensational than any ascent into the stratosphere. The precarious thread of chance on which hung his own life and Loretta's seemed temporarily of slight importance beside the steel cable which was sliding down into the depths through the concentric ripples dilating out from it across the surface.

After fifteen minutes which might have been an hour, the cable swayed with the first trace of slackness and the loud speaker suddenly squeaked: "Whoa!" The burring of the winch died away, and the man who was chalking the cable in ten-foot lengths as it slipped over the boom looked at his figures and called a guttural "Five hundred seventy-five."

"Five hundred and seventy-five feet," Vogel relayed impassively over the phone.

"Splendid. I'm on the bottom." It was indescribably eerie to listen to Yule's matter-of-fact voice speaking from the eternal windless night of the sea bed. "Everything's working perfectly. The heating arrangement makes a lot of difference—I'm not a bit cold."

"Can you move about?"

"Yes, I think so. This bathystol is a lot lighter than the last one."

"Could you bend down to pick anything up in it?"

There was a brief pause. Glancing at Kurt Vogel in a moment's recollection of what this preliminary experiment stood for besides its contribution to scientific knowledge, Simon saw that the man's face was taut and shining with the same curiously waxen glaze which he had noticed on that hair-raising search of the *Corsair*.

Then the Professor's voice came through again. "Yes—I got hold of a bit of rock. Quite easy . . . Phew! That was a small fish nosing the window, and I nearly caught him. A bit too quick for me, though . . . Now I'm going to try and walk a bit. Give me another twenty feet of cable."

The winch thrummed again for a few seconds, and then there was absolute silence on deck. The engineer wiped his hands mechanically on a piece of cotton waste, and thrust it back in his pocket. The man who had been checking off the lengths of cable put away his chalk and pulled reflectively at his ear. The carpenter tied a last linking hitch between the cable and the telephone line, and clambered down from his perch. The other seamen drew together at the stern and stood in a taciturn and inexpressive group, oddly reminiscent of a knot of miners waiting at the pit-head after a colliery explosion.

There was the same sullen stoicism, the same brooding intensity of imagination. Simon felt his pulses beating and the palms of his hands turning moist. He flashed another glance at Vogel. The pirate was standing stiff and immobile, his head thrust a little forward so that he looked more than ever like a pallid vulture, his black eyes burning vacantly into space; his face might have been carved in ivory, a macabre mask of rapt attention.

The Saint's gaze turned to catch Loretta's, and he saw an infinitesimal tremor brush her shoulders—twin brother to the ballet of ghostly spiders that were curveting up his own spinal ganglions. He felt exactly as if he were waiting for the initial heart-releasing crash of a tropical thunderstorm, and he did not know why. Some faint whisper of warning was trying to get through to his brain in that utter silence of nerve-pulping expectation, but all he could hear was the stertorous breathing of Otto Arnheim and the swish and gurgle of the swell under the counter . . .

"I can walk quite comfortably." The sharp stridency of the loud speaker crackled abruptly into the stillness, somehow without breaking the suspense. "I've taken about thirty steps in two directions. It is a bit slow, but not excessively fatiguing. There is no sign of a leak, and the reading of the humidity recorder is still normal."

One of the seamen spat a cud of tobacco over the side, and the engineer pulled out his cotton waste and rubbed introspectively at an invisible speck on a chromium-plated cleat. Vogel's gaunt figure seemed to grow taller as he raised his head. His eyes swept round over Arnheim, Loretta, and the Saint, with a sudden blaze of triumph.

Then the loud speaker clattered again.

"Something seems to have gone wrong with the oxygen supply. One of the cylinders has just fizzled out, although the gauge still shows it three-quarters full. The valve must have been damaged in packing and started a slow leak. I'm turning on the other cylinder. I think you might bring me up now."

The slight fidgeting of the cluster of seamen stopped altogether. The engineer looked round.

"Up!" snapped Vogel.

Loretta was gripping the Saint's arm. Simon was only numbly aware of the clutch of her fingers: for a perceptible space of time his mind was half deadened with incredulity. His reactions were momentarily out of control, while his brain reeled to encompass the terrific adjustment that Vogel had sprung on him. Even then he was uncertain, unconvinced by that horrible leap of foresight—until the rumble of the winch stopped again almost as soon as it had started, and left a frightful stillness to force its meaning back into his unbelieving ears.

Vogel was watching the engineer with a faint frown.

"What is the matter?"

"A fuse, I think."

The man left his controls and vanished down a companion, and Vogel spoke into the telephone mouthpiece in his clear flat voice.

"They're just fixing the winch, Professor. We'll have you up in a few minutes." There was a short interval before Yule's calm reply.

"I hope it isn't anything serious. The reserve cylinder seems to be worse than the first.

The pressure is falling very rapidly. Please don't be long."

The Saint's eyes were freezing into chips of ultramarine. Every instinct he possessed was shrieking at him for action, and yet he was actually afraid to move. He had straightened up off the rail, and yet some twisted doubt within him still held him from taking the first step forward. So successfully had the cunning of Kurt Vogel insinuated itself into his mind.

Professor Yule had made his descent, established the safety and mobility of the new bathystol, stooped down and picked up rocks and walked in it—proved practically everything that Vogel needed to know. True, the tests had not been made at any impressive depth, but Vogel's previous experience of the invention might have satisfied him to dispense with that. And yet Simon was still trying to make himself believe that he was standing by, watching in silence, while Yule was being murdered in cold blood.

He saw it at once as the practically perfect crime, the incontrovertible accident—an automatic provision for fatalistic obituaries and a crop of leading articles on the martyrs of science. And yet the nerveless audacity of the conception, in the circumstances in which he was seeing it, had to fight its way up to the barricades of his reason. The inward struggle was tearing him apart, but while it went on he was gripped in a paralysis more maddening than any physical restraint. The torturing question drummed sickeningly through his brain and rooted him to the deck: *Was this only another of Vogel's satanically deep-laid traps?*

Vogel had walked across to the companion down which the engineer had disappeared. He was standing there, looking down, tapping his fingers quietly on the rail. He hadn't even seemed to look at the Saint.

"Can't we do anything?" Loretta was pleading. Vogel glanced at her with a shrug.

"I know nothing about machinery," he said, and then he stepped back to make way for the returning engineer.

The man's face was perfectly wooden. His gaze flickered over the circle of expectant faces turned towards him, and he answered their unspoken questions in a blunt staccato like a rolling drum.

"I think one of the armature windings has burnt out. They're working on it."

Another hush fell after his words, in which Otto Arnheim emptied his lungs with a gusty sigh. Loretta was staring at the taut cable swaying slightly from the nose of the boom as the *Falkenberg* tilted in the swell, and her face had gone paler under the golden tan. A gull turned in the bright sky and went gliding soundlessly down a long air-slope towards the east.

Simon's fists were clenched till the nails bit into his palms, and there was a kind of dull nausea in his stomach. And the loud speaker clacked through the silence.

"The reserve cylinder seems to be worse than the first. I don't think it will last much longer. What is the matter?"

"We are trying to repair the winch," Vogel said quietly.

Then he looked at the Saint. Was that intended to be a tragic appeal, or was it derision and sinister watchfulness in the black eyes? Simon felt his self-command snapping under the intolerable strain. He turned to the loud speaker and stared at it in the most vivid torment of mind that he had ever known. Was it possible that some expert manipulation of the wiring might have made it possible to cut off the Professor's voice, while one of Vogel's crew somewhere on the ship spoke through it instead?

"The cylinder has just given out."

Yule's voice came through again unfalteringly, almost casually. The Saint saw that Loretta's eyes were also fixed on the loud speaker: her chest was scarcely moving, as if her own breathing had stopped in sympathy with what those six words must have meant to the man helplessly imprisoned in his grotesque armour five hundred feet below the bountiful air.

"Can't you put the cable on to another winch?" asked the Saint, and hardly recognised his own voice.

"There's no other winch on the ship that would take the load."

"We can rig up a tackle if you've got a couple of large blocks."

"It takes more than twenty minutes to raise the bathystol from this depth," Vogel said flatly. "With a block and tackle it would take over an hour."

Simon knew that he was right. And his brain worked on, mechanically, with its grim computation. In that confined space it would take no more than a few minutes to consume all the oxygen left in the air. And then, with the percentage of carbon dioxide leaping towards its maximum . . .

"I'm getting very weak and giddy." The Professor's voice was fainter, but it was still steady and unflinching. "You will have to be very quick now, or it will be no use."

Something about the scene was trying to force itself into the Saint's attention. Was he involuntarily measuring his distances and marking down positions, with the instinct of a seasoned fighter? The group of seamen at the stern. One of them by the drum of insulated cable, further up the deck. Vogel at the head of the companion. Arnheim . . . Why had Arnheim moved across to stand in front of the winch controls, so that his broad squat bulk hid them completely?

There was another sound trying to break through the silence—a queer jerky gasping sound. A second or two went by before the Saint traced it to its source and identified it. The terrible throaty sound of a man battling for breath, relayed like every other sound from the bathystol by the impersonal instrument on the table . . .

In some way it wiped out the last of his indecision. He was prepared to be wrong, prepared also not to care. Any violence, whatever it might bring, was better than waiting for his nerves to be slowly racked to pieces by that devilish inquisition.

He moved slowly forwards—towards the bulkhead where the winch controls were.

Towards Arnheim. And Arnheim did not move. The Saint smiled for the first time since the Professor had gone down, and altered his course a couple of points to pass round him. Arnheim shifted himself also, and still blocked the way. His round pouting mouth with the bruise under it opened like a trout's.

"It isn't easy to wait, is it?" he said.

"It isn't," agreed the Saint, with a cold and murderous precision, and the automatic flashed from his pocket to grind its muzzle into the other's yielding belly. "So we'll stop waiting. Walk backwards a little way, Otto."

Arnheim's jowl dropped. He looked down at the gun in his stomach, and looked up again with his eyes round as saucers and his wet mouth sagging wider. He coughed. "Really, Mr Tombs—"

"Have you gone mad?"

Vogel's dry monotone lanced across the feeble protest with calculated contempt. And the Saint grinned mirthlessly.

"Not yet. But I'm liable to if Otto doesn't get out of my way in the next two seconds. And then you're liable to lose Otto."

"I know this is a ghastly situation." Vogel was still speaking calmly, with the soothing and rather patronising urbanity with which he might have tried to snub a drunkard or a lunatic. "But you won't help it by going into hysterics. Everything possible is being done."

"One thing isn't being done," answered the Saint, in the same bleak voice, "and I'm going to do it. Get away from those controls. Otto, and watch me start that winch!"

"My dear Mr Tombs—"

"Behind you!"

Loretta's desperate cry pealed in the Saint's ears with a frantic urgency that spun him round with his back to the deckhouse. He had a glimpse of a man springing at him with an upraised belaying-pin, and his finger was tightening on the trigger when Arnheim dragged down his wrist and struck him a terrific left-handed blow with a rubber truncheon. There was an instant when his brain seemed to rock inside his skull. Then darkness.

4

"I trust you are feeling better," said Vogel.

"Much better," said the Saint. "And full of admiration. Oh, it was smooth, very smooth, Birdie—you don't mind if I call you Birdie, do you? It's so whimsical."

He sat in an armchair in the wheelhouse, with a brandy and soda in one hand and a cigarette in the other. Both of them had been provided by Kurt Vogel. He was not even tied up. But there the free hospitality ended, for Vogel kept one hand obtrusively in his jacket pocket, and so did Arnheim.

Simon Templar allowed himself a few more moments to digest the profound smoothness of the ambush. He had been fairly caught, and he admitted it—caught by a piece of machiavellian strategy that was ingenious enough to have netted even such a wary bird as himself without disgrace. Oh, it had been exceedingly smooth; a bait that flesh and blood and human feeling could scarcely have resisted. And the climax had supervened with an accuracy of co-ordination that could hardly have been slicker if it had been rehearsed—from which he deduced that it probably had. If he had been unprepared, the seaman with the belaying-pin would have got him; if he was warned, Arnheim had his chance . . .

"And the Professor?" he asked. Vogel lifted his shoulders.

"Unfortunately the fault was traced too late, Mr Templar."

"So you knew," said the Saint softly. The other's thin lips widened.

"Of course. When you were photographed in Dinard—you remember? I received the answer to my inquiry this morning. You were with us when I opened the telegram. That was when I knew that there would have to be an accident."

Naturally. When once the Saint was known, a man like Vogel would not have run the risk of letting the Professor be warned, or snatched out of his power. He had been ready in every detail for the emergency—was there anything he had not been ready for? . . . Simon had a moment's harrowing vision of that naïve and kindly man gasping out his life down there in the cold gloom of the sea, and the steel frosted in his blue eyes . . .

He thought of something else. Loretta's piercing cry, the last voice he had heard before he was knocked down, still rang through his aching head. If he had been known since the morning, the stratagem had had no object in making him give himself away. But it had provided a subsidiary snare for Loretta while it was achieving the object of disarming him. And she also had been caught. Simon acknowledged every refinement of the conspiracy with inflexible resolution. Kurt Vogel had scooped the pool in one deal, with the most perfectly stacked deck of cards that the Saint had ever reviewed in a lifetime of going up against stacked decks.

He realised that Vogel was watching him, performing the simple task of following his thoughts, and smiled with unaltered coolness.

"So where," he murmured, "do you think we go from here?"

"That depends on you," said Vogel.

He put a match to his cigar and sat on the arm of a chair, leaning forward until the Saint was sitting under the shadow of his great eagle's beak. Looking at him with the same lazy smile still on his lips, Simon was aware of the vibration of the powerful engines, and saw out of the corner of his eye that a seaman was standing at the wheel, with his back to them, his eyes intent upon the compass card. Wherever they were going, at any rate they were already on their way . . .

"You have given me a good deal of trouble, Templar. Not by your childish interference—that would be hardly worth talking about—but by an accident for which it was responsible."

"You mean the Professor?" Simon suggested grittily. Vogel snapped his fingers.

"No. That's nothing. Your presence merely caused me to get rid of him a little earlier than I should otherwise have done. He would have come to the same end, anyway, within the next few weeks. The accident I am referring to is the one which happened last night."

"Your amateur burglar?"

"My burglar. I should hardly call him an amateur—as a matter of fact he was one of the best safe-breakers in Europe. An invaluable man . . . And therefore I want him back."

The Saint sipped his brandy.

"Birdie," he said gently, "you're calling the wrong number. What you want is a spiritualist."

"You were telling the truth, then?"

"I always do. My Auntie Ethel used to say—"

"You killed him?"

"That's a crude way of putting it. If the Professor had an unfortunate accident this afternoon, so did your boyfriend last night."

"And then you took him ashore?"

"No. That was the only part of my story where I wandered a little way from the truth. A bloke with my reputation can't afford to deliver dead bodies at police stations, even if they died of old age—not without wasting a lot of time and answering a lot of pointed questions. So we gave him a sailor's funeral. We rowed him out some way from the harbour and fed him to the fish."

The other's eyes bored into him like splinters of black marble, as if they were trying to split open his brain and impale the first fragment of a lie, but Simon met them with the untroubled steadiness of a clear conscience. And at last Vogel drew back a little.

"I believe you. I suspected that there was some truth in your story when you first told it. That is why you are alive now."

"You're too generous, Birdie."

"But how long you will remain alive is another matter."

"I knew there was a catch in it somewhere," said the Saint, and inhaled thoughtfully from his cigarette.

Vogel got up and walked over to one of the broad windows, and Simon transferred his contemplative regard to Otto Arnheim, estimating how long it might take him to bridge the distance between them. While Vogel and the man at the wheel both had their backs turned to the room, could a very agile man . . .?

And Simon knew that he couldn't. Reclining as he was in the depths of one of those luxuriously streamlined armchairs, he couldn't even hope to get up on his feet before he was filled full of lead. He tried hauling himself up experimentally, as if in search of an ashtray, and Arnheim had a gun thrusting out at him before he was even sitting upright. The Saint dropped his ash on the carpet and lay back again, scratching his leg ruminatively. At least the knife strapped to his calf was still there—if it came to a pinch and the opportunity offered, he might do something with that. But even while he knew that his life would be a speculative buy at ten cents in the open market, he was being seized with an overpowering curiosity to know why Vogel had left it even that nominal value.

After about a minute Vogel turned round and came back.

"You are responsible for the loss of one of my best men," he said with peremptory directness. "It will be difficult to replace him, and it may take considerable time. Unfortunately, I cannot afford to wait. But fortunately, I have you here instead."

"So we can still play cut-throat," drawled the Saint.

Vogel stood looking down at him impassively, the cigar glowing evenly between his teeth.

"Just now you wanted to know where we were going, Templar. The answer is that we are going to a point a little way south-west of the Casquet Lighthouse. When we stop again there, we shall be directly over the wreck of the *Chalfont Castle*—you will remember the ship that sank there in March. There are five million pounds' worth of bullion in her strong-room which I intend to remove before the official salvage operations are begun. The only difficulty is that your clumsiness has deprived me of the only member of my crew who could have been relied upon to open the strong-room. I'm hoping that that is where your interference will prove to have its compensations. I said that the man you killed was one of the best safe- breakers in Europe. But I have heard that the Saint is one of the greatest experts in the world."

So that was it . . . Simon dropped his cigarette-end into his empty glass, and took out his case to replace it. A miniature power plant was starting up under his belt and sending a new and different tingle along his arteries.

It was his turn to follow Vogel's thoughts, and the back trail was blazed and signposted liberally enough.

"You want me to go down and give a demonstration?" he said lightly, and Vogel nodded.

"That is what I intend you to do."

"In the bathystol?"

"That won't be necessary. The *Chalfont Castle* is lying in twenty fathoms, and an ordinary diving suit will be quite sufficient."

"Are you offering me a partnership?"

"I'm offering you a chance to help your partner."

Something inside the Saint turned cold. Perhaps it was not until he heard that last quiet flat sentence that he had realised how completely Vogel had mastered the situation. Every twist and turn of strategy fitted together with the geometrical exactitude of a jigsaw puzzle. Vogel hadn't missed one finesse. He had dominated every move of the opposition with the arrogant ease of a Capablanca playing chess with a kindergarten school.

Simon Templar had never known the meaning of surrender, but at that moment, in the full appreciation of the supreme generalship against which he had pitted himself, the final understanding of how efficiently the dice had been cogged, he was as near to admitting the hopelessness of his challenge as he would ever be. All he had left was the indomitable spirit that would keep him smiling and fighting until death proved to his satisfaction that he couldn't win all the time. It hadn't been proved yet . . . He looked fearlessly into the alabaster face of the man in front of him, and told himself that it had still got to be proved.

"And what happens if I refuse?" he asked quietly.

Vogel shrugged.

"I don't need to make any melodramatic threats. You are intelligent enough to be able to make them for yourself. I prefer to assume that you will agree. If you do what I tell you, Loretta will be put ashore as soon as it is convenient—alive."

"Is that all?"

"I don't need to offer any more."

The answer was calm, uncompromising, blood-chilling in its ruthless economy of detail. It left volumes unsaid, and expressed every necessary word of them.

Simon looked at him for a long time.

"You've got all these situations down to their lowest common denominator, haven't you?" he said, very slowly. "And what inducement have I got to take your word for anything?"

"None whatever," replied Vogel carelessly. "But you will take it, because if you refuse you will certainly be dead within the next half-hour, and while you are alive you can always hope and scheme and believe in miracles. It will be interesting to watch a few more of your childish manoeuvres." He studied his watch, and glanced out of the forward windows. "You have about fifteen minutes to make your choice."

CHAPTER SEVEN:

HOW SIMON AND LORETTA TALKED TOGETHER AND LORETTA CHOSE LIFE

1

"Once upon a time," said the Saint, "there was a lugubrious yak named Elphinphlopham, who grazed on the plateaus of Tibet and meditated over the various philosophies and religions of the world. After many years of study and investigation he eventually decided that the only salvation for his soul lay in the Buddhist faith, and he was duly received into the Eightfold Path by the Grand Lama, who was fortunately residing in the district. It was then revealed to Elphinphlopham that the approved method of attaining Nirvana was to spend many hours a day sitting in a most uncomfortable position, especially for yaks, whilst engaging in an ecstatic contemplation of the navel. Dutifully searching for this mystic umbilicus, the unhappy Elphinphlopham discovered for the first time that his abdomen was completely over grown with the characteristic shaggy mane of his species, so that it was physically impossible for him to fix his eyes upon the prescribed organ, or indeed for him to discover whether nature had ever endowed him with this indispensable adjunct to the Higher Thought. This awful doubt worried Elphinphlopham so badly—"

"Nothing worries you very much, does it?" said Loretta gently.

The Saint smiled.

"My dear, I gave that up after the seventh time I was told I had about ten minutes to live. And I'm still alive."

He lay stretched out comfortably on the bunk, with his hands behind his head and the smoke spiralling up from his cigarette. It was the same cabin in which he had knocked out Otto Arnheim not so long ago—the same cabin from which he had so successfully rescued Steve Murdoch. With the essential difference that this time he was the one in need of rescuing, and there was no one outside who would be likely to do the job. He recognised it as Kurt Vogel's inevitable crowning master-stroke to have sent him down there, with Loretta, while he made the choice that had been offered him. He looked at the steady humour in her grey eyes, the slim vital beauty of her, and knew by the breathless drag of his heart how accurately that master-stroke had been placed, but he could never let her know.

She sat on the end of the bunk, leaning against the bulkhead and looking down at him, with her hands clasped across her knees. He could see the passing of time on her wrist watch.

"How long do you think we shall live now?" she said.

"Oh, indefinitely—according to Birdie. Until I'm a toothless old gaffer dribbling down my beard, and you're a silver-haired duenna of the Women's League of Purity. If I do this job for him, he's ready to send us an affectionate greeting card on our jubilee."

"If you believe him."

"And you don't?"

"Do you?"

Simon twitched his shoulders. He thought of the bargain which he had really been offered, and kept his gaze steadfastly on the ceiling.

"Yes. In a way I think he'll keep his word."

"He murdered Yule."

"For the bathystol. So that nobody else should have it. But no clever crook murders without good reason, because that's only adding to his own dangers. What would he gain by getting rid of us?"

"Silence." she said quietly. He nodded.

"But does he really need that anymore? You told me that some people had known for a long time that this racket existed. The fact that we're here tells him that we've linked him up with it. And that means that we've got friends outside who know as much as we know."

"He knows who I am, then?"

"No. Only that you've been very inquisitive, and that you tried to warn me. Doubtless he thinks you're part of my gang—people always credit me with a gang."

"So he'd let you go, knowing who you are?"

"Knowing who I am, he'd know I wouldn't talk about him to the police."

"So he'd let you go to come back with some more of your gang and shoot him up again?"

Simon turned his head to cock an eye at her. She must not know. He must not be drawn further into argument. Already, with that cool courageous wit of hers, she had him blundering.

"Are you cross-examining me, woman?" he demanded quizzically.

"I want an answer."

"Well, maybe he thinks that I'll have had enough."

"And maybe he believes in fairies."

"I do. I saw a beautiful one in Dinard. He had green lacquered toe-nails."

"You're not very convincing."

The Saint raised himself a little from the pillow, and shook the ash from his cigarette.

He met her eyes without wavering.

"I'm convinced, anyway," he said steadily. "I'm going to do the job." She looked at him no less steadily.

"Why are you going to do the job?"

"Because it's certain death if I don't, and by no means certain if I do. Also because I'll go a long way for a new sensation, and this will be the first strong-room I've ever cracked in a diving suit."

Her hands unclasped from her knees, and she opened her bag to take out a cigarette. He propped himself up on one elbow to light it for her. Then he took her hand and held it. She tilted her golden-chestnut head back against the bulkhead, and a shaft of sunlight through the porthole lay across her face so that she looked like a fallen angel catching the last light from heaven. He had no regrets.

"We have had one or two exciting days," she said.

"Probably we've had exciting lives."

"You have."

"And you. If I can imagine all you haven't told me . . . You're not a bit like a detective, Loretta."

"What should I be?"

He shrugged.

"Tougher?" he said.

"Don't you think I'm tough?"

"Yes. I know you are. But not all through."

"Ought I to be an ogre?"

"You couldn't. Not with a mouth like yours. And yet . . ."

"I oughtn't to have a heart."

"Perhaps."

"I know. I must get rid of it. Do you think there'd be any second-hand market for it?"

"I could introduce you to a second-rate buccaneer who'd make a bid."

She laughed.

"And yet you're not everything that a second-rate buccaneer ought to be—not as I've known them."

"Tell me."

She considered him for a while, with a shadow of wistfulness in her mocking gaze that made him aware of his own hunger, through her parted lips still smiled.

"You're kind," she said simply, "and you want so much that you can never have. You have an honour that honest people couldn't understand. You're not fighting against laws: you're fighting against life. You'd tear the world to pieces to find something that's only in your own mind, and when you'd got it you'd find it was just a dream . . . Besides, you don't talk out of the side of your mouth enough."

He was silent for a moment.

"I expect I could cultivate that," he said at length, and sat up so that he could put her hand to his lips. "Otherwise, we aren't so different. We both wanted something that wasn't there, and we set out to find it—in our own ways."

"And now we've found plenty." She glanced out of the porthole, and turned back to him thoughtfully. "We'll probably both be down somewhere in the sea before the sun comes up again. Saint . . . It's a funny sort of thought, isn't it? I've always thought it must be so exasperating to die. You must always leave so much unfinished."

"You're not afraid."

"Neither are you."

"I've so much less to be afraid of."

She closed her eyes for a second.

"Oh, dishonour! I think I should hate that, with death after it."

"But suppose it had been a choice," he said conversationally. "You know the old story-book formula. The heroine always votes for death. Do you think she really would?"

"I think I should like to live," she said slowly. "There are other things to live for, aren't there? You can keep your own honour. You can rebuild your pride. Life can go on for a long while. You don't burn your house down because a little mud has been trodden into the floor."

Simon looked over his shoulder. The sea had turned paler in the glassy calm of the late afternoon, and the sky was without a cloud, a vast howl of blue-tinted space stretching through leagues of unfathomable clearness beyond the sharp edge of the horizon.

"Meanwhile," he said flippantly, "we might get a bit more morbid if I told you some more about the horrible dilemma of Elphinphlopham."

She shook her head.

"No."

"You're right," he said soberly. "There are more important things to tell you."

"Such as?"

"Why I should fall in love with you so quickly."

"Weren't you just taking advantage of the garden?" she said, with her grey eyes on his face.

"It may have been that. Or maybe it was the garden taking advantage of me. Or maybe it was you taking advantage of both. But it happened."

"How often has it happened before?"

He looked at her straightly.

"Many times."

"And how often could it happen again?"

His lips curved with the fraction of a sardonic grin. Vogel had never promised him life—had never even troubled to help him delude himself that his own life would be included in the bargain. Whether he opened the strong-room of the *Chalfont Castle* or not, Vogel had given his sentence.

Simon Templar had had the best of outlawry. He had loved and romanced, dreamed and philandered and had his fling, and loved again, and he had come to believe that love shared the impermanence of all adventures. Of all the magnificent madnesses of youth he had lost only one—the power to tell himself, and to believe, that the world could be summed up and completed in one love. Yet, for the first time in his life, he could tell the lie and believe that it could be true.

"I don't think it'll happen again," he said.

But she was laughing quietly, with an infinite tenderness in her eyes. "Unless a miracle happens," she said. "And who's going to provide one?"

"Steve Murdoch?" he suggested, and glanced round the bare white cabin. "This is the dungeon I fished him out of. He really ought to return the compliment."

"He'll be in St Peter Port by now . . . But this boat is the only address he's got for me, and he won't know where we've gone. And I suppose Vogel won't be going back that way."

"Two friends of mine back there have some idea where we've gone. Peter Quentin and Roger Conway. They're staying at the Royal. But I forgot to bring my carrier pigeons."

"So we'll have to provide our own miracle?"

"Anyway," said the Saint, "I don't like crowds. And I shouldn't want one now."

He flicked his cigarette-end backwards through the porthole and turned towards her. She nodded.

"Neither should I," she said.

She threw away her own cigarette and gave him both her hands. But she stayed up on her knees, as she had risen, listening to the sounds which had become audible outside. Then she looked out, and he pulled himself up beside her.

The *Falkenberg* was hove to, no more than a long stone's throw from the Casquet Rocks. The lighthouse, crowning the main islet like a medieval castle, a hundred feet above the water, was so close that he could see one of the lighthouse-keepers leaning over the battlements and looking down at them.

For a moment Simon was puzzled to guess the reason for the stop, and then the sharp clatter of an outboard motor starting up, clear above the dull vibration, of the *Falkenberg's* idling engines, made him glance down towards the water, and he understood. The *Falkenberg's* dinghy had been lowered, and it was even then stuttering away towards the landing stage, manned by Otto Arnheim and three of the crew. As it drew away from the side the *Falkenberg* got under way again, sliding slowly through the water towards the south.

Simon turned away from the porthole, and Loretta's eyes met him. "I suppose the lighthouse overlooks the wreck," she said.

"I believe it does," he answered, recalling the chart which he had studied the night before.

Neither of them spoke for a little while. The thought in both their minds needed no elaborating. The staff on the lighthouse might see too much—and that must be prevented. The Saint wondered how drastically the prevention would be done, and had a grim suspicion of the answer. It would be so easy for Arnheim, landing with, his crew in the guise of an innocent tripper asking to be shown over the plant . . .

Simon sat down again on the bunk. His lips were drawn hard and bitter with the knowledge of his helplessness. There was nothing that he could do. But he would have liked, just once, to feel the clean smash of his fists on Vogel's cold sneering face . . .

"I guess it's nearly time for my burglary," he said. "It's a grand climax to my career as a detective."

She was leaning back, with her head on his shoulder. Her cheek was against his, and she held his hands to her breasts.

"So you signed on the dotted line, Simon," she said softly.

"Didn't you always know I would?"

"I hoped you would."

"It's been worth it."

She turned her face a little. Presently she said, "I told you I was afraid, once. Do you remember?"

"Are you afraid now?" he asked, and felt the shake of her head.

"Not now."

He kissed her. Her lips were soft and surrendering against his. He held her face in his hands, touched her hair and her eyes, as he had done in the garden. "Will you always remember me like this?" she said.

"Always."

"I think they're coming."

A key turned in the lock, and he stood up. Vogel came in first, with his right hand still in his side pocket, and two of his crew framed themselves in the doorway behind him. He bowed faintly to the Saint, with his smooth face passive and expectant and the great hook of his nose thrust forward. If he was enjoying his triumph of scheming and counter-plot, the exultation was held in the same iron restraint as all his emotions. His black eyes remained cold and expressionless.

"Have you made up your mind?" he asked.

Simon Templar nodded. In so many ways he was content. "I'm ready when you are," he said.

2

They were settling the forty-pound lead weights over his shoulders, one on his back and one on his chest. He was already encased in the heavy rubber-lined twill overall, which covered him completely from foot to neck, with the vulcanised rubber cuffs adjusted on his wrists and the tinned copper corselet in position, and the weighted boots, each of them turning the scale at sixteen pounds, had been strapped on his feet. Another member of the crew, similarly clad, was explaining the working of the air outlet valve to him before the helmet was put on.

"If you screw up the valve you keep the air in the dress and so you float. If you unscrew it you let out the air, and you sink. When you get to the bottom, you adjust the valve so that you are comfortable. You keep enough air to balance the weights without lifting you off your feet, until it is time to come up. You understand?"

"You have a gift for putting things plainly," said the Saint.

The man grunted and stepped back, and Kurt Vogel stood in front of him.

"Ivaloff will go down with you—in case you should be tempted to forget your position," he explained. "He will also lead you to the strong-room, which I have shown him on the plans of the ship. He will also carry the underwater hydro-oxygen torch, which will cut through one and a half inches of solid steel—to be used as and when you direct him."

Simon nodded, and drew at the cigarette he was smoking. He fingered an instrument from the kit which he had been examining.

"Those are the tools of the man you killed," said Vogel. "He worked well with them. If there is anything else you need, we will try to supply you."

"This looks like a pretty adequate outfit."

Simon dropped the implement back in the bag from which he had taken it. The brilliance of the afternoon had passed its height, and the sea was like oiled crystal under the lowering sun. The sun was still bright, but it had lost its heat. A few streaks of cloud were drawing long streamers towards the west.

The Saint was looking at the scene more than at Vogel. There was a dry satirical whim in him to remember it—if memory went on to the twilight where he was going. Death in the afternoon. He had seen it so often, and now he had chosen it for himself. There was no fear in him, only a certain cynical peace. It was his one regret that Vogel had brought Loretta out on to the deck with him. He would rather have been spared that last reminder.

"I shall be in communication with both of you by telephone all the time, and I shall expect you to keep me informed of your progress." Vogel was completing his instructions, in his invariable toneless voice, as if he were dealing with some ordinary matter of business. "As soon as you have opened the strong-room, you will help Ivaloff to bring out the gold and load it on to the tackle which will be sent down to you . . . I think that is all?"

He looked at the Saint inquiringly, and Simon shrugged.

"It's enough to be going on with," he said, and Vogel stood aside and signed to the man who waited beside him with the helmet.

The heavy casque was put over the Saint's head, settled in the segmental neck rings on the corselet, and secured with a one-eighth turn, after which a catch on the back locked it against accidental unscrewing. Through the plate-glass window in the front Simon watched the same process being performed on Ivaloff, and saw two seamen take the handles of the reciprocating air pump which had been brought out on deck. His breathing became tainted with a faint odour of oil and rubber . . .

"Can you hear me?"

It was Vogel's voice, reverberating metallically through the telephone.

"Okay," answered the Saint mechanically, and heard his own voice booming hollowly in his ears.

Ivaloff beckoned to him, and he stood up and walked clumsily to the stern. A section of the taffrail had been removed to give them a clear passage, and a sort of flat cradle had been slung from the end of the boom from which the bathystol had been lowered. They stepped on to it and grasped the ropes, and in another moment they were swinging clear of the deck and coming down over the water.

Taking his last look round as they went down, Simon caught sight of the outboard coming back, a speck creeping over the sea from the north-west, and he watched it with an arctic stillness in his eyes. So, doubtless, the lighthouse had been dealt with, and two more innocent men had gone down perplexedly into the shadows, not knowing why they died. Before long, probably, he would be able to tell them . . .

Then the water closed over his window, and, as it closed, seemed to change startlingly from pale limpid blue to green. In an instant all the light and warmth of the world were blotted out, leaving nothing but that dim emerald phosphorescence. Looking up, he could see the surface of the water like a ceiling of liquid glass rolling and wrinkling in long slow undulations, but none of the crisp warm sparkle which played over it under the sun came through into the weird viridescent gloaming through which they were sinking down. Up over his head he could see the keel of the *Falkenberg* glued in bizarre truncation to that fluid awning, the outlines growing vaguer and darker as it receded.

They were sinking through deeper and deeper shades of green into an olive-green semi-darkness. There was a thin slight singing in his ears, an impression of deafness: he swallowed, closing his nasal passages, exactly as he would have done in coming down in an aeroplane from a height, and his ear-drums plopped back to normal. A long spar rose out of the green gloom to meet them, and he realised suddenly that it was a mast: he looked down and saw the dim shapes of the funnels rising after it, slipping by . . . the white paintwork of the upper decks.

The grating on which they stood jarred against the rail of the promenade deck, and their descent ceased. Ivaloff was clambering down over the rail, and Simon followed him. In spite of all the weight of his gear, he felt curiously light and buoyant—almost uncomfortably so. Each time he moved he felt as if his whole body might rise up and float airily away.

"Unscrew your valve."

Ivaloff's gruff voice crackled in his helmet, and he realised that the telephone wiring connected them together as well as keeping them in communication with the *Falkenberg*. Simon obeyed the instruction, and felt the pressure of water creeping up his chest as the suit deflated until Ivaloff tapped on his helmet and told him to stop.

The feeling of excessive buoyancy disappeared with the reduction of the air. As they moved on, he found that the weights with which he was loaded just balanced the buoyancy of his body, so that he was not conscious of walking under a load, and the air inside his helmet was just sufficient to relieve his shoulders of the burden of the heavy corselet. Overcoming the resistance of the water itself was the only labour of movement, and that was rather like wading through treacle.

In that ghostly and fatiguing slow-motion they went down through the ship to the strong-room. It was indescribably eerie, an unforgettable experience, to trudge down the carpeted main stairway in that dark green twilight, and see tiny fish flitting between the balusters and sea-urchins creeping over a chandelier, to pick his way over scattered relics of tragedy on the floor, and see queer creatures of the sea scuttle and crawl and rocket away as his feet disturbed them, to stand in front of the strong-room door, presently, and see a limpet firmly planted beside the lock. To feel the traces of green scum on the door under his finger-tips, and remember that a hundred and twenty feet of water was piled up between him and the frontiers of human life. To see the uncouth shape of Ivaloff looming beside him, and realise that he was its twin brother—a weird, lumbering, glassy-eyed, cowled monster moving at the dictation of Simon Templar's brain . . .

The Saint knelt down and opened his kit of tools, and spoke into the telephone transmitter: "I'm starting work."

Vogel was reclining in a deck chair beside the loud speaker, studying his finger-nails. He gave no answer. The slanting rays of the sun left his eyes in deep shadow and laid chalky high-lights on his cheekbones: his face was utterly sphinx-like and inscrutable. Perhaps he showed neither anxiety nor impatience because he felt none.

Arnheim had returned, clambering up from the dinghy like an ungainly bloated frog, and the three hard-faced seamen with him had hauled it up on the davits and brought it inboard before moving aft to join the knot of men at the taffrail.

Vogel had looked up briefly at his lieutenant. "You had no trouble?"

"None."

"Good."

And he had gone back to the idle study of his finger-nails, breathing gently on them and rubbing them slowly on the palm of the opposite hand, while Arnheim rubbed a handkerchief round the inside of his collar and puffed away to a chair in the background. The single question which Vogel had asked had hardly been a question at all, it had been more of a statement challenging contradiction; his acceptance of the reply had been simply an expression of satisfaction that the statement was not contested. There was no suggestion of praise in it. His orders had been given, and there was no reason why they should have miscarried.

Loretta stared down into the half-translucent water and felt as if she was watching the inexorable march of reality turn into the cold deliberateness of nightmare. Down there in the sunless liquid silence under her eyes, under the long measured roll of that great reach of water, men were living and moving, incredibly, unnaturally, linked with the life-giving air by nothing but those fragile filaments of rubber hose which snaked over the stern; the Saint's strong lean hands, whitened with the cold and pressure, were moving deftly towards the accomplishment of their most fantastic crime. Working with skilled sure touches to lay open the most fabulous store of plunder that could ever have come in the path even of his amazing career—while his life stood helpless at the mercy of the two men who bent in monotonous alternation at the handles of the air compressor, and waited on the whim of the impassive hook-nosed man who was polishing his nails in the deck chair. Working with the almost certain knowledge that his claim to life would run out at the moment when his errand was completed.

She knew . . . What had she told him, once? "To do your job, to keep your mouth shut, and to take the consequences" . . . And in her imagination she could see him now, even while he was working towards death, his blue eyes alert and absorbed, the gay fighting mouth sardonic and unafraid, as it had been while they talked so quietly and lightly in the cabin . . . She could smile, in the same way that he had smiled goodbye to her—a faint half-derisive half-wistful tug at the lips that wrote its own saga of courage and mocked it at the same time . . .

She knew he would open the strong-room, knew that he had made his choice and that he would go through with it. He would never hesitate or make excuses.

A kind of numbness had settled on her brain, an insensibility that was a taut suspension of the act of living rather than a dull anaesthesia. She had to look at her watch to pin down the leaden drag of time in bald terms of minutes and seconds. Until his voice came through the loud speaker again to announce the fulfilment of his bargain, the whole universe stood still. The *Falkenberg* lifted and settled in the stagnant swell, the two automatons at the air-pump bent rhythmically at the wheels, Vogel rubbed his nails gently on his palms, the sun climbed fractionally down the western sky, but within her and all around her there seemed to be a crushing stillness, an unbearable quiet.

It was almost impossible to believe that only forty minutes went by before the Saint's voice came again through the loud speaker, ending the silence and the suspense with one cool steady sentence:

"The strong-room is open."

3

Arnheim jumped as if he had been prodded, and got up to come waddling over. Vogel only stopped polishing his nails, and turned a switch in the telephone connection box beside him. His cairn check-up went back over the line.

"Everything is all right, Ivaloff?"

"Yes. The door is open. The gold is here."

"What do you want us to send down?"

"It will take a long time to move—there is a great deal to carry. Wait . . ."

The loud speaker was silent. One could imagine the man twenty fathoms down, leaning against the water, working around in laboured exploration. Then the guttural voice spoke again.

"The strong-room is close to the main stairway. Above the stairway there is a glass dome. We can go up on deck again and break through the glass, and you can send down the grab. That way, it will not be so long. But we cannot stay down here more than a few minutes. We have been here three quarters of an hour already, which is too long for this depth."

Vogel considered this for a moment.

"Break down the glass first, and then we will bring you up," he directed, and turned to the men who were standing around by the winch. "Calvieri—Orbel—you will get ready to go down as soon as these two come up. Grondin, you will attend to the grab . . ."

For some minutes he was issuing detailed orders, allotting duties in his cold curt voice with impersonal efficiency. He shook off the lassitude in which he had been waiting without losing a fraction of the dispassionate calm which laid its terrifying detachment on everything he did. He became a mere organising brain, motionless and almost disembodied himself, lashing the cogs of his machine to disciplined movement.

And as he finished, Ivaloff's voice came through again.

"We have made a large enough opening in the dome. Now we should come up." Vogel nodded, and a man stepped to the controls of the winch. And at last Vogel got up.

He got up, straightening his trousers and settling his jacket with the languid finickiness of a man who has nothing much to do and nothing of importance on his mind. And as casually and expressionlessly as the same man might have wandered towards an ashtray to dispose of an unconsidered cigarette-end, he strolled over the yard or two that separated him from the air pump, and bent over one of the rubber tubes.

His approach was so placid and unemotional that for a moment even Loretta, with her eyes riveted mutely on him, could not quite believe what she was seeing. Only for a moment she stared at him, wondering, unbelieving. And then, beyond any doubt, she knew . . .

Her eyes widened in a kind of blind horror. Why, she could never have said. She had seen death before, had faced it herself only a little while ago, had lived with it, had stood pale and silent on that same deck while Professor Yule died. But not until then had she felt the same frozen clutch on her heart, the same dumb stab of anguish, the same reckless annihilation of her restraint. She didn't know what she was doing, didn't think, made no conscious movement, and yet suddenly, somehow, in another instant of time, she was beside Vogel, grasping his wrist and arm, tearing his hand away. She heard someone sobbing: "No! No! Not that!"—and realised in a dazed sort of way that she was hearing her own voice.

"No! No!"

"My dear Loretta!"

He had straightened up, was looking down at her with his hooked waxen face cold and contemptuously critical. She became aware that she was breathing as if she had just run to him from a great distance, that her heart was pounding against her ribs like a deliriously wielded hammer, that there must have been a wild stupidity in her gaze. And she realised at the same time that the winch had stopped again.

"Why have you done that?" she gasped.

"Done what?"

She was shaking his arm unconsciously. "Stopped bringing them up."

"My dear girl!" His tone was bland and patronising. "That is the normal process. When a man has been working for three quarters of an hour at the depth where they have been, his blood becomes saturated with nitrogen. If he was brought up quickly and the pressure was suddenly taken off, the gas would form bubbles in his blood like it does in champagne when the cork is drawn. He would get a painful attack of diver's paralysis. The pressure has to be relieved gradually—there is a regular time-table for it. Our divers have been stopped at thirty feet. They will rest there for five minutes, then for ten minutes at twenty feet, then for fifteen minutes—"

She knew that he was trying to make her feel foolish, but she was too sure of her knowledge to care.

"That's not all you were doing," she said.

"What else?"

"You were going to take one of those airlines off the pump."

"My dear—"

"Weren't you?"

He looked at her impassively, as if he was playing with the possible answers at his disposal, deliberating their probable effect on her rather than their accuracy. She shrugged bitterly.

"Oh, I know. You don't need to lie. You were going to kill him."

A faint flicker of expression, the gleam of passionless calculating cruelty which she had seen before, passed over his face.

"And if I was? How deeply will his death hurt you?"

"I should be hurt in a way you couldn't understand."

He waited. She had an uncanny spine-chilling feeling that he was not sane—that he was giving rein to the solitary sadistic megalomania that was branded on all his actions, playing with her like a cat and savouring the lustful pleasure of watching her agony. Searching for his eyes under the heavy shadow of his brows, she suddenly found them devouring her with a weird rigidity that struck her cold. She found herself speaking disjointedly, breathlessly again, trying to drown the new horror in a babble of words that she would never be able to utter unless she let them pour blindly out.

"I know why he went down. I know why he opened that strong-room for you. He wouldn't have done that to save his life—not his own life. He wouldn't have believed you. He tried to tell me that that was why he was going to do it, but couldn't make me believe it. He knew you meant to kill him as soon as it was done. He wasn't afraid. I saw him. I talked to him. He lied to me. He was splendid. But I knew. You offered him something that he could believe. You made him do it for me!"

"Really, my dear Loretta, this is so dramatic. I must have misunderstood our friend Templar. So he becomes the perfect gentle knight, dying to save a lady's honour—"

"Yes. I told you that you wouldn't understand."

He gave a short harsh exhalation of breath that could not have been called a laugh. "You little fool! He never did anything of the kind."

Then she remembered.

"No. But I told him that I should like to live. He did it to save my life."

"The perfect knight again!"

"Something that you could never understand. I know now. That's the truth, isn't it? You made that bargain with him. My life against his—and a little work. Didn't you?"

He sighed.

"It would have been such a pity not to give such a classical chivalry its chance," he said.

The sneer brought the blood to her cheeks. She felt a disgust that was almost petrifying. The mask which he had worn since she had first known him was gone altogether now. The smooth imperturbability of his face was no longer the veneer of impenetrable self-possession—it was the fixed grimace of a demon gloating over its own inhumanity. Now she had seen his eyes . . .

"He never had any right to bargain for me," she said, and tried not to let her voice tremble. "I didn't ask him for any sacrifice—I wouldn't take any. I'm here, and I can make my own bargain. The Saint's done all you wanted him to. Why not let him go?"

"To come back presently and interfere with me again?"

"You could make it a condition that he said nothing—that he forgot everything he knew. He'd keep his word."

"Of course—the perfect knight . . . How ridiculous you are!"

"Did you always think that?"

He stopped short, with his head on one side. Then his cold reptilian hand went up and slowly touched her face.

"You know what I think of you, my dear. I told you, once. You were trying to deceive me. You tried to destroy me with your beauty, but you would have given me nothing. And yet for you I took risks—I placed myself in fantastic danger—I gambled everything—to keep you beside me and see how treacherous you could be. But!"—his hand suddenly dropped on her arm in a grasp so brutal that she almost cried out—"I had my own idea about how treacherous I would allow you to be, and how you would make amends for it later."

He dragged her up against him and ravished her mouth, briefly, cold-bloodedly. She stood unresisting and still as death until he thrust her away.

"Now," he said, "you are not in a position to make bargains."

He stooped over the air-line again. She tore at his hand, and he stood up.

"If you are going to be a nuisance," he said in his supercilious expiring voice, "I shall have you taken away."

"You can't do it!" she panted. "You haven't everything you want yet. If you kill him, you could never have it."

"I have you."

"Only as a prisoner. You can do what you like with me, I suppose. What you want, you can take by force. If that's all you want—"

"It will be enough."

"But I could give . . ."

"What?"

He was staring at her, seized with a new stillness. There was a thread of moisture on his thin lips, and the high glaze on his cheekbones shone with a dull white lustre. His eyes squinted slightly, smouldering like dark coals. His soft clammy hands gripped her shoulders.

"What?" he repeated.

She could not look at him, or her courage would not be enough. Already she felt defiled, shuddering at the dank chill of his touch. She closed her eyes.

"If you let him go I will stay with you willingly—I will be to you anything that you like."

4

Altogether they took over forty minutes to come up—nearly as long as they had spent on the bottom. It was a wearisome business going through the gradual decompression, hanging suspended in the green void through the lengthening pauses, rising a little further and halting for another interregnum of blank inactivity. The Saint felt no ill effects from his long submersion other than a growing fatigue, which had become almost overpowering in the last ten minutes when they had been breaking through the glass dome above the stairway. He had never realised that the resistance of the water which had to be overcome with every smallest movement could eat up so much strength; fit and strong as he was, he had a dull ache in every limb and a nervous hunger for unhampered movement in all his muscles which made the exasperatingly slow ascent harder to endure than anything that had preceded it. He would have given half the millions which he had uncovered down there for a cigarette, but even that solace was unattainable.

He realised at the same time that he was lucky to be able to experience discomfort. When he stood back from the open door of the strong-room and announced the completion of his work into the microphone beside his mouth, he had waited for the quick blotting out of all sensation. He did not know exactly how it would come, but he believed that it would be swift and certain. He had done all that Vogel required of him, and, beyond that, he survived only as a potential menace, to be logically obliterated as soon as possible, before he could do any further damage. Like Loretta, he felt that it must be infuriating to die, leaving so much unfinished, down there in the lonely dark, with none of the drunken exaltation of battle to give it a persuasive glory, but that was what he had gone down to do. When he still lived, he wondered what could have happened to bring him the reprieve.

Had Vogel changed his mind? That was more than the Saint could make himself believe. Or had Vogel begun to wonder whether it would be safe to kill him, when he must be presumed to have associates somewhere who knew as much as he knew and knew also where he had gone, who would make inquiries and take action when he didn't come back? The Saint could see practical difficulties in the way of casually bumping himself off which might have made even Kurt Vogel stop to think, and yet he couldn't quite convince himself that Vogel's strategic talents had at last been baffled.

He was alive without knowing why—without knowing how long that delicious surprise could last, but believing that it could not possibly last for long. And yet the instinct of life is so strong that he was more occupied with wondering how he would turn the reprieve to the most profit. Even when he was working down there on the strong-room door, believing that he had no hope of seeing the light again, that same queer instinct of survival had made him prepare for the impossible chance. Now, when he moved his arm, he could feel a wet discomfort in his sleeve that was more than compensated by the small steel instrument which slithered against his wrist—an instrument which he had not possessed when he left the deck of the *Falkenberg,* which might yet be worth more to him than all the gold of the *Chalfont Castle . . .*

The water above his head thinned and lightened, became a mere film which broke against his helmet. The weight on his shoulders became real again, and the massive boots dragged at his feet. Then expert hands unlocked the helmet and detached it from the breastplate, and he filled his lungs with the clean sea air and felt the breath of the sea on his face.

Vogel stood in front of him.

"Perhaps you were justified in calling my former assistant an amateur," he remarked urbanely. "Judged by your own exceptional standard, I fear he was not so efficient as I used to think."

"It's hardly fair to compare anyone with me," murmured the Saint modestly. "And so where do we go after the compliments, Birdie?"

"You will go to your cabin below while I consider what is to be done with you."

He left the Saint with a satirical bow, and went on to give further instructions to the two replacement divers who were waiting to have the straps tightened on their corselets. Simon sat on a stool and loosened the cords and straps of his boots, while his own breastplate was taken off. As he wriggled out of the cumbersome twill and rubber suit he managed to get the instrument in his sleeve into his hand, and during the process of peeling off the heavy woollen sweater and pants with which he had been provided to protect him against the cold of the water he managed to transfer it undetected into an inside pocket of his clothes. He was not dead yet—not by a million light-years . . .

He fished out a crumpled packet of cigarettes and lighted one while he sought a sign from Loretta. The smoke caressed the hungry tissue of his lungs and sent its narcotic balm stealing gratefully along his nerves, and over by the rail he saw her, slim and quiet and desirable in her scanty white dress, so that it was all he could do not to go over and take her quietly into his arms. Even to see her and to desire her in helpless silence was a part of that supreme ecstasy of the return to life, a delight of sensual survival that had its place with the smell of the sea and the reddening retreat of the sun, a crystallisation of the voluptuous rapture of living, but she only looked at him for a moment, and then turned away again. And then he was seized by the arms and hurried down the companion.

Loretta heard him go, without looking round. She heard the feet of men on the deck, and the whine of the winch as the second pair of divers were lowered. Presently she heard Arnheim's fat voice:

"How much longer will this take?"

And Vogel's reply : "I don't know. Probably we shall have to send Ivaloff down again, with someone else, when Orbel and Calvieri are tired. I expect it will be dusk before we can reach St Martin."

"Are they expecting us?"

"I shall have to tell them. Will you attend to the telephone?"

Loretta rested her elbows on the rail and her chin on her hands. Her face slid down between her hands till her fingers combed through her hair. She heard without hearing, gazed over the sea and saw nothing.

A touch on her shoulder roused her. She shivered and straightened up, shaking the hair out of her eyes. Her face was white with a sort of lifeless calm.

Vogel stood beside her, with his hands in his pockets. "You are tired?" he said, in his cold grating voice.

She shook her head.

"Oh, no. It's just—rather dull, waiting, isn't it? I suppose you're interested in the work, but—I wish they'd be quick. We've been here for hours . . ."

She was talking aimlessly, for the sake of talking, for the sake of any distraction that would reassure her of her own courage. His thin lips edged outwards in what might have been a smile.

"Would you like a drink?"

"Yes."

He touched her arm. "Come."

He led her into the wheelhouse and pressed the bell for a steward. As the man entered silently, he said, "A highball?—I think that would be your national prescription."

She nodded, and he confirmed the order with a glance.

He held out an inlaid cigarette-box and struck a match. She inhaled the smoke and stood up to him without recoiling, with her head lifted in that white lifeless pride. Her heart was beating in quick leaden strokes, but her hand was steady.

Was it to be so soon? She wished it could be over before she was weakened by her fear, and yet the instinct of escape prayed for a respite, as if time could give cold logic a more crushing mastery of her revulsion. What did it amount to after all, this physical sacrifice, this brief humiliation? Her mind, her self that made her a living personality, her soul or heart or whatever it might be called, could not be touched. It was beyond reach of all the assailments of the body for so long as she chose to keep it so. "You don't burn your house down because a little mud has been trodden into the floor." She, her essential self, could triumph even in the defeat of the flesh. What a lot of exaggerated nonsense was talked about that one crude gesture . . . And yet her heart throbbed with that leaden pulse before the imminent reality.

"Excuse me a moment."

Either he had observed nothing, or he was insensible to her emotions. Without touching her, he turned away and moved over to the bookcases at the after end of the room.

She had her respite. The steward returned, and put down a tray on the table beside her; he poured out a drink and went out again without speaking. Loretta took up the glass and tasted it: after she had sipped, it occurred to her that it might be drugged, and she almost put it down.

And then her lips moved in the ghost of a wry grimace. What did it matter?

She looked to see what Vogel was doing. He had taken a chair over to the bookcase and sat down in front of it. The upper shelves had opened like a door, carrying the books with them, and in the aperture behind was the compact instrument panel of a medium-powered radio transmitting station. Vogel had clipped a pair of earphones over his head, and his long white fingers were flitting delicately over the dials—pausing, adjusting, timing his station with quick and practised touches. Somewhere in the stillness she could hear the faint whirr of a generator . . . And then she heard a clearer, sharper, intermittent tapping, Vogel had found his correspondent, and he was sending a message.

The staccato rhythm of the transmitter key pattered into her brain and translated itself almost automatically into letters and words. Like everyone else in Ingerbeck's, she had studied the Morse code as part of her general training: it was second nature to interpret the rattle of dots and dashes, as effortless a performance as if she had been listening to Vogel talking. She did it so instinctively, while the active part of her mind was too turbulent with other thoughts to pay attention, that it was a few seconds before she coordinated what she was hearing.

Dot-dot-dash-dot . . . *dot-dot-dash* . . . *dash-dot-dash-dot* . . . She searched through her memory: wasn't that the call signal of the radio station at Cherbourg? Then he was giving his own call signal. Then, with the swift efficiency of a professional operator, he was tapping out his message. A telegram. *"Baudier, Herqueville . . . Arrive ce soir vers 9 heures demi. Faites préparer phares . . ."*

The names meant nothing to her; the message was unimportant— obviously Vogel must have a headquarters somewhere, which he would head for at such a time as this. But the fact that was thundering through her head was the radio itself. It wasn't merely in touch with a similar station at his headquarters—it could communicate openly with Cherbourg, and therefore presumably with any other wireless telegraph receiving station that it could reach. The Niton station in the Isle of Wight, for instance, might easily be within range; from which a telegram might be relayed by cable to St Peter Port . . . There seemed to be no question about the acceptance of the message. Obviously the *Falkenberg* was on the list of registered transmitters, like any Atlantic liner. She almost panicked for a moment in trying to recall the signal by which Vogel had identified himself, but she had no need to be afraid. The letters were branded on her memory as if by fire. Then, if she could only gain five minutes alone in the chair where Vogel was sitting . . .

He had finished. He took off the headphones, swung over the main switch in the middle of the panel, turned out the light which illuminated the cupboard, and closed the bookshelf door. It latched with a faint click, and he came towards her again.

"I didn't know you were so well equipped," she said, and hoped he would not notice her breathlessness.

He did not seem to notice anything—perhaps because he was so confident that he did not care. He shrugged.

"It is useful sometimes," he said. "I have just sent a message to announce that we shall soon be on our way."

"Where?"

"To Herqueville—below Cap de la Hague, at the northern end of the Anse de Vauville. It is not a fashionable place, but I have found it convenient for that reason. I have a château there where you can be as comfortable as you wish—after tomorrow. Or, if you prefer, we can go for a cruise somewhere. I shall be entirely at your service."

"Is that where you'll put the Saint ashore?" He pressed up his under lip.

"Perhaps. But that will take time. You understand—I shall have to protect myself."

"If he gives you his word—"

"Of course, that word of a gentleman!" Vogel smiled sarcastically. "But you must not let yourself forget the other knightly virtue: Chivalry . . . He might be unwilling to leave you."

Loretta had put down her glass. Her head ached with the tumultuous racing of her brain, and yet another part of her mind was numb and unresponsive. She had reached a stage of nervous exhaustion where her thoughts seemed to be torn between the turmoil of fever and the blank stupor of collapse. What did anything matter? She passed a hand over her forehead, pushing back her hair, and said hazily: "But he mustn't know."

"Naturally. I should not attempt to reconcile him to our bargain. But he will want to know why you are staying with us, and we shall have to find a way to satisfy him. Besides, I have too much to risk . . ."

She half turned her head towards a window, so that she need not look at his smooth gloating face. Her head was throbbing with disjointed thoughts that she could not discipline. Radio. Radio. Peter Quentin. Roger Conway. Orace. Steve Murdoch. The *Corsair*. At St Peter Port. The Royal Hotel. If only a message could get through to them . . . And Vogel was still talking, with leisured condescension.

"You understand that I cannot go about with such a cargo as we shall have on board. And there have been other similar cargoes. The banks are no use to me, and they take time to dispose of. Therefore I have my own bank. Down at the bottom of the sea off Herqueville, under thirty feet of water, where no one could find it who did not know the exact bearing, where no one could reach it who did not possess equipment which would be beyond the understanding of ordinary thieves, I have such a treasure in gold and jewels as you have never dreamed of. When I have added today's plunder to it there will be nearly twelve millions, and I shall think that it may be time to take it away somewhere where I can enjoy it. It is for you to share—there is nothing in the world that you cannot have. Tonight we shall drop anchor above it, and the gold of the *Chalfont Castle* will be lowered to the same place. I think that perhaps that will be enough. You shall go with me wherever you like, and queens will envy you. But I must see that Templar cannot jeopardise this treasure."

He was looking at her sidelong, and she knew with a horrible despair that all his excuses were lies. Perhaps she had always known it. There was only one way in which the Saint could cease to be a danger, by Vogel's standards, and that was the way which Vogel would inevitably dictate in the end. But first he would play with them while it pleased him; he would let the Saint live—so long as in that way she might be made easier to enjoy.

"I suppose you must," she said, and she was too weary to argue.

"You will not be sorry."

He was coming closer to her. His hands touched her shoulders, slipped round behind her back, and she felt as if a snake had crawled over her flesh. He was drawing her up to him, and she half closed her eyes. It was a nightmare not to struggle, not to hit madly out at him and feel the clean shock of her young hands striking into his face, but it would have been like hitting a corpse. And what was the use? Even though she knew that he was mocking her with his promises and excuses, she must submit, she must be acquiescent, just as a man obeys the command of a gun even though he knows that it is only taking him to his death—because until the last dreadful instant there is always the delusion of life.

His lips were an inch from hers; his black stony eyes burned into her. She could see the waxen glaze of his skin, flawless and tight-drawn as if it had been stretched over a skull, filling her vision. Something seemed to break inside her head—it might have been the grip of the fever—and for a moment her mind ran clear as a mountain stream. And then her head fell back and she went limp in his arms.

Vogel held her for a second, staring at her, and then he put her down in a chair. She lay there with her head lolling sideways and her red lips open, all the warm golden life of her tempting and unconscious, and he gazed at her in hungry triumph for a moment longer before he rang the bell again for the steward.

"We will dine at eight," he said, and the man nodded woodenly. "There will be smoked salmon, *langoustine Grand Duc, Suprême de volaille Bergerette, fraises Mimosa.*"

"Yes, sir."

"And let us have some of that Château Lafitte 1906."

He dismissed the man with a wave of his hand, and carefully pierced the end of a cigar. On his way out on to the deck he stopped by Loretta's chair and stroked her cheek.

All the late afternoon Simon Templar heard the occasional drone of the winch, the heavy tramp of feet on the deck over his head and the mutter of hoarse voices, the thuds and gratings of the incredible cargo coming aboard and being manhandled into place, and he also thought of Peter and Roger and Orace and the *Corsair*, back in St Peter Port, as Loretta had done. But most of all he was thinking of her, and tormenting himself with unanswerable questions. It was nearly eight o'clock when at last all the noises ceased, and the low-pitched thrum of the engines quivered again under his feet. He looked out of the porthole, over the sheen of the oily seas streaming by, and saw that they were heading directly away from the purple wall of cloud rimmed with scarlet where the sun was dipping to its rest. A seaman guarded by two others who carried revolvers brought him a tray of food and a glass of wine, and half an hour later the same cortège came back for the tray and removed it without speaking. Simon lighted a cigarette and heard the key turn in the lock after them. For the best part of another hour he sat on the bunk with his knees propped up, leaning against the bulkhead, smoking and thinking, while the shadows spread through the cabin and deepened towards darkness, before he ventured to take out the instrument which Fortune had placed in his hands so strangely while he was opening the strong-room of the *Chalfont Castle* in the green depths of the sea.

CHAPTER EIGHT:
HOW SIMON TEMPLAR USED HIS KNIFE AND KURT VOGEL WENT DOWN TO HIS TREASURE

1

The lock surrendered after only five minutes of the Saint's silent and scientific attack.

Not that it had ever had much chance to put up a fight. It was quite a good reliable lock by ordinary domestic standards, a sound and solid piece of mechanism that would have been more than adequate for any conventional purpose, but it had never been constructed to resist an expert probing with the sort of tool which Simon Templar was using.

Simon kissed the shining steel implement ecstatically before he put it away again in his pocket. It was much more than a scrap of cunningly fashioned metal. At that moment it represented the consummation of Vogel's first and only and most staggering mistake—a mistake that might yet change the places of victory and defeat. By sending him down to open the strong-room, Vogel had given him the chance to select the instrument from the burglar's kit with which he had been provided, and to slip it under the rubber wristbands into the sleeve of his diving dress; by letting him come up alive, Vogel had given him the chance to use it; by giving him the chance to use it, Vogel had violated the first canon of the jungle in which they both lived—that the only enemy from whom you have nothing to fear is a dead enemy . . . It was all perfectly coherent and logical, as coherent and logical as any of Vogel's own tactical exercises, lacking only the first cause which set the rest in motion. For two hours Simon had been trying to discover that first cause, and even then he had only a fantastic theory to which he trembled to give credence. But he would find out . . .

A mood of grim and terrible exhilaration settled on him as he grasped the handle of the door and turned it slowly and without sound. At least, whatever the first cause, he had his chance, and it was unlikely that he would have another. Within the next hour or so, however long he could remain at large, his duel with Kurt Vogel must be settled one way or the other, and with it all the questions that were involved. Against him he had all Vogel's generalship, the unknown intellectual quantity of Otto Arnheim, and a crew of at least ten of the toughest twentieth-century pirates who ever sailed the sea; for him he had only his own strength of arm and speed of wit and eye, and the advantage of surprise. The odds were enough to set his mouth in a hard fighting line, and yet there was a glimmer of reckless laughter in his eyes that would have flung defiance at ten times the odds. He had spent his life going up against impossible hazards, and he had the knowledge that he could have nothing worse to face than he had faced already.

The latch turned back to its limit, and he drew the door stealthily towards him. It came back without a creak, and he peered out into the alleyway through the widening aperture. Opposite him were other doors, all of them closed. He put his head cautiously out and looked left and right. Nothing. The crew must have been eating, or recuperating from the day's work in their own quarters: the alleyway was an empty shaft of white paint gleaming in the dim lights which studded it at intervals. And in another second the Saint had closed the door of his prison silently behind him and flitted up the after companion on to the deck.

The cool air struck refreshingly on his face after the stuffiness of the cabin. Overhead, the sky was growing dark, and the first pale stars were coming out; down towards the western horizon, where the greyness of the sky merged indistinguishably into the greyness of the sea, they were becoming brighter, and among them he saw the mast-head lights of some small ship running up from the south-west, many miles astern. The creamy wake stretched away into the darkness like a straight white road.

He stood there for a little while in the shadow of the deckhouse and absorbed the scene. The only sounds he could hear there were the churning rush of the water and the dull drone of the engines driving them to the east. Above him, the long boom of the grab jutted out at a slight angle, with the claw gear dangling loosely lashed to the taffrail, and all around him the wet wooden cases of the bullion from the *Chalfont Castle* were stacked up against the bulkheads. He screwed an eye round the corner and inspected the port deck. It was deserted, but the air-pump and telephone apparatus were still out there, and he saw four diving suits on their stretchers laid out in a row like steam-rollered dummies with the helmets gathered like a group of decapitated heads close by. Further forward he could see the lights of the wheelhouse windows cutting the deck into strips of light and darkness; he could have walked calmly along to them, but the risk of being prematurely discovered by some member of the crew coming out for a breather was more than he cared to take. Remembering the former occasion on which he had prowled over the ship, he climbed up over the conveniently arranged stairway of about half a million pounds on to the deckhouse roof, and went forward on all fours.

A minute or so later he was lying flat on his tummy on the roof of the streamlined wheelhouse, with the full wind of their twenty knots blowing through his hair, wondering if he could risk a cigarette.

Straight ahead, the scattered sights of the French coast were creeping up out of the dark, below the strip of tarnishing silver which was all that was left of the daylight. He could just see an outline of the black battlements of a rocky coast; there was nothing by which he could identify it, but from what he knew of their course he judged it to be somewhere south of Cap de la Hague. Down on the starboard beam he picked up a pair of winking lights, one of them flashing red and the other red and white, which might have belonged to Port de Diélette . . .

"Some more coffee, Loretta?"

Vogel's bland toneless voice suddenly came to him through one of the open windows, and the Saint drew a deep breath and lowered his head over the edge of the roof to peep in. He only looked for a couple of seconds, but in that time the scene was photographed on his brain to the last detail.

They were all there—Vogel, Arnheim, Loretta. She had put on a backless white satin dress, perfectly plain, and yet cut with that exquisite art which can make ornament seem garish and vulgar. It set off the golden curve of her arms and shoulders with an intoxicating suggestion of the other curves which it concealed, and clung to the slender sculpture of her waist in sheer perfection; beside her, the squat paunchy bulk of Otto Arnheim with his broad bulging shirtfront looked as if it belonged to some obscene and bloated toad. But for the set cold pallor of her face she might have been a princess graciously receiving two favoured ministers, the smooth hawk-like arrogance of Kurt Vogel, in a blue velvet smoking-jacket, pouring out coffee on a pewter tray at a side table, fitted in completely with the illusion. The man standing at the wheel, gazing straight ahead, motionless except for the occasional slight movements of his hands, intruded his presence no more than a waiting footman would have done. They were all there—and what was going to be done about it?

Simon rolled over on his back, listening with half an ear to the spasmodic mutter of absurdly banal conversation, and considered the problem. Almost certainly they were heading for Vogel's local, if not his chief, headquarters: the stacks of bullion left openly on the after deck, and the derrick not yet lashed down and covered with its tarpaulin, ruled out the idea that they were putting into any ordinary port. Presumably Vogel had a house or something close to the sea; he might unload the latest addition to his loot and go ashore himself that night, or he might wait until morning. The Saint realised that he could plan nothing until he knew. To attempt to burst into the wheelhouse and capture the brains of the organisation there without an alarm of any sort being raised was a forlorn hope; to think of corralling the crew, one by one or in batches as he found them, armed only with his knife, without anyone in the wheelhouse hearing an outcry, was out of the question even to a man with Simon Templar's supreme faith in his own prowess. Therefore he must wait for an opportunity or an inspiration, and all the time there was a thread of risk that some member of the crew might have been detailed to keep an eye on him and might discover that he had vanished out of his prison . . .

"The lights, sir."

A new voice jarred into his divided attention, and he realised that it must be the helmsman speaking. He turned over on his elbow and looked out over the bows. The lights of the shore were very close now, and he saw that two new pairs of lights had appeared on the coast ahead, red and very bright, one pair off the port bow and one pair off the starboard. He guessed that they had been set by Vogel's accomplices on shore to guide the *Falkenberg* between the tricky reefs and shoals to its anchorage.

"Very well." Vogel was answering, and then he was addressing Loretta: "You will forgive me if I send you below, my dear? I fear you might be tempted to try and swim ashore, and you gave us a lot of trouble to find you last time you did that."

"Not with the Saint?"

There was a sudden pleading tremor of fear in her voice which the Saint had never heard there before, and Simon hung over the edge again to see her as Vogel replied.

"Of course, that would be difficult for you. Suppose you go to your own cabin? I will see that you are not locked in any longer than is necessary."

She nodded without speaking, and walked past the steward who had appeared in the doorway. Before she went, Simon had seen the mute embers of that moment's flare of fear in her eyes, and the veiled smirk which had greased through Vogel's reassurance of her told him the rest. Once again he stood before the open strong-room of the *Chalfont Castle*, twenty fathoms down under the tide, wondering why the death that he was expecting did not come, and all the questions that had been fermenting in his mind since then were answered. He could no longer shut out belief from what his brain had been telling him. He knew, and his bowels turned to water. He knew, and the understanding made his knuckles whiten where they gripped the edge of the roof, and burned in his mind like molten lead as he crushed his eyes for a moment into his arm. He was bowed down with an unutterable humility and pride.

He half-rose, with the only thought of following and finding her. She at least must be free, whatever he did with his own liberty . . .

And then he realised the madness of the idea. He had no knowledge of where her cabin was, and while he was searching for it he was just as likely to open a cabin occupied by some member of the crew—even if no steward or seaman caught sight of him while he was prowling about below decks. And once he was discovered, whatever hope the gods had given him was gone again. Somehow he must still find the strength to wait, though his muscles ached with the frightful discipline, until he had a chance to take not one trick alone but the whole grand slam.

"Will you unload the gold tonight?"

It was Arnheim's fat throaty voice, and Simon waited breathlessly for the reply. It came.

"Yes—it will be safer. The devil knows what information this man Templar has given to his friends. He is more dangerous than all the detective agencies in the world, and it would be fatal to underrate him. Fortunately we shall need to do nothing more for a long time . . . It will be a pity to sink the *Falkenberg*, but I think it will be wise. We can easily fit out a trawler to recover the gold . . . As for disposing of it, my dear Otto, that will be your business."

"I made the final arrangements before we left Dinard."

"Then we have very little cause for anxiety."

Vogel's voice came from a different quarter, and the Saint treated himself to another cautious glimpse of the interior set. Vogel had taken over the wheel and was standing up to the open glass panel in the forward bay, a fresh cigar clipped between his teeth and his aquiline black-browed face intent and complacent. He pushed forward the throttle levers, and the note of the engines faded with the rush of the water.

Simon glanced forward and saw that they were very near the shore. The granite cuffs loomed blackly over them, and he could see the white line of foam where they met the sea. The lights of a village were dotted up the slope beyond, and to the left and right the pairs of red lights which he had noticed before were now nearly in line. Closer still, another light danced on the water.

So unexpectedly that it made the Saint flatten himself on the roof like a startled hare, a searchlight mounted close to his head sprang into life, flooding the foredeck and the sea ahead with its blazing beam. As they glided on over the black water, the dancing light which he had observed proved to be a lantern standing on one of the thwarts of a dinghy in which a solitary man was leaning over the gunnel fishing for a cork buoy. The helmsman came forward into the drench of light and took the mooring from him with a boathook, making it fast on one of the forward bollards, and the dinghy bumped along the side until the boatman caught the short gangway and hauled himself dexterously on board, while the *Falkenberg's* engines roared for a moment in reverse. Then the engines stopped, and the searchlight went out again.

"Ah, mon cher Baudier!" Vogel greeted his visitor at the door of the wheelhouse. *"Ça va bien? Entrez, entrez—"*

He turned to the helmsman.

"Tell Ivaloff to be ready to go down in a quarter of an hour. And tell Calvieri to have a dress ready for me. I shall be along in a few minutes."

"Sofort."

The seaman moved aft along the deck, and Vogel rejoined Baudier and Arnheim in the wheelhouse. And the Saint drew himself up on his toes and fingertips and shot after the helmsman like a great ghostly crab.

Only the Saint's own guardian angel could have said what was in the Saint's mind at that moment. The Saint himself had no very clear idea. And yet he had made one of the wildest and most desperate decisions of his life in an immeasurable fraction of a second—a decision that he probably would not have dared to make if he had stopped to think about it. He hadn't even got the vaguest idea of the intervening details between the first movement and the final result which he had visioned in that microscopical splinter of time. They could be filled in later. The irresistible surge of inspiration had taken all those petty trivialities in its stride, outdistancing logic and coherent planning . . . Without knowing very clearly why, the Saint found himself spread-eagled on the roof again in front of the unsuspectingly ambulating seaman, and as the man passed underneath him Simon's arm shot out and grasped him by the throat . . .

Before the cry which the man might have uttered could gain outlet it was choked back into his gullet by the merciless clutch of those steel fingers, and before he could tear the fingers away the Saint's weight had dropped silently on his shoulders and borne him down to the deck. Staring up with shocked and dilated eyes as he fought, the man saw the cold flash of a knife-blade in the dim light, and then the point of the knife pricked him under the chin.

The Saint's fierce whisper sizzled in his ear.

"*Wenn du einen Laut von dir gibst, schneide ich dir den Kopf ab.*"

The man made no sound, having no wish to feel the hot bite of that vicious blade searing through his neck. He lay still, and the Saint slowly released the grip on his throat and used his freed hand to take the automatic from the man's hip pocket. Then he took his knee out of the man's chest.

"Get up."

The man worked himself slowly to his feet, with the muzzle of the gun grinding into his breastbone and the knife still under his eyes.

"Do you want to live to a ripe old age, Fritz?" asked the Saint gently.

The man nodded dumbly, licking his lips. And the Saint's white teeth flashed in a brief and cheerless smile.

"Then you'd better listen carefully to what I'm saying. You're not going to take all of that message to Ivaloff. You're going to take me along, and tell him that Vogel says *I'm* to go down. That's all. You won't see this gun anymore, because it'll be in my pocket, but it'll be quite close enough to hit you. And if you make the slightest attempt to give me away, or speak one word out of your turn, I'll blow the front out of your stomach and let your dinner out for some air. Do you get my drift or shall I say it again?"

2

As they moved on, Simon amplified his instructions. He replaced his knife in its sheath and put it inside his shirt; the gun he slipped into his trouser pocket, turning it up so that he could fire fairly easily across his body. He was still building up his plan while he was giving his orders. Crazy? Of course he was. But any man who was going to win a fight like that had to be crazy anyhow.

And now he could fill in the steps of reasoning which the wild leap of his inspiration had ignored. The sight of those cases of bullion stacked around the after deck had started it; the grab not yet dismantled and lashed down had helped. Vogel's talk about unloading the gold had fitted in. And then, when he had heard Vogel speak about "going down" again, and gathered that Vogel himself was going to accompany Ivaloff, the complete and incontestable explanation had opened up in his mind like an exploding bomb. Loretta had told him—how many hundred years ago?—that Vogel must have some fabulous treasure-house somewhere, where much of the proceeds of his astounding career of piracy might still be found, which Ingerbeck's had been seeking for five years. And now the Saint knew where that treasury was. He knew it as certainly as if he could have seen down through the thirty feet of stygian water over the side. Where else could it have been? Where else, in the name of all the sublime and extravagant gods of piracy, could Kurt Vogel, taking his loot from the trackless abysses of the sea, have found a more appropriate and inviolable depository for it than down there in the same vast lockers of Davy Jones from which it had been stolen?

And the Saint was going down there to find it. Vogel was going down with him to show him the last secret. And down there, in the heavy silence of that ultimate underworld, where no other soul could interfere, their duel would be fought out to its finish.

As they came to the companion, Simon was ripping off his tie and threading it through the trigger-guard of his automatic. He steadied the helmsman as they reached the lower deck.

"Hold my arm."

The man looked at him and obeyed. The Saint's blue eyes held him with a wintry dominance that would not even allow the idea of disobedience to come to life.

"And don't forget," added that smouldering undertone, which left no room for doubt in its audience that every threat it made would be unhesitatingly fulfilled. "If they even begin to suspect anything, you'll never live to see them make up their minds. Move on."

They moved on. The helmsman stopped at a door a little further up the alleyway and on the opposite side from the cabin in which Simon had been locked up, and opened it.

Ivaloff and the two men who had dressed the Saint before were there, and they looked up in dour interrogation.

Simon held his breath. His forefinger took up the first pressure on the trigger, and every muscle in his body was keyed up in terrible suspense. The second which he waited for the helmsman to speak was the longest he could remember. It dragged on through an eternity of pent-up stillness while he watched his inspiration trembling on a balance which he could do no more to control.

"The Chief says Templar is to go down again . . ."

Simon heard the words through a haze of relief in which the cabin swam round him. The breath seeped slowly back out of his thawing lungs. His spokesman's voice was practically normal—at least there was not enough shakiness in it to alarm listeners who had no reason to be suspicious. The Saint had been sent down once already; why not again?

Without a question, the two dressers got to their feet and stumped out into the alleyway, as the helmsman completed the order.

"He says you, Calvieri, see that there is a dress ready for him. He goes down himself also. He will be along in a few minutes—you are to be quick."

"Okay."

The two dressers went on, and Ivaloff was coming out to follow them when the helmsman stopped him.

"You are to stay here. You change into your shore clothes at once, and then you stay below here to see that none of the others come out on deck. No one except the engineer and his assistant must come out for any reason, he says, until this work is finished. Then you will go ashore with him."

"*Boje moy*," grumbled the other. "What is this?"

The helmsman shrugged.

"How should I know? They are his orders."

Ivaloff grunted and turned back, unbuckling his belt, and the helmsman closed the door on him.

It had worked.

The stage was set, and all the cues given. With that last order, the remainder of the crew were immobilised as effectively as they could have been by violence, and far more simply, while the one man whose unexpected appearance on deck would have blown everything apart was detailed to look after them. A good deal of jollification and whoopee might take place on deck while the authority of Vogel's command kept them below as securely as if they had been locked up—he had no doubt that a man like Vogel would have thoroughly impressed his underlings with the unpleasant consequences of disobedience. And the exquisite strategy of the idea traced the first glint of a purely Saintly smile in the depths of Simon Templar's eyes. He only hoped that Kurt Vogel, that refrigerated maestro of generalship, would appreciate it himself when the time came . . .

As he drew the helmsman, now white and trembling with the knowledge of what he had done, further along the alleyway, Simon flashed a lightning glance over the details of his organisation, and found no flaw. There remained only the helmsman himself, who could undo all the good work with the speech which he would undoubtedly make as soon as he had the chance. It was, therefore, essential that the chance should not come for a long time . . . Simon halted the man opposite the cabin where he had been imprisoned, and grinned at him amiably. And then his fist smoked up in a terrific uppercut.

It was a blow that carried with it every atom of speed and strength and science which the Saint had at his disposal. It impacted with surgical accuracy on the most sensitive spot of the helmsman's jaw with a clean crisp smack like the sound of a breaking spar, and the man's head snapped back as if it had collided with an express train. Beyond that single sharp crack of collision it caused no sound at all—certainly the recipient was incapable of making any, and the Saint felt reasonably sure that he would not become audible again for a full hour. He caught the man as he fell, lowered him to the ground inside the cabin which he should have been occupying himself, and silently shut the door.

As he hurried up the companion, Simon was rapidly knotting his tie behind his neck and stuffing it under his shirt. The automatic, already threaded on it by the trigger-guard, hung at his collar-bone, where he could reach it in full diving kit so long as the helmet was off.

Calvieri and his assistant had been out of sight when the Saint struck that one vital blow, and they showed no surprise when he appeared on deck alone. In point of time only a few seconds had elapsed since they stumped up the companion before the Saint followed them, and the helmsman had had a separate message to give to Ivaloff. Probably they thought nothing about it, and the Saint's demeanour was so tractable that it would have seemed quite safe for him to be moving about without a close guard.

He sat down on the stool and unlaced his shoes. His experience that afternoon had made him familiar with the processes of dressing for the dip, and every second might be precious. As quickly as he could without seeming to be in frantic haste, he tucked the legs of his trousers inside his socks, pulled on the heavy woollen pants, and wriggled into the woollen sweater. They helped him on with the long coarse woollen overstockings which came up to his thighs, and steered his feet into the legs of the diving suit. Calvieri rubbed soft soap on his wrists, and he gripped the sleeve of the dress between his knees and forced his hands through the vulcanised rubber cuffs with the adroitness of a seasoned professional. They slipped on the strong rubber bands to tighten the fit of the wrists, and then, while Calvieri laced and strapped on the heavy boots, the other man was putting the cushion collar over his head and wrestling the rim of the suit on to the bolts of the breastplate.

While they were tightening down the wing-nuts around the straps he slipped a cigarette out of the packet which he had put down beside him, and lighted it while they hitched on the lead weights back and front of the corselet. All the time he was listening tensely for the first warning of Vogel's approach, but Calvieri had stepped back from the job before he heard footsteps and voices on the deck behind him.

"Alors . . . à demain."

"À demain, m'sieu."

Simon stood up. He heard the wooden clumping of Baudier climbing down into his dinghy, and then the double steps of Vogel and Arnheim coming along the deck. The hazards were not yet past.

A complete diving outfit weighs one hundred and eighty pounds, which is not the handiest load to walk and lounge about in on land, but Ivaloff was husky enough, and the Saint had to risk making him seem eccentric. He walked laboriously to the taffrail and leaned on it, smoking and watching the man in the dinghy pull slowly away out of range of the deck lights towards the shore. Behind him he heard the vague sounds of Vogel being encased in his suit, but there was no conversation. On his dip that afternoon, Simon had noticed that Vogel encouraged no unnecessary speech from his crew, and he had been hoping that the rule would still hold good. And once again the bet had come off. The Saint had been sent down before—why should the dressers comment on his being sent down again?

At last he heard the *chuff-chuff* of the air pump, and the slow thudding tramp of heavy boots behind him, and Calvieri appeared beside him with his helmet. He stooped for it to be put on, without turning his head, and waited for the front window to be screwed on before he looked round.

Then, safely hidden behind the small panel of reflecting plate glass, he turned round to the ladder which had been fitted into sockets on the counter, and saw Vogel following cumbrously after him. And at the same moment a three-hundred-watt submarine lamp suspended from the boom was switched on, deluging the after deck and the sea over the stern with light.

They sank down in the centre of its cone of brilliance. There was the sudden shock of air pressure thumping into the eardrums, the sudden lifting of the load of the heavy gear, and then the eerie silence and loneliness of the deep. The lamp, lowered into the water after them, came to rest at the same time as they reached the bottom, and hung six feet over their heads, isolating them in its little zone of light. The effect of that night descent was stranger even than the twenty-fathom plunge which the Saint had taken in daylight. The lamp gave more light within its circumscribed radius than he had had in the *Chalfont Castle* even when the sun was blazing over the surface of the sea, and the water was so clear that they might have been in a tank. The contours of the rocky bottom within the narrow area in which vision was possible were as plain as if they had been laid out under the sun. The Saint could see scattered fronds of weed standing erect and writhing in the stir of imperceptible currents, and a few small surprised pollack darted under the light and hung poised in fishy puzzlement at the unceremonious invasion of their sleep.

Vogel was already ploughing away towards a huge rounded boulder that was dimly visible on the blurred outskirts of their field of light, and Simon adjusted his escape valve and waded after him. Again he had to adapt himself to the tedious struggle which the water forced upon every movement: it was rather like a nightmare in which invisible tentacles dragged against all his limbs and reduced progress to a snail-like crawl which no effort could hasten. It seemed to take several minutes to cover the few yards which he had to go, and as he got nearer he noticed that Vogel seemed to be trying to wave him away. He turned clumsily aside and swayed up towards the other side of the rock.

It occurred to him with a sudden clutch of anxiety that the lamp by whose light they were moving might make everything that happened down on the sea floor as plainly visible to the men on the deck of the *Falkenberg* as it was to him. And then, with his lips twisting in a faint curve of grim and unrelaxed relief, he realised that he had no cause for alarm. The ripples and tiny wavelets scampering across the surface of the water above would break up all details into a confused eddy of indistinguishable shapes. They would hardly be able to see any more than a swirling nimbus of light down in the opaque surge of the deep. Why else would Vogel go down himself with one trusted man to keep the secret of his fantastic treasure- house?

He saw that Vogel was looking upwards, his helmet tilted back like the face of some weird dumb monster of the sea lifted to a blind pre-historic sky, Simon looked up also, and saw that the grab was coming down through the roof of the tent of light over them. Vogel began to work himself out to meet it, and the Saint did the same. Following what he could divine of Vogel's intention, he helped to drag the great claw over and settle it around the rock by which they had been standing. Then they moved back, and he heard Vogel's voice reverberating in his helmet.

"All ready. Lift!"

The wire cables straightened, became taut and rigid as steel bars. A little cloud of disturbed sediment filtered out like smoke from the base of the rock. It was going up, rolling over to follow the diagonal drag . . .

"Stop!"

The boulder lurched once, and settled; the hawsers became slack again. Looking down breathlessly through the wispy grey fog that curled sluggishly up around his legs, the Saint saw that where the stone had once rested was now an irregular black oval crater in the uneven floor. At first he could make out no more than the hazy outlines of it, but even then he knew that the shifting of that rock had laid open the last of Kurt Vogel's secrets, the most amazing Aladdin's cave that the hoards of piracy had ever known.

3

Vogel was floundering to the edge of the hole in the awkward slow-motion which was the best that either of them could achieve down there, his arms waving sprawlingly like the feelers of an octopus in an attempt to help himself along. He sank down on his knees and lowered his legs into the pit; there seemed to be a ladder fixed to the rock inside, for presently his feet found the rungs and he began to descend step by step.

Simon started to follow him, but again Vogel waved him back. He heard the muffled clatter of the telephone.

"Stay there and guide the cases down to me."

The Saint hesitated. Down there in that narrow cavern at his feet, beyond any doubt, was Vogel's outlandish strong-room, and down there must lie the stupendous booty for which so much had been risked and suffered—for which three men had already set out on a quest from which they never returned, for which Wesley Yule had gone down into the silence and died without knowing why, for which Loretta and himself had stood under the sentence of death and more than death.

Having fought his way to it so far, at such a cost, it was almost as much as he could do to hold himself back from the last step.

And then he realised that the step could wait. The murky smokiness under his feet was settling down, and he could see Vogel's helmet gleaming below him. The boulder which had just been lifted away was protection enough for the treasure. There would be no more doors to open . . .

A vague bulk swaying into the margins of his vision made him turn with a start. The grab had released the boulder and gone up, and now it was descending again with a stack of bullion cases clutched in its giant grip.

"Steady!" snapped the Saint into his telephone, and heaved himself unwieldily towards it.

The descent stopped, and he got his hands to the load and pushed it towards the hole. It was hard work against the resistance of the water, and he needed all his strength. At last it was in position, and he ventured to give the order for it to go on.

"Lower slowly."

The grab descended again, while he strained against it—the *Falkenberg* was not quite vertically overhead, and the five or six feet which the load had to be held out seemed like a hundred yards. He kept his weight thrusting against it till it was below the lip of the hole, and presently Vogel gave the order to stop. Simon recovered his balance with an effort. He could feel a prickle of sweat breaking out over his body, and his vision seemed to have become obscured. He realised that a film of steam had condensed inside the glass panel of his helmet, and he opened the air cock on the left of his helmet and sucked in a mouthful of water, blowing it out over the glass as Ivaloff had told him to do that afternoon. It ran down into the collar of the dress, and he could see better.

The claw opened when Vogel gave the word, and presently came up again empty.

Simon helped it over the edge of the hole and let it go by. He tried to estimate how much had gone down on its first voyage. Half a million? A million? It was difficult to calculate, but even the roughest guess staggered the imagination. It is one thing to talk airily in such astronomical figures; it is something else again to see them made concrete and tangible, to push and toil against a load of solid wealth which even a millionaire himself might never see. It dawned upon the Saint that he had always been too modest in his ambitions. With all his fame and success, with all the amazing coups which he had engineered and seen blazoned across the front pages of the world's press, he had never touched anything that was not beggared by this prodigious plunder of which the annals of loot might never see the like again.

But he could judge time better than he could judge the value of bar gold. About four minutes, he concluded, was all that went by between the time when the grab vanished empty out of the light and the time when it came sinking down again with the second load. Therefore it would be wise to prepare the setting for the last scene at once.

Again he toiled and struggled to steer the laden grab over the hole. But this time, as soon as it had gone below his reach, he groped round for Vogel's life-line and drew down a fathom of slack from the hands that held it up on the deck.

Then he took the keen heavy-bladed diver's knife out of its sheath on his belt.

He knew exactly what he was doing, but he was without pity. He thought of Professor Yule, with the winch inactive and the oxygen failing, waiting for death in the grey-green darkness of the Hurd Deep, while his voice spoke through the loud speaker in the blessed light and air without fear. He remembered himself standing in the wreck of the *Chalfont Castle*, waiting with a cold and cynical detachment for the monotonous chuffing of the air driving into his helmet to give place to the last silence in which death would come. He remembered Loretta, and the price for which he had done Vogel's work—a price which she had chosen, he knew now, a different way to pay. And he was without pity. In his own way, in all his buccaneering, he had been just, and it seemed to him that this was justice. He began to cut through the fibres of Vogel's life-line. Load after load of gold came down, and he had to put his knife away while he fought it over to the hold and held it clear while it went down to Vogel, but in the four-minute intervals between those spasms of back-breaking labour he sawed away at the tough manila with his heart cold and passionless as iron. He cut through Vogel's life-line until only the telephone wires were left intact. Then he cut through his own line till it only hung together by the same slender link. When he had finished, either line could be severed completely with one powerful slash of the knife-blade. It had to be done that way; because while the loud speaker would not tell which line a voice came over, and the telephonic distortion combined with the reverberation inside the helmet would make it practically impossible to identify the voice, the man who held the other ends of the lines would still know which was which when the time came to haul them up.

Altogether six loads came down, and the Saint's nerves were strained to the uttermost pitch of endurance while he waited for the last two of those loads. Even then, he could still lose everything; he could still die down there and leave Loretta helpless, with the only satisfaction of knowing that Kurt Vogel at least would never gloat over his defeat or her surrender. If the helmsman recovered too soon from that volcanic punch under the jaw . . . He rubbed his cold right fist in the palm of his left hand, wondering. His knuckles were still sore and his wrist still ached from the concussion; he was sure that never in his life had he struck such a blow. And yet, if Fate still had the cards stacked against him . . . He wondered what sort of a bargain he could strike, with Vogel at his mercy down there . . .

"That's all."

It must have been Arnheim's voice. The Saint heard it through a sort of muffling fog for which the acoustics of the helmet could not have been entirely responsible. He saw that the empty grab was coming up out of the pit for the last time. It bumped over the rocky floor, swung clear, and rose up under the steadily blazing lamp. The gold was all down, and only the account remained for settlement.

The thudding beat of the Saint's pulses which had crept up imperceptibly to a pounding crescendo during those last minutes of nerve-splitting suspense suddenly died down. Only then did he become aware, from the void left by its cessation, that it had ever reached such a height. But his blood ran as cool and smooth as a river of liquid ice as he folded Vogel's telephone wires over his knife-blade and snapped them through with one powerful jerk of his arm.

Quietly and steadily as if he had been dressing himself in costume for a dance, he brought the end of Vogel's lifeline round his own waist and knotted it in a careful bowline. He spoke into the telephone in a sufficient imitation of the flat rhythm of Vogel's accent.

"Wait a moment."

He drew down some more of his own life-line and hitched it round a jagged spur of granite above the cut be had made in it, so that it would still be anchored there after he broke the telephone wires.

The top of Vogel's helmet was coming to the surface as he climbed up the ladder.

Simon went down on one knee at the edge of the hole. His right hand dabbed round and found a large loose stone, twice the size of his fist. He picked it up.

"No," he said, still speaking with Vogel's intonation. "You stay here. I have something else for you to do. I shall come down again in a few minutes."

Vogel's hand came over the top of the hole and clutched for a hold. His head rose above the surface, and he waved the Saint impatiently back to make room for him to clamber out.

Simon did not move.

The broken end of Vogel's life-line trailed away from its lashing on his helmet, but he did not seem to have noticed it. His head turned up towards the light, and his lips moved in some words which no one would ever hear.

The Saint stayed where he was.

Perhaps it was the fact that he received no answer to whatever he had said that started the first wild and ghastly doubt in Vogel's mind. Perhaps it was the absolute immobility of the grotesque shape crouching over him. Whatever it may have been, he stopped. And then he brought his helmet slowly nearer to the Saint's, until barely six inches separated their front windows.

The Saint let him look. It had never been part of his plan that Vogel should be spared that final revelation. For the first time he held up his head and turned it so that the other could get a straight view into his helmet. The light above them reflected into his face from Vogel's upturned casque and filtered through the side panels to outline his features. The effect must still have been dim and shadowy, but at that close range it would still be recognisable.

And Vogel recognised it. His black burning eyes widened into fathomless pools of horror, and the thin bloodless lips drew back from his teeth in a kind of snarl. For the first time the smooth waxen mask was smashed away from his face, and only the snarl of the wolf remained. Then he began to speak. His mouth twisted in the shape of soundless words that no human ears would ever hear. Until he found that there was no answer and no obedience, and one of his hands groped round and found the loose trailing end of his severed line . . .

God knows what thoughts, what roaring maelstroms of incredulous understanding, must have gone thundering through his brain in those infinite seconds. He must have known even then that the death which he had meted out to others had found him in his turn, but he would never know how it had come about. He had been on the peaks of triumph. He had won every point, and this last descent should have been no more than a stereotyped epilogue to a finished history. He had left Simon Templar a prisoner, outwitted and disarmed and beaten, locked up to await the moment when he chose to remove him forever from the power of interference. And yet the Saint was there, smiling at him with set lips and bleak steel-blue eyes, where Ivaloff should have been. The Saint had come back, not beaten, but free and inescapable. The crew had dressed him and sent him down without a word. That was the last bitter dreg of realisation which he had to accept. The Saint had reversed their weapons. But how it had been done, how the crew had been bribed or intimidated, by what inconceivable alchemy the Saint had turned the tables, remained a riddle that he would never solve.

He fought. As if the shock had wiped away the last fragments of that more than human self-control, his hand shot out and clawed at the Saint's shoulder. His fingers slipped on the coarse twill, and the Saint grasped his wrist and twisted it away.

From the distance of a foot, which might have been the breadth of the Atlantic, Simon Templar looked at him through the wall of water which cut them off, and his blue eyes smiled with a soundless and terrible laughter into the wild distorted face. And he brought down the stone he was holding in a fearful blow on the fingers of Vogel's right hand where they clung to the rock.

A spasm of agony crawled across Vogel's features. And as the crushed hand released its hold, Simon slashed his knife clean through Vogel's air pipe and pushed him away.

Vogel fell, absurdly slowly, toppling backwards from the ladder very gradually and deliberately, with his arms waving and his hands clutching spasmodically at the yielding water. He went down, and the darkness of his own treasure-cave closed on his gleaming helmet. A slender trickle of bubbles curled up out of the gloom . . .

The Saint climbed lumberingly to his feet.

"Otto," he said curtly, still imitating Vogel's voice, and in a moment Arnheim answered.

"Yes?"

"Bring me up alone."

Vogel's life-line, knotted around his waist, tightened against his body. And at once he slashed through the telephone wires which were his last link with his own line.

His feet dragged off the ground, and he rose up through the light, past the lamp, up through the deep green shadowiness beyond. The circle of illuminated sea floor dwindled below him. Down, in the darkness of the crypt into which Vogel had fallen, he seemed to catch a glimpse of a moving sheen of metal, as if Vogel was trying to fight his way up again. But all that was very far away. He went up alone, up through the darkening shadows and the silence.

4

Coming up from that depth, there was no need for a gradual decompression. In three minutes he was getting his feet on to the rungs of the ladder. There was the sudden release of pressure from his body, and the pull of the weights on his shoulders. He climbed up into the light.

Hands helped him up on to the deck, tapped on his helmet and pointed, guiding him to the stool that was placed behind him. He sat down, facing the sea, and they unscrewed the porthole in the front of his helmet. He felt the sweet freshness of the natural air again.

The round opening where the porthole had been slid sideways across his vision as the helmet was released. He bent his head for it to be lifted off, and at the same time he slipped his knife out of its sheath into his left hand. As the helmet came off, he kept his head bowed and felt for the automatic inside his collar. He found it, and the knife flashed momentarily as he cut through the tie on which he had slung the gun. Then he turned round and faced the deck.

"I think this is the end, boys," he said quietly.

At the sound of his voice, those who had not been looking at him turned round, Calvieri, who was putting down the helmet, dropped it the last six inches. It fell with a deep hollow thud. And then there was utter stillness.

Arnheim had got up out of his chair and had been advancing towards him. He stopped, as if a brick wall had suddenly materialised in front of his toes, and his pink fleshy face seemed to turn yellow. His gross paunch quivered. A glassy film spread over his small pig eyes, turning them into frozen buttons of ink, and his soft moist mouth drooped open in a red "O" of fluttering unbelief. The Saint spoke principally to him.

"Kurt Vogel is dead. Or he soon will be. I believe there's enough air in a diving suit to last a man about five minutes after his air-line is cut. That is my justice . . ." The Saint paused for a moment, and his calm gaze swept over the rest of them there with the timeless impassivity of a judge. "As for the rest of you," he said, "some of you may get away with a nice long rest in prison—if you live long enough to stand your trial. But to do that you will have to put your hands high up above your heads and take great care not to annoy me, because if any of you give me a scare—"

The automatic in his hand cracked once, a sudden sharp splash of sound in the persuasive flow of his words, and Otto Arnheim, with his hand halfway to his pocket, lurched like a drunken man. A stupid blankness spread across his face, and his knees folded. He went down limply on to the deck, rolled over, and lay still, with his staring eyes turned to the winking stars.

"—this gun is liable to go off," said the Saint.

None of the men moved. They looked down at the motionless body of Otto Arnheim, and kept their hands stretched well above their heads. And the Saint smiled with his lips.

"I think we shall have to put you away for a while," he said. "Calvieri, you take some of that life-line and tie your playmates together. Lash 'em by the waists about a yard apart, and then add yourself to the string. Then we'll all go below, with you leading the way and me holding the other end of the line, and see about rounding up the rest of the herd."

"That's already been done, old boy," murmured Roger Conway, stepping out on to the deck from the after companion, with a gun in each hand and Steve Murdoch following him.

FINALE

"It was quite easy really," said Roger Conway patronisingly. "When we got Loretta's radiogram we set off at once, straight for here. We nearly piled your boat up on several rocks on the way, but Orace managed to see us through. Took us about three hours. The *Falkenberg* passed us about halfway, somewhere in the distance, and we just managed to keep her in sight. Luckily it was getting dark, so we turned out our lights after a bit and crept up as close as we dared. We dropped our hook about a quarter of a mile away, and as soon as we'd given the *Falkenberg* time to get well settled in we manned the dinghy and paddled over to reconnoitre. Everybody on deck seemed to be pretty busy with the diving business, so we came aboard on the other side and went below. We collected seven specimens altogether on the round-up, including a bloke who seems to have got a broken jaw. Anyway he's still asleep. The rest of 'em we gagged and tied up and left for inspection. We made a pretty thorough job of it, if I may say so."

With which modest summary of his activities, Roger helped himself to one of Vogel's cigars, threw another to Peter Quentin, and subsided exhausted into the most comfortable armchair.

Simon Templar regarded them disparagingly.

"You always were frightfully efficient at clearing up the battlefield after all the troops had gone home," he remarked appreciatively. "And where did you collect the American Tragedy?"

"Oh, him? He crashed on to the *Corsair* while we were having a drink with Orace, earlier in the afternoon," Peter explained. "Seemed to be all steamed up about something, and flashed a lot of badges and things at us, so we brought him along. He seemed to be very excited about Loretta batting off on this party, so I suppose he's her husband or something. Are you the co-respondent?"

Steve Murdoch dug his fists into his coat pockets and glowered round with his square jaw thrust out. His rugged hard-boiled face made the luxurious furnishings of the wheelhouse seem faintly effeminate.

"Yeah, I'm here," he stated truculently. "And this time I'm stayin'. I guess I owe you something for helpin' me clean up this job, Saint, an' maybe it's good enough to account for those two punches you hung on me. But that's as far as it goes. I'll see that Ingerbeck's hear about what you've done, and probably they'll offer you a share of the reward. If they do, you can go up an' claim it honest. But for the time being I'll look after things myself."

Simon looked at the ceiling.

"What a lot of modest violets there are around here," he sighed. "Of course I wouldn't dream of trying to steal your curtain, Steve, after all the brilliant work you've put in. But what exactly are you going to do?"

"I'm goin' to ask one of you boys to go ashore an' see if you can knock up the gendarmerie. If you can find a telegraph office, you can send one or two cables for me as well. The gendarmes can grab this guy Baudier before he skips, an' come on down to post a guard on board here. That'll do till I can start things movin' from the top. But until I've got that guard posted I'm going to sit over the diving gear myself, in case one of you thought he might go down an' see what he could pick up. I guess you've done enough diving for one day, Saint, an' you're not goin' down again while I can stop you. An' just in case you're thinkin' you can put me to sleep again like you did before, let me tell you that if you did get away with anything like that you'd have to shoot me to stop me puttin' every police organisation in the world on your trail as soon as I woke up. Do you get it?"

"Oh, I get you, Steve," said the Saint thoughtfully. "And I did tell Loretta I was tempted to come in for a share of the commission. Although it does sort of go against the grain to earn money honestly. It's such an anti-climax . . ."

He slid off the edge of the table and stood up, stroking his chin meditatively for a moment. And then, with a rueful shrug, he turned and grinned cheerfully at the detective.

"Still, it's always a new experience, and I suppose you've got to earn your living the same as I have," he drawled. "We'll let you have your fun. Peter, be a good boy and toddle along and do what Mr Murdoch asks you to."

"Right-ho," said Peter doubtfully.

"Roger, you can keep Steve company on his vigil. You'll have lots of fun telling each other how clever you are, but I'd much rather not listen to you."

The ineradicable suspicion darkened again in Murdoch's eyes.

"If you think you're goin' to talk Loretta round again," he began growlingly, "let me tell you—"

"Write it all down and post it to me in the morning, dear old bird," said the Saint affably and opened the door for them.

They filed out, Murdoch going last and most reluctantly, as if even then he couldn't believe that it was safe to let the Saint out of his sight. But Simon pushed him on, and closed the door after them.

Then he turned round and came towards Loretta.

She sat in her chair, rather quiet and still, with her lips slightly parted and the hint of mischief hushed for the moment into the changing shadows of her grey eyes. The lines of her slim body fell into a pattern of unconscious grace that made him almost hold his breath in case she moved, although he knew that in moving she would only take on a new beauty. He knew that, when all was said and done, in the last reckoning it was only the queer hunger which she could give a man that had tempted Kurt Vogel into his first and fatal mistake. She had so much that a man dreams about sometimes in the hard lonely trails of outlawry. She had so much that he himself had desired. In the few overcrowded hours since they had been thrown together, they had met in an understanding which no words could cover. They had walked in a garden, and talked together before the doors of death. He had known fear, and peace.

He stood looking down at her, half smiling. And then, with, a sudden soft breath of laughter, she took both his hands and came up into his arms. "So you don't like your dotted line?" she said.

"Maybe it grows on one."

She shook her head.

"Not on you."

He thought for a moment. Between them, who had lived so much, a lie had no place. "This job is finished," he said. "Steve Murdoch's mounting guard over the diving gear, and I promise I won't touch him. We can start again. Wash out the dotted line."

"And then?"

"For the future?" he said carelessly. "I shall still have the fun of being chivvied by every policeman in the world. I shall steal and fight, win and lose, go on—didn't you say it?— wanting so much that I can never have, fighting against life. But I shall live. I shall get into more trouble. I may even fall in love again. I shall end up by being hanged, or shot, or stabbed in the back, or something—if I don't find a safe berth in prison first. But that's my life. If I tried to live any other way, I'd feel like a caged eagle."

"But tomorrow?"

He laughed.

"I suppose I'll have to dump Peter and Roger somewhere. But the *Corsair*'s still ready to go anywhere. She's not so luxurious as this, but she's pretty comfortable. And about a hundred years ago I was in the middle of a vacation."

His hands were on her shoulders, and she smiled into his eyes.

"What do either of us know about the day after tomorrow?" she said.

Nearly an hour later he came out on deck, as half a dozen palpitating gendarmes were scrambling up the gangway. Murdoch had met the leader of them and was struggling to converse with him in a microscopical vocabulary of French delivered in a threatening voice with an atrocious accent. Simon left him to perspire alone, and drew Peter and Roger to one side.

"We're going back to the *Corsair*," he said.

"Without the heroine?" protested Peter. "Why, I was only just getting to know her." The Saint took him by the arm.

"You'll be able to improve the acquaintance tomorrow," he said kindly. "For as long as it takes us to sail back to St Peter Port and get rid of you. On your way."

They dropped into the dinghy, and Simon settled himself lazily in the stern, leaving the others to take the oars. He lighted a cigarette and gazed up at the star-dusted sky.

The lights of the *Falkenberg* drifted away behind them, and the cool quietness of the night took them in. The voices died away, and there was only the creak of the rowlocks and the gentle plash of the water. The Saint watched his smoke floating in gossamer veils across the stars, and let his mind stray through the lanes of memory. There was the only real knowledge, and all other doubt and disbelief could steal nothing from it. What did either of them know about the day after tomorrow? . . .

Roger's voice broke into his thoughts.

"Well, that's goodbye to those millions you promised us," he remarked glumly, and Simon sat up with the old buccaneering glint wakening in his eyes.

"Who said goodbye? My dear Roger, we're not going to bed yet! We're going to bring the *Corsair* up closer and unpack those nice new diving suits we've got on board. And then one of you drawing-room heroes is coming down with me on a little treasure-hunt. Steve and his gendarmes can mount guard over Vogel's diving gear all night for all I care. But they don't know how much boodle is stowed away down there, and what they don't know about they'll never miss. We're going to make sure of our share of the reward tonight," said the Saint.

PUBLICATION
HISTORY

Like so many previous Saint adventures the origins of this novel can be found in a magazine, but unlike so many it was not in *The Thriller* but an American magazine called, surprisingly enough, *The American Magazine*. Charteris had met the editor, Sumner Blossom, in a New York speakeasy on one of his first trips to the United States. By the mid-1930s Blossom, who as Charteris would later say "had conceived the even more reckless notion that I might bring a new breath of something to American crime fiction with a British approach," had placed the writer under contract and this was one of several stories he would ultimately write for the magazine. It first appeared in the November 1935 edition under the title *The Pirate Saint*.

British readers had to wait until the New Year to get their first opportunity to read the story when it was serialized—under the title *Saint Overboard*—in the *Daily Mirror* from January 6 to February 15. This coincided with the first hardback edition, which Hodders published in January with the Doubleday Crime Club publishing an American edition shortly afterwards. By May that year, Hodders were already on their fourth printing of the hardback.

Sales of the book were good, and continued in subsequent years. By 1952 Hodders were on their nineteenth printing of this title—an average of more than one a year. But it didn't hit the mark for some reviewers with *The Observer*'s anonymous contributor suggesting, "If Mr Charteris would allow his Saga hero to join all those other Saints in the hymn, I think his own great energy and undoubted skill might give us something better."[1] With sixteen books in eight years though, the Saint and Leslie Charteris had reached the ranks of assured success with new Saint books guaranteed to find a big audience.

Well, at least in his home bases of England and America. Foreign translations took a while; the French were quick off the mark with *La Justice du Saint* in 1938 and the Swedes followed in 1942 with *Helgonet härjar i havet* (though as of a 1957 reprint changed it to *Helgonet överbord*). A Turkish edition, *Kaplan gülüyor*, appeared in 1946 whilst Germany and Italy—both countries which had banned Charteris's books during the war—finally discovered the novel in 1957 and the late 1970s, respectively.

Adaptations of the book are few and far between; in the early 1940s RKO studios bought the film rights to the novel, however any possible production fell afoul of Charteris's developing displeasure with the studio and consequently no film was ever made. In 1995 BBC Radio adapted the novel for their short series of dramatizations which starred Paul Rhys as the Saint and were first aired on BBC Radio 4 in 1995.

---

1 *The Observer,* 8 March 1936

ABOUT THE AUTHOR

*I'm mad enough to believe in romance. And I'm sick and
tired of this age—tired of the miserable little mildewed
things that people racked their brains about, and wrote
books about, and called life. I wanted something more
elementary and honest—battle, murder, sudden death, with
plenty of good beer and damsels in distress, and a complete
callousness about blipping the ungodly over the beezer. It
mayn't be life as we know it, but it ought to be.*

—*Leslie Charteris in a 1935 BBC radio interview*

Leslie Charteris was born Leslie Charles Bowyer-Yin in Singapore on
12 May 1907.

He was the son of a Chinese doctor and his English wife, who'd
met in London a few years earlier. Young Leslie found friends hard to
come by in colonial Singapore. The English children had been told not
to play with Eurasians, and the Chinese children had been told not to
play with Europeans. Leslie was caught in between and took refuge in
reading.

"I read a great many good books and enjoyed them because
nobody had told me that they were classics. I also read a great many
bad books which nobody told me not to read . . . I read a great many

popular scientific articles and acquired from them an astonishing amount of general knowledge before I discovered that this acquisition was supposed to be a chore."[1]

One of his favourite things to read was a magazine called *Chums*. "The Best and Brightest Paper for Boys" (if you believe the adverts) was a monthly paper full of swashbuckling adventure stories aimed at boys, encouraging them to be honourable and moral and perhaps even "upright citizens with furled umbrellas."[2] Undoubtedly these types of stories would influence his later work.

When his parents split up shortly after the end of World War I, Charteris accompanied his mother and brother back to England, where he was sent to Rossall School in Fleetwood, Lancashire. Rossall was then a very stereotypical English public school, and it struggled to cope with this multilingual mixed-race boy just into his teens who'd already seen more of the world than many of his peers would see in their lifetimes. He was an outsider.

He left Rossall in 1924. Keen to pursue a creative career, he decided to study art in Paris—after all, that was where the great artists went—but soon found that the life of a literally starving artist didn't appeal. He continued writing, firing off speculative stories to magazines, and it was the sale of a short story to *Windsor Magazine* that saved him from penury.

He returned to London in 1925, as his parents—particularly his father—wanted him to become a lawyer, and he was sent to study law at Cambridge University. In the mid-1920s, Cambridge was full of Bright Young Things—aristocrats and bohemians somewhat typified in the Evelyn Waugh novel *Vile Bodies*—and again the mixed-race Bowyer-Yin found that he didn't fit in. He was an outsider who preferred to make his own way in the world and wasn't one of the privileged upper class. It didn't help that he found his studies boring and decided it was more fun contemplating ways to circumvent the law. This inspired him to write a novel, and when publishers Ward Lock & Co. offered him a three-book deal on the strength of it, he abandoned his studies to pursue a writing career.

When his father learnt of this, he was not impressed, as he considered writers to be "rogues and vagabonds." Charteris would later recall that "I wanted to be a writer, he wanted me to become a lawyer. I was stubborn, he said I would end up in the gutter. So I left home. Later on, when I had a little success, we were reconciled by letter, but I never saw him again."[3]

X Esquire, his first novel, appeared in April 1927. The lead character, X Esquire, is a mysterious hero, hunting down and killing the businessmen trying to wipe out Britain by distributing quantities of free poisoned cigarettes. His second novel, *The White Rider*, was published the following spring, and in one memorable scene shows the hero chasing after his damsel in distress, only for him to overtake the villains, leap into their car . . . and promptly faint.

These two plot highlights may go some way to explaining Charteris's comment on *Meet—the Tiger!*, published in September 1928, that "it was only the third book I'd written, and the best, I would say, for it was that the first two were even worse."[4]

Twenty-one-year-old authors are naturally self-critical. Despite reasonably good reviews, the Saint didn't set the world on fire, and Charteris moved on to a new hero for his next book. This was *The Bandit*, an adventure story featuring Ramon Francisco De Castilla y Espronceda Manrique, published in the summer of 1929 after its serialisation in the *Empire News*, a now long-forgotten Sunday newspaper. But sales of *The Bandit* were less than impressive, and Charteris began to question his choice of career. It was all very well writing—but if nobody wants to read what you write, what's the point?

"I had to succeed, because before me loomed the only alternative, the dreadful penalty of failure . . . the routine office hours, the five-day week . . . the lethal assimilation into the ranks of honest, hard-working, conformist, God-fearing pillars of the community."[5]

However his fortunes—and the Saint's—were about to change. In late 1928, Leslie had met Monty Haydon, a London-based editor who was looking for writers to pen stories for his new paper, *The Thriller*— "The Paper with a Thousand Thrills." Charteris later recalled that "he said he was starting a new magazine, had read one of my books and would like some stories from me. I couldn't have been more grateful, both from the point of view of vanity and finance!"[6]

The paper launched in early 1929, and Leslie's first work, "The Story of a Dead Man," featuring Jimmy Traill, appeared in issue 4 (published on 2 March 1929). That was followed just over a month later with "The Secret of Beacon Inn," starring Rameses "Pip" Smith. At the same time, Leslie finished writing another non-Saint novel, *Daredevil*, which would be published in late 1929. Storm Arden was the hero; more notably, the book saw the first introduction of a Scotland Yard inspector by the name of Claud Eustace Teal.

The Saint returned in the thirteenth issue of *The Thriller*. The byline proclaimed that the tale was "A Thrilling Complete Story of the Underworld"; the title was "The Five Kings," and it actually featured Four Kings and a Joker. Simon Templar, of course, was the Joker.

Charteris spent the rest of 1929 telling the adventures of the Five Kings in five subsequent *The Thriller* stories. "It was very hard work, for the pay was lousy, but Monty Haydon was a brilliant and stimulating editor, full of ideas. While he didn't actually help shape the Saint as a character, he did suggest story lines. He would take me out to lunch and say, 'What are you going to write about next?' I'd often say I was damned if I knew. And Monty would say, 'Well, I was reading something the other day . . .' He had a fund of ideas and we would talk them over, and then I would go away and write a story. He was a great creative editor."[7]

Charteris would have one more attempt at writing about a hero other than Simon Templar, in three novelettes published in *The Thriller* in early 1930, but he swiftly returned to the Saint. This was partly due to his self-confessed laziness—he wanted to write more stories for *The Thriller* and other magazines, and creating a new hero for every story was hard work—but mainly due to feedback from Monty Haydon. It seemed people wanted to read more adventures of the Saint . . .

Charteris would contribute over forty stories to *The Thriller* throughout the 1930s. Shortly after their debut, he persuaded publisher Hodder & Stoughton that if he collected some of these stories and rewrote them a little, they could publish them as a Saint book. *Enter the Saint* was first published in August 1930, and the reaction was good enough for the publishers to bring out another collection. And another . . .

Of the twenty Saint books published in the 1930s, almost all have their origins in those magazine stories.

Why was the Saint so popular throughout the decade? Aside from the charm and ability of Charteris's storytelling, the stories, particularly those published in the first half of the '30s, are full of energy and joie de vivre. With economic depression rampant throughout the period, the public at large seemed to want some escapism.

And Simon Templar's appeal was wide-ranging: he wasn't an upper-class hero like so many of the period. With no obvious background and no attachment to the Old School Tie, no friends in high places who could provide a get-out-of-jail-free card, the Saint was uniquely classless. Not unlike his creator.

Throughout Leslie's formative years, his heritage had been an issue. In his early days in Singapore, during his time at school, at Cambridge University or even just in everyday life, he couldn't avoid the fact that for many people his mixed parentage was a problem. He would later tell a story of how he was chased up the road by a stick-waving typical

English gent who took offence to his daughter being escorted around town by a foreigner.

Like the Saint, he was an outsider. And although he had spent a significant portion of his formative years in England, he couldn't settle.

As a young boy he had read of an America "peopled largely by Indians, and characters in fringed buckskin jackets who fought nobly against them. I spent a great deal of time day-dreaming about a visit to this prodigious and exciting country."[8]

It was time to realise this wish. Charteris and his first wife, Pauline, whom he'd met in London when they were both teenagers and married in 1931, set sail for the States in late 1932; the Saint had already made his debut in America courtesy of the publisher Doubleday. Charteris and his wife found a New York still experiencing the tail end of Prohibition, and times were tough at first. Despite sales to *The American Magazine* and others, it wasn't until a chance meeting with writer turned Hollywood executive Bartlett McCormack in their favourite speakeasy that Charteris's career stepped up a gear.

Soon Charteris was in Hollywood, working on what would become the 1933 movie *Midnight Club*. However, Hollywood's treatment of writers wasn't to Charteris's taste, and he began to yearn for home. Within a few months, he returned to the UK and began writing more Saint stories for Monty Haydon and Bill McElroy.

He also rewrote a story he'd sketched out whilst in the States, a version of which had been published in *The American Magazine* in September 1934. This new novel, *The Saint in New York*, published in 1935, was a significant advance for the Saint and Leslie Charteris. Gone were the high jinks and the badinage. The youthful exuberance evident in the Saint's early adventures had evolved into something a little darker, a little more hard-boiled. It was the next stage in development for the author and his creation, and readers loved it. It became a bestseller on both sides of the Atlantic.

Having spent his formative years in places as far apart as Singapore and England, with substantial travel in between, it should be no surprise that Leslie had a serious case of wanderlust. With a bestseller under his belt, he now had the means to see more of the world.

Nineteen thirty-six found him in Tenerife, researching another Saint adventure alongside translating the biography of Juan Belmonte, a well-known Spanish matador. Estranged for several months, Leslie and Pauline divorced in 1937. The following year, Leslie married an American, Barbara Meyer, who'd accompanied him to Tenerife. In early 1938, Charteris and his new bride set off in a trailer of his own design and spent eighteen months travelling round America and Canada.

The Saint in New York had reminded Hollywood of Charteris's talents, and film rights to the novel were sold prior to publication in 1935. Although the proposed 1935 film production was rejected by the Hays Office for its violent content, RKO's eventual 1938 production persuaded Charteris to try his luck once more in Hollywood.

New opportunities had opened up, and throughout the 1940s the Saint appeared not only in books and movies but in a newspaper strip, a comic-book series, and on radio.

Anyone wishing to adapt the character in any medium found a stern taskmaster in Charteris. He was never completely satisfied, nor was he shy of showing his displeasure. He did, however, ensure that copyright in any Saint adventure belonged to him, even if scripted by another writer—a contractual obligation that he was to insist on throughout his career.

Charteris was soon spread thin, overseeing movies, comics, newspapers, and radio versions of his creation, and this, along with his self-proclaimed laziness, meant that Saint books were becoming fewer and further between. However, he still enjoyed his creation: in 1941 he indulged himself in a spot of fun by playing the Saint—complete with monocle and moustache—in a photo story in *Life* magazine.

In July 1944, he started collaborating under a pseudonym on Sherlock Holmes radio scripts, subsequently writing more adventures for Holmes than Conan Doyle. Not all his ventures were successful—a screenplay he was hired to write for Deanna Durbin, "Lady on a Train," took him a year and ultimately bore little resemblance to the finished film. In the mid-1940s, Charteris successfully sued RKO Pictures for unfair competition after they launched a new series of films starring George Sanders as a debonair crime fighter known as the Falcon. But he kept faith with his original character, and the Saint novels continued to adapt to the times. The transatlantic Saint evolved into something of a private operator, working for the mysterious Hamilton and becoming, not unlike his creator, a world traveller, finding that adventure would seek him out.

"I have never been able to see why a fictional character should not grow up, mature, and develop, the same as anyone else. The same, if you like, as his biographer. The only adequate reason is that—so far as I know—no other fictional character in modern times has survived a sufficient number of years for these changes to be clearly observable. I must confess that a lot of my own selfish pleasure in the Saint has been in watching him grow up."[9]

Charteris maintained his love of travel and was soon to be found sailing round the West Indies with his good friend Gregory Peck. His forays abroad gave him even more material, and he began to write true-crime articles, as well as an occasional column in *Gourmet* magazine.

By the early '50s, Charteris himself was feeling strained. He'd divorced his second wife in 1943 and got together with a New York radio and nightclub singer called Betty Bryant Borst, whom he married in late 1943. That relationship had fallen apart acrimoniously towards the end of the decade, and he roamed the globe restlessly, rarely in one place for longer than a couple of months. He continued to maintain a firm grip on the exploitation of the Saint in various media but was writing little himself. The Saint had become an industry, and Charteris couldn't keep up. He began thinking seriously about an early retirement.

Then in 1951 he met a young actress called Audrey Long when they became next-door neighbours in Hollywood. Within a year they had married, a union that was to last the rest of Leslie's life.

He attacked life with a new vitality. They travelled—Nassau was a favoured escape spot—and he wrote. He struck an agreement with *The New York Herald Tribune* for a Saint comic strip, which would appear daily and be written by Charteris himself. The strip ran for thirteen years, with Charteris sending in his handwritten story lines from wherever he happened to be, relying on mail services around the world to continue the Saint's adventures. New Saint books began to appear, and Charteris reached a height of productivity not seen since his days as a struggling author trying to establish himself. As Leslie and Audrey travelled, so did the Saint, visiting locations just after his creator had been there.

By 1953 the Saint had already enjoyed twenty-five years of success, and *The Saint Detective Magazine* was launched. Charteris had become adept at exploiting his creation to the full, mixing new stories with repackaged older stories, sometimes rewritten, sometimes mixed up in "new" anthologies, sometimes adapted from radio scripts previously written by other writers.

Charteris had been approached several times over the years for television rights in the Saint and had expended much time and effort during the 1950s trying to get the Saint on TV, even going so far as to write sample scripts himself, but it wasn't to be. He finally agreed a deal in autumn 1961 with English film producers Robert S. Baker and Monty Berman. The first episode of *The Saint* television series, starring Roger Moore, went into production in June 1962. The series was an immediate success, though Charteris himself had his reservations. It reached second place in the ratings, but he commented that "in that distinction it was topped by wrestling, which only suggested to me that the competition may not have been so hot; but producers are generally cast in a less modest mould." He resented the implication that the TV series had finally made a success of the Saint after twenty-five years of literary obscurity.

As long as the series lasted, Charteris was not shy about voicing his criticisms both in public and in a constant stream of memos to the producers. "Regular followers of the Saint saga . . . must have noticed that I am almost incapable of simply writing a story and shutting up."[10] Nor was he shy about exploiting this new market by agreeing to a series of tie-in novelisations ghosted by other writers, which he would then rewrite before publication.

Charteris mellowed as the series developed and found elements to praise too. He developed a close friendship with producer Robert S. Baker, which would last until Charteris's death.

In the early '60s, on one of their frequent trips to England, Leslie and Audrey bought a house in Surrey, which became their permanent base. He explored the possibility of a Saint musical and began writing some of it himself.

Charteris no longer needed to work. Now in his sixties, he supervised the Saint from a distance whilst continuing to travel and indulge himself. He and Audrey made seasonal excursions to Ireland and the south of France, where they had residences. He began to write poetry and devised a new universal sign language, Paleneo, based on notes and symbols he used in his diaries. Once Paleneo was released, he decided enough was enough and announced, again, his retirement. This time he meant it.

The Saint continued regardless—there was a long-running Swedish comic strip, and new novels with other writers doing the bulk of the work were complemented in the 1970s with Bob Baker's revival of the TV series, *Return of the Saint.*

Ill-health began to take its toll. By the early 1980s, although he continued a healthy correspondence with the outside world, Charteris felt unable to keep up with the collaborative Saint books and pulled the plug on them.

To entertain himself, Leslie took to "trying to beat the bookies in predicting the relative speed of horses," a hobby which resulted in several of his local betting shops refusing to take "predictions" from him, as he was too successful for their liking.

He still received requests to publish his work abroad but had become completely cynical about further attempts to revive the Saint. A new Saint magazine only lasted three issues, and two TV productions—*The Saint in Manhattan*, with Tom Selleck look-alike Andrew Clarke, and *The Saint*, with Simon Dutton—left him bitterly disappointed. "I fully expect this series to lay eggs everywhere . . . the only satisfaction I have is in looking at my bank balance."[11]

In the early 1990s, Hollywood producers Robert Evans and William J. Macdonald approached him and made a deal for the Saint to return to cinema screens. Charteris still took great care of the Saint's reputation and wrote an outline entitled *The Return of the Saint* in which an older Saint would meet the son he didn't know he had.

Much of his time in his last few years was taken up with the movie. Several scripts were submitted to him—each moving further and further away from his original concept—but the screenwriter from 1940s Hollywood was thoroughly disheartened by the Hollywood of the '90s: "There is still no plot, no real story, no characterisations, no personal interaction, nothing but endless frantic violence . . ." Besides, with producer Bill Macdonald hitting the headlines for the most un-Saintly reasons, he was to add, "How can Bill Macdonald concentrate on my Saint movie when he has Sharon Stone in his bed?"

The Crime Writers' Association of Great Britain presented Leslie with a Lifetime Achievement award in 1992 in a special ceremony at the

House of Lords. Never one for associations and awards, and although visibly unwell, Leslie accepted the award with grace and humour ("I am now only waiting to be carbon-dated," he joked). He suffered a slight stroke in his final weeks, which did not prevent him from dining out locally with family and friends, before he finally passed away at the age of 85 on 15 April 1993.

His death severed one of the final links with the classic thriller genre of the 1930s and 1940s, but he left behind a legacy of nearly one hundred books, countless short stories, and TV, film, radio, and comic-strip adaptations of his work which will endure for generations to come.

> *I was always sure that there was a solid place in escape literature for a rambunctious adventurer such as I dreamed up in my youth, who really believed in the old-fashioned romantic ideals and was prepared to lay everything on the line to bring them to life. A joyous exuberance that could not find its fulfilment in pinball machines and pot. I had what may now seem a mad desire to spread the belief that there were worse, and wickeder, nut cases than Don Quixote.*
>
> *Even now, half a century later, when I should be old enough to know better, I still cling to that belief. That there will always be a public for the old-style hero, who had a clear idea of justice, and a more than technical approach to love, and the ability to have some fun with his crusades.*[12]

---

1 *A Letter from the Saint,* 30 August 1946
2 "The Last Word," *The First Saint Omnibus,* Doubleday Crime Club, 1939
3 *The Straits Times,* 29 June 1958, page 9

4 Introduction by Charteris to the September 1980 paperback reprint of *Meet—the Tiger!* (Charter), the last ever print edition.

5 *The Saint: A Complete History,* by Burl Barer (McFarland, 1993)

6 PR material from the 1970s series *Return of the Saint*

7 From "Return of the Saint: Comprehensive Information" issued to help publicise the 1970s TV show

8 *A Letter from the Saint,* 26 July 1946

9 Introduction to "The Million Pound Day," in *The First Saint Omnibus*

10 *A Letter from the Saint,* 12 April 1946

11 Letter from LC to sometime Saint collaborator Peter Bloxsom, 2 August 1989

12 Introduction by Charteris to the September 1980 paperback reprint of *Meet—the Tiger!* (Charter).

WATCH FOR THE SIGN

OF THE SAINT!

THE SAINT CLUB

And so, my friends, dear bookworms, most noble fellow drinkers, frustrated burglars, affronted policemen, upright citizens with furled umbrellas and secret buccaneering dreams that seems to be very nearly all for now. It has been nice having you with us, and we hope you will come again, not once, but many times.

Only because of our great love for you, we would like to take this parting opportunity of mentioning one small matter which we have very much at heart . . .

—Leslie Charteris, *The First Saint Omnibus* (1939)

Leslie Charteris founded The Saint Club in 1936 with the aim of providing a constructive fanbase for Saint devotees. Before the War, it donated profits to a London hospital where, for several years, a Saint ward was maintained. With the nationalisation of hospitals, profits were, for many years, donated to the Arbour Youth Centre in Stepney, London.

In the twenty-first century, we've carried on this tradition but have also donated to the Red Cross and a number of different children's charities.

The club acts as a focal point for anyone interested in the adventures of Leslie Charteris and the work of Simon Templar, and offers merchandise that includes DVDs of the old TV series and various Saint-related publications, through to its own exclusive range of notepaper, pin badges, and polo shirts. All profits are donated to charity. The club also maintains two popular websites and supports many more Saint-related sites.

After Leslie Charteris's death, the club recruited three new vice-presidents—Roger Moore, Ian Ogilvy, and Simon Dutton have all pledged their support, whilst Audrey and Patricia Charteris have been retained as Saints-in-Chief. But some things do not change, for the back of the membership card still mischievously proclaims that . . .

> *The bearer of this card is probably a person of hideous antecedents and low moral character, and upon apprehension for any cause should be immediately released in order to save other prisoners from contamination.*

To join . . .

Membership costs £3.50 (or US$7) per year, or £30 (US$60) for life. Find us online at www.lesliecharteris.com for full details.